E.R. PUNSHON
NIGHT'S CLOAK

ERNEST ROBERTSON PUNSHON was born in London in 1872.

At the age of fourteen he started life in an office. His employers soon informed him that he would never make a really satisfactory clerk, and he, agreeing, spent the next few years wandering about Canada and the United States, endeavouring without great success to earn a living in any occupation that offered. Returning home by way of working a passage on a cattle boat, he began to write. He contributed to many magazines and periodicals, wrote plays, and published nearly fifty novels, among which his detective stories proved the most popular and enduring.

He died in 1956.

The Bobby Owen Mysteries

E.R. PUNSHON

NIGHT'S CLOAK

With an introduction
by Curtis Evans

DEAN STREET PRESS

Published by Dean Street Press 2016

Copyright © 1944 E.R. Punshon

Introduction copyright © 2016 Curtis Evans

All Rights Reserved

Published by licence, issued under the
UK Orphan Works Licensing Scheme.

First published in 1944 by Victor Gollancz

Cover by DSP

ISBN 978 1 911413 37 0

www.deanstreetpress.co.uk

INTRODUCTION

ON 1 DECEMBER 1942 the British wartime coalition government led by Prime Minister Winston Churchill published "Social Insurance and Allied Services," a report authored by Liberal economist and social reformer Sir William Beveridge, in which Beveridge called for the provision in the United Kingdom of a comprehensive system of cradle-to-grave social insurance. The Beveridge Report, as it became known, quickly sold 70,000 copies and its ambitious agenda was embraced by much of the British public, although there were naysayers to be found as well, including certain British crime writers. For decades it has been contended of most British Golden Age detective novelists that they leaned toward the Right and supported the Conservative Party, popularly known as the Tories. Indeed, the late leftist mystery writer and critic Julian Symons in his popular mystery genre history *Bloody Murder* sweepingly characterized as politically and socially reactionary the British detective novelists belonging to the generation that preceded his, memorably declaring that "[u]npleasant things were ignored in almost all the detective stories in the Golden Age. ... The social order in these stories was as fixed and mechanical as that of the Incas." Yet E.R. Punshon was, like Sir William Beveridge, a member of the Liberal Party and he supported many of the progressive aspirations for a more equitable society that were outlined in the Beveridge Report. In his Bobby Owen detective novels Punshon had long criticized social privilege and satirized reactionary members of the business and gentry classes. These long-familiar elements in Punshon's mysteries were given greater prominence than usual in *Night's Cloak* (1944), the first detective novel entirely written by the author after the publication and popular dissemination of the Beveridge Report.

Night's Cloak opens with Bobby grumbling about having been imperiously summoned for an ambiguous evening audience at the mansion of William Weston, a former Midwych Lord Mayor and MP and the current "chairman, managing director and virtual dictator" of the Weston West Mills, as well as a millionaire ("or at least a 'near millionaire'"), "with all that implies," Punshon notes sardonically, "in our present-day civilization of power, prestige and influence." Bobby's meeting with Weston at the misleadingly named Weston Lodge Cottage (an "enormous building, though more like a factory than a house") gets off to rather a bad start, with the industrialist, seemingly in expectation of some favor, ham-handedly referencing Bobby's aristocratic background, ironically a status which the policeman had fondly hoped had gone undetected in Wychshire, his having "done his best to live down his connection with one of Britain's most impecunious peers."

From there things get even worse. Weston darkly implies that Bobby has socialist leanings, menacingly adding that "[s]ome of the County Watch Committee are a bit—well, worried," while Bobby bluntly reminds Weston that in Wychshire the industrialist enjoys no greater privileges in relation to the police than any other citizen. The meeting abruptly ends with Weston promising Bobby, "Young man, you'll hear more of this." In this prediction Weston proves gravely wrong, for the next morning Bobby receives a telephone call informing him that his wealthy antagonist has been found stabbed to death in the very study where he and Bobby had their stormy altercation. Bobby reflects that in this particular murder, he might be considered a suspect.

Fatally obnoxious millionaires (or "near millionaires") done to death in their studies may at times seem a dime-a-dozen in Golden Age country house mysteries, yet Punshon's novel is distinguished not only by an intricate problem and interesting characters (the *Saturday Review* judged it the "very best British brand," with a "deftly portrayed" background and characters and an "air-tight" plot), but by the originality of the plot's political and social elements. One of the suspects in the murder of Mr. Weston is Dan Edwardes, a major Weston West Mills shareholder who has turned to socialism in an attempt to find meaning in his life after the deaths of his three sons in the current war. In a long speech to Bobby which echoes popular sentiment of the day, Edwardes explains that he learned from his late sons that the common people of Britain, having labored so dutifully for victory in the war and made so much personal sacrifice, deserve, after the war has ended, a far greater say in the way things are run in their country: "Churchill has got to answer to the dustman; and if the dustman isn't satisfied, Churchill has got to go." Edwardes wants to concede control over the factory to the Weston West Mills workers and he had passed along to Weston a socialist political pamphlet, "What It Will Be Like", explaining his views; but in doing so he only incurred the late manufacturer's wrath.

Night's Cloak initially may seem to adhere more to Golden Age norms in its treatment of the retinue of house servants at Weston Lodge Cottage. After the murder is discovered we are informed, for example, that the "women servants were having hysterics by turn in the kitchen." And Hargreaves, Weston's elderly, white-haired butler, is a domestic picture of perfection, looking "so much like the English butler in an American film that Bobby was almost inclined to ask him if he took other roles." Yet with the servants as well cracks are discernible in the purportedly immutable Golden Age mystery social order. Hargreaves complains to Bobby that the two prewar footmen have been called up ("Mr Weston was refused exemption for them"), forcing him to resort to the services of William, who is "less a footman than a boot-and-knife boy masquerading as such." And even the deplorable William "has been directed to join the Home Guard, though that will interfere seriously with his duties," Hargreaves adds gloomily.

Although Hargreaves has every semblance of the perfect butler ("I can picture the admirable Hargreaves appearing on the Day of Judgment to announce 'Dinner is served,'" quips Dan Edwardes), in truth he presents something of a false front to the privileged elite for whom he labors. First, there is the matter of names:

> "Let's see, your name is Hargreaves, isn't it?" Bobby asked when the butler appeared. "First names?"
>
> ...
>
> "Well, sir, when applying for a situation, I generally give it as Thomas. Ladies seem to consider it more suitable."
>
> "Do you mean it's not your real name?"
>
> ..."I was christened Lancelot Galahad. My father, sir, was a great admirer of Tennyson."

Then there is the matter of Hargreaves's dignified mane of white hair:

> "Ladies, sir, frequently display a preference for white hair in those holding a position as butler. It seems to be a general belief among ladies that a sense of responsibility and

discretion is thus indicated. So it has been my habit, sir, to rub in each morning a certain—er—bleaching preparation, so to say, of my own invention. In my profession, sir, if I may so, is it often necessary to play up to the gentry's most fat-headed ideas."

"I expect it is," agreed Bobby. ...

Traditional—if not to say fatheaded—ideas were being roundly challenged in the United Kingdom during the years of the Second World War, both in weighty political documents like the Beveridge Report and the light crime fiction of E. R. Punshon. In the 1945 UK general election Winston Churchill's Conservative Party, having failed, one might say, to satisfy the dustman, was resoundingly turned out of power and replaced by Clement Atlee's Labour Party, which began energetically implementing the proposals contained in the Beveridge Report. (Punshon's Liberal Party collected only 9% of the vote in 1945, compared to 48% for Labour and 36% for the Tories.) Many prominent Golden Age mystery writers of the time, such as Dorothy L. Sayers, Agatha Christie, John Dickson Carr and Henry Wade, viewed the state of the UK under the Labour government, which held power into 1951, with mounting pessimism. In future Dean Street Press reprints we shall judge what E.R. Punshon's attitude was.

Curtis Evans

CHAPTER I
IMPERIOUS SUMMONS

"AND WHO," demanded Inspector Bobby Owen, addressing his question to the universe in general and to the Wychshire County Police in particular, "who is Mr William Weston, if you please?"

The question was purely rhetorical, for Bobby knew perfectly well—as did every one in the city of Midwych and most in the county of Wychshire and many elsewhere—all about that great man. Was he not a former Lord Mayor of the city; a former M.P. for the Stimmell Division of Midwych; the present chairman, managing director and virtual dictator of the Weston West Mills and its subsidiary undertakings, above all, was he not a millionaire, or at least a "near millionaire", with all that implies in our present-day civilization of power, prestige and influence? Did not his position therefore resemble that of one of those great feudal lords who, in the Middle Ages, were the powers behind the throne—and not so very much behind, either? True, he did not wield the power of the High Justice, the Middle, and the Low, but he did wield the power of job or no job, which comes to much the same thing.

A great man, then, but none the less, as the great and the powerful so often are, a disappointed man. He had expected at least a knighthood—stepping-stone to the peerage—on the conclusion of his term of office as Lord Mayor of Midwych. He had not received it, whereon in a fit of pique he had resigned from the City Council. Again at the last general election, though Tory successes had been widespread, he had lost his seat for the Stimmell Division in spite of the fact that the Stimmell Division was largely inhabited by his own workpeople.

This misfortune Mr Weston was accustomed to cite, not without bitterness, as a classic example of working-class ingratitude—a "biting of the hand that fed them"—and as a not surprising result of recent political pampering. And he would quote figures from the annual reports of the Weston West Company to show how much money had been spent on such amenities as a canteen where meals were provided at a cost that showed only a trifling profit, as a playing-field laid out on a site purchased cheaply for that purpose and possibly one day useful for an extension of the mill buildings. Indeed, as Mr Weston was accustomed to say, on a thousand and one other benefits that were neither more nor less than free gifts. Why, there was even a welfare officer, if you please, a Miss Olga Severn, though the fact that she was a rather charming girl, fresh and lively, certainly counted as an alleviating factor. Nor was it necessary to pay too much attention to her recommendations, even though old Dan Edwardes, another director, and holder of as many ordinary shares as were held by Mr Weston himself, had recently gone all sappy and sentimental. Age, and the loss of all his three sons on active service in the early stages of the war, no doubt accounting for this, and indicating, Mr Weston felt, a sad loss of mental stability, as shown in certain suggestions recently put forward by him for the future control of the business.

And that at a time, Mr Weston would add quietly, when the shareholders, thanks to the former general business depression and present war-time difficulties, had received no dividend for some years, though certainly their property was of great potential value.

Furthermore, Mrs Weston, expressing a pedantic disapproval of a certain largeness of heart that could refuse a welcome to no—feminine—visitant, had departed to the south of England, where she had recently died, leaving a will which bequeathed all her possessions—these were both few and small—to her husband, with the exception of a block of five thousand one-pound ordinary shares in the Weston West Mills Company. These she had left to young Martin Weston Wynne, her husband's first cousin once removed and his nearest living relative in England, though there were other cousins in the Dominions.

Not that this bequest seemed of any great pecuniary value, since not only had no dividend been paid on the shares for some years, but none could be paid until the very heavy arrears on the preference shares had been entirely cleared off. But it was an open secret that Mr Weston's feelings had been much hurt, and that he had expressed himself as being entirely unable to understand what had induced his wife to do such a thing.

"Not that I mind her remembering the boy and leaving him anything she wanted to," he had been heard to remark. "But why these shares in my company that the young man has never shown any interest in? He was with us for a time. I meant him to take my place some day. Threw it all up and went off on his own!"

All this Bobby knew well, and Sergeant Payne, his chief assistant in the much-depleted Wychshire County C.I.D., knew he knew it. Which did not prevent a very shocked tone appearing in Payne's voice as he said:—

"Mr Weston, sir? Mr Weston? Why, sir . . . well, sir . . . the Weston West Mills, sir. ..."

"Yes, I know," snapped Bobby, somewhat illogically. "Look at that."

"That" was a note from Mr William Weston, requesting, indeed demanding, that Inspector Owen should call at Weston Lodge Cottage at eight o'clock that evening.

Payne read it gravely, but made no comment. No comment annoyed Bobby still more. He said:—

"Does the fellow think we have nothing to do but run about after him?"

Payne coughed.

"Well, sir," he said, "you know, sir—very influential gentleman, Mr Weston. Mayor a few years back. Very friendly with Sir Merrick Templemore, and you know yourself, sir, Sir Merrick—well, he just is the County Watch Committee."

"No reason," growled Bobby, "why this Weston bloke should think we've got to be at his beck and call. Seems to think he can give us orders—he might be our chief, from the way he writes."

"I expect it's only his way," Payne suggested placatingly. "Very autocratic gentleman, Mr Weston, I've always heard. Used to giving orders and expects to be obeyed."

"Oh, does he?" said Bobby, the light of battle beginning to gleam in his eyes.

"Colonel Glynne," murmured Payne, apparently changing the subject and gazing in an abstracted way at the ceiling, "thinks Sir Merrick will be likely to approve of the plans for the new headquarters going through."

Bobby nearly choked. New headquarters for the county police was the pet dream of the Chief Constable, Colonel Glynne. He had even spent some of his own money in getting plans prepared for the projected building. By careful diplomacy, strengthened by the discreet use of a special port, Sir Merrick Templemore had been induced to promise support when the scheme came before the

Wychshire Watch Committee, notorious for turning down every suggestion even remotely threatening an increase in the rates. If Mr Weston got to work on Sir Merrick and Sir Merrick withdrew his support, then the project would certainly be wrecked and Colonel Glynne's heart broken—which would be a pity. Moreover, the county police would lose their nice new headquarters Bobby wanted as much as any one—and that would be an even greater pity.

He picked up the note again.

"Written in the third person," he grumbled. "Not a hint what it's all about. Miles out of the way, his place. Suppose a dustman wrote to us like that, what would you do?"

Payne looked very shocked. Not but that he knew very well what he would do if a dustman had written in such terms. He said:—

"Must be something important, sir. Mr Weston's a very responsible gentleman. Might be something to do with the war."

"Well, if it is, why can't he come here and say so?" demanded Bobby. "I'll ring him up and ask him what it's all about," he decided.

Payne looked alarmed this time. He had a very lively sense of Mr Weston's position in the scheme of things, and of both the power and the will of that gentleman to make himself unpleasant when so minded. He looked relieved when Bobby failed to get his call through.

"Sure to be a good reason," Payne repeated. "Mr Weston isn't the gentleman to waste his own time or other people's either."

An hour or so later Bobby tried again, and this time with better success, even though it was only to learn that Mr Weston was out and had not said when he would return. The voice over the 'phone was, however, sure that Mr Weston would be back in time for any appointment he had made. The voice evidently considered that any failure on Mr Weston's part to keep an appointment he had made was quite inconceivable.

An interesting voice, this he was listening to, Bobby thought. A woman's voice, a contradictory voice, low and husky and yet clear, decided, compelling even, and yet within it an oddly soft, caressing note as well. It made him think somehow of the purr of a contented cat that might in a moment change to something very different.

The voice belonged, it informed him, to Miss Thomasine Rowe, Mr Weston's private secretary. Miss Thomasine had no idea what the purpose of the suggested interview might be. But—the husky voice sounded both a little amused and a little shocked—the inspector might be very sure it was important. Mr Weston was not in the habit of making appointments without good reason.

Bobby hung up the receiver and supposed gloomily that he would have to go. No doubt whatever it was all about might be important from the point of view of Mr William Weston, of the Weston West Mills and all the rest of it. But it by no means followed that such importance would appear equally important in the eyes of the police in general or of Inspector Bobby Owen in particular. However, one could not take risks in these days. It might be something in some way affecting public security. It might be something important affecting black-market activities, for instance. Or, for that matter, something affecting even more vital public interests. It would be awkward if it turned out that he had neglected some such opportunity. A policeman soon learns that nothing may be overlooked, since anything may lead anywhere.

But Bobby promised himself that unless the reason was sufficient, Mr William Weston, great man as he might be, would hear quite plainly what one inspector of police at least thought of people who in these days of trial and difficulty put officials to unnecessary trouble.

CHAPTER II
BARMAID BESSIE BELL

THAT EVENING, then, saw a still-disgruntled Bobby Owen driving along the road that led to Weston Lodge Cottage, a designation modest or pretentious according to the point of view. He came to the great iron gates of the drive. They stood always open in these days, for the former lodge-keeper had been called up and his wife had somewhat inconsiderately gone into munitions, but at any rate the push for scrap iron had spared these enormous productions by reason of their "artistic value". Artistic value is a matter of taste, and if Bobby thought the gates heavy and clumsy, that again was a matter of taste.

The drive on which they opened provided, however, a lovely approach to the house, lined as it was by fine old trees, with here and there clumps of flowering shrubs. In spring its show of daffodils and hyacinths gave it additional beauty. Very pleasantly the drive pursued its curving way through an ancient and gracious park, till at last there came into sudden view the great house itself.

An enormous building, though more like a factory than a house, Bobby thought, and indeed when Mr Weston decided to rebuild from cellar to roof he employed the same firm of architects as had designed for him the new Weston West Mills building as well as that for Weston Industries, of which Mr Weston was also chairman and managing director. In long, straight lines the house stretched its length across that green and pleasant countryside. All very much, no doubt, in that modern style which believes the tee-square to be the line of beauty, but also very much, to Bobby's mind at least, as if some giant child had been playing with a box of bricks.

Nothing more out of harmony with its ancient, quiet background could Bobby imagine. Not that in itself it was actually displeasing, merely deadly dull with its regular monotony of line and angle. Or rather it would have been deadly dull had it not so challengingly screamed its defiance of all established tradition.

"I am new and, by definition, new is best," it seemed to be shouting, and if Bobby fancied that the old, old land around listened to the strident shout with the faintest of faint ironic smiles, that was merely the imaginative side of his nature asserting itself for once.

With these thoughts running through his mind, Bobby—for he was a little before his time—remained seated a moment or two in his car he had brought to a standstill in order to survey the scene before him. He heard approaching steps, a murmur of voices, one voice unmistakable in its deep husky undertone with the purring note that might so easily, one felt, turn to menace. Miss Thomasine Rowe, Mr Weston's secretary, who had spoken over the 'phone, Bobby was certain. Possibly Mr Weston wished her to be present at the coming interview, or possibly he was in the habit of working her late. Or it might be that she lived at Weston Lodge Cottage and was enjoying a stroll in the park before dinner.

Not alone, though, for there was another voice, a male voice, Bobby thought, though a voice much lower and less distinctive. The voices ceased abruptly, the footsteps died away. Bobby wondered vaguely if he had been seen and if that accounted for this sudden silence and retreat. He was a trifle disappointed. He felt interested in the owner of that distinctive voice and wondered if it belonged to a personality as distinctive. Probably not. Probably Miss Thomasine Rowe would turn out to be the most ordinary commonplace little typist who ever sat tapping all day long the keys of her machine.

He started the car again, and when he knocked at the front door it was opened by an elderly, white-haired butler, who looked so much like the English butler in an American film that Bobby was almost inclined to ask him if he ever took other roles. Instead Bobby explained that Mr Weston was expecting him and gave his name, and the butler, looking gravely disappointed that Bobby had neither hat nor gloves nor stick for him to take possession of, led the way with severe dignity down a thickly carpeted corridor—Mr Weston had a passion for thick carpetings, the thicker, closer, softer, the better, so that all movement in the house was nearly noiseless—into a small, severely furnished room that only needed a few out-of-date illustrated papers on the table in the centre to resemble any dentist's waiting-room.

"I will acquaint Mr Weston, sir, with your presence," the butler announced—should one say, intoned?—and so retired.

For the first moment Bobby supposed the room was unoccupied. But then there was a movement by the heavily curtained windows and a woman who had before been hidden by them turned round and stepped back into the room.

She was a big, handsome young woman. Younger still, she must have been remarkably handsome in what is called the Nordic style, with fair complexion, blue sleepy eyes, and golden hair that owed, Bobby thought, all to Nature and nothing to art. But though she was still young, the fair complexion had already need of powder to hide small blotches and pimples, the blue eyes were no longer so clear as they had been at eighteen, the golden hair had lost much of its early soft, enchanting shine, the once-graceful, lissom form was beginning to spread and lose its grace and lightness. But it was still a fine animal physically and one not easily forgotten.

Bobby knew her at once. Bessie Bell, barmaid at the Wych and Wych Arms in the city. The Wych and Wych Arms was something of an institution in Midwych and Bessie was something of an institution at the Wych and Wych Arms. Bobby had seen her there more than once, a tumultuous, noisy priestess of the bar. Also he had seen her in court when two or three rowdy Dublin Irishmen, who had been gloating over British reverses in France, had been thrown out in a violent affray in which it was rumoured Bessie had taken an active part. However, that detail had been glossed over. A complaint by one of the Irishmen that his broken nose was the result of a collision between it and a pewter pot wielded by Bessie's own fair hand had been set aside for lack of corroborative evidence, and subsequently a charge that might have been preferred of drunk and disorderly that same evening somehow or another failed to find its way into court.

Now Bessie was apt to take her revenge on any customer she thought came from Eire by telling him a story she had picked up somewhere. It was a variation of the old tale of the Irishman who, seeing a fight in progress in the street, asked if it were a private fight, or could he join in? In Bessie's version the Irishman was represented as asking if it were a public fight, or could he be neutral? She had grown less fond of this amusement, though, since she had told the tale to two young men in plain clothes, both evidently very Irish indeed, and both of whom she subsequently discovered were fighter pilots in the R.A.F.

Recognition was apparently as quick on her side as it had been on Bobby's, for Bessie was staring at him with wide-open, slightly glassy eyes. A distinct odour of whisky now perceptible, suggested strongly that she had been fortifying herself for her visit here. And to Bobby's surprise, for as far as his knowledge went she was a fairly law-abiding person, it was sheer, stark terror that sprang into her eyes with her recognition of him.

"Oh, my God," she muttered, "you—has that old devil got you here?"

"What do you mean?" Bobby asked. "Anything wrong?"

She did not answer, but began to back away towards the window. She almost had the air of being about to jump out and take to flight.

"If there's anything wrong, you had better tell me," Bobby said. "You know who I am?"

"What about it if I do?" she muttered.

"What's frightening you?" Bobby asked. "Why are you afraid?"

She had reached the window now. The house, built on the crest of a slight slope, was higher here than at the front, where most of the windows opened directly on the ground level. This window, of the sash variety, was some six feet from the ground. Bobby followed her. The window was wide open. He remembered she had been standing there, half hidden by the curtains, when he came in. It struck him that perhaps she had been leaning out, talking to some one. Beneath was a flower-bed, and when Bobby looked he was confirmed in this belief by seeing footprints in the soft mould to show some one had been standing there.

"Talking to some one, weren't you?" Bobby asked.

"What's it to do with you if I was?" she retorted.

"Nothing that I know of," agreed Bobby pleasantly. "In a general way any one can talk to any one else out of windows all day long for all I care, and all night long, too. But it is plain enough you are frightened about something. And what frightens people may well turn out to be very much police business."

"I'm not frightened of anything, not me," she declared vehemently. "Not of him, anyhow."

"Who is 'him'?" Bobby asked.

"I tell you straight," she said, "if he tries to interfere with me—" She gulped. "Never you mind, Mr Policeman," she said hoarsely, with difficulty, indeed. "I'll handle this," she burst out in a voice that now had changed almost to a scream.

The door opened and the old butler hurried in, not quite so dignified now. Disturbed, one would have said, or even scared, and even more so, apparently, when he saw how Bobby and Bessie were facing each other.

"Oh, I beg your pardon," he stammered, looking at Bobby. "Oh, excuse me, would you please come this way at once?"

CHAPTER III
COUSINS

As he followed the butler out of the room, Bobby glanced approvingly at his wrist watch. It showed the exact hour appointed for the interview with Mr Weston. Bobby was pleased. He liked punctuality—a virtue both rare and admirable. He became inclined to forget that his dignity had been slightly ruffled by the peremptory tone of Mr Weston's message. Perhaps after all it was something really pressing and important, and he wondered if the presence of Miss Bessie Bell could have anything to do with it. Certainly that young lady had shown herself to be in a disturbed state of mind. Curious, he thought, her presence, and he began to be aware that the white-haired old butler was now also looking very disturbed. Scared, indeed. Something had happened apparently in the last few moments to give him a bad fright. His habitual dignity had almost entirely deserted him. Holding half open the door of the room to which he had conducted Bobby, he said nervously:—

"You won't think it necessary to mention it, sir, I hope?"

Bobby hardly heard. He was aware of a curious impression that as the door opened, some one left hurriedly by the window. Hard to say exactly what made him think so. A kind of movement in the air. A faint trembling of the window-curtains. A chair between window and door that looked out of place. One side of the open french window swinging back into position. But that might have been the result of a passing gust of wind. Bobby crossed the room. The window opened directly on the garden—"grounds" was the word Mr Weston preferred. Bobby was just in time to catch a glimpse of some one vanishing amidst the ornamental bushes opposite. A swift mover, evidently.

Presumably it had been some one who had no business there and who had been startled by their appearance. Bobby glanced round the room. Evidently devoted to business and to business alone. Comfortably, even luxuriously, fitted up, though. An enormous writing-table. A silver inkstand with an inscription thereon. No doubt a presentation piece. Superb easy-chairs, magnificent alike in comfort and in size. A safe like a young strong room, so big it was, so ponderous its mighty door and sides. Over the fireplace— in it an electric fire pretending for some reason to be a log fire—a portrait in oils, life size, by a popular and much-respected member of the Royal Academy, of Mr Weston in his mayoral robes. In one corner another smaller desk, evidently for a secretary or typist. Telephones. One—a separate line—on the great walnut desk. One— an extension—on the smaller desk. On the floor a carpet into which the feet sank. Near the window the soft, seldom-trodden pile still retained the quickly fading impress of what might, Bobby thought, have been the heel of a woman's shoe. Impossible to be sure. The mark had already almost disappeared. He said to his companion:—

"Somebody just gone out in a hurry. Who would it be?"

But the question passed by the butler's attention as the butler's own recent remark had passed by Bobby unheeded. It was repeated now.

"You won't think it necessary to mention it, sir, I hope?"

"Mention what?" demanded Bobby. "That some one was in here and skedaddled in a hurry when we came in?"

As he spoke he moved to glance behind the great writing-table. It showed nothing out of place, no drawers left open, no trace of disturbed papers. He went across to the enormous safe, and found it securely locked. The butler, though looking slightly puzzled now, was too much engrossed by his thoughts and fears to do more than repeat for the third time:—

"You won't think it necessary to mention it, sir, I hope? Mr Weston would be much annoyed. As much as my place is worth, sir. He gave the most particular instructions, sir. A most unfortunate oversight."

"What was?" demanded Bobby.

"Mr Weston's instructions were most emphatic," the butler explained. "He said the young person was to be shown into the sewing-room. He wished her to wait there alone. And then William shows her into the small garden room. Mr Weston will blame me if he knows."

"Oh, yes. Will he?" Bobby murmured, finding this desire to keep Miss Bessie Bell in a kind of semi-privacy even more curious. Some sort of connection with that imperative summons to Bobby seemed indicated. All very curious, very curious indeed. "Who is William?" he asked.

"Our footman, sir," explained the butler. "Most incompetent," he added severely. "But owing to the war we have to put up with him. Both the other men on our staff have been called up. Mr Weston was refused exemption for them, though much of Mr Weston's business activities centre here." He paused for a sympathy he did not receive, Bobby failing to perceive that the loss of even two footmen would seriously impede Mr Weston's business activities, and not caring if it did. "And William," the butler went on gloomily, "has been directed to join the Home Guard, though that will interfere seriously with his duties." He sighed. "William," he announced, "is less a footman than a boot-and-knife boy masquerading as such. And I have told him so."

Bobby supposed the unfortunate William must—or must not—have been cut to the quick by this bitter saying. Deciding to drop the subject, since to say more would be a mere anti-climax, he repeated:—

"Some one was here when we came in. Who would it be?"

"In here, sir?" asked the butler. "Oh, no, sir. Mr Weston would be most annoyed—most annoyed." He repeated the phrase. Evidently to him the words spelt doom. Bobby was beginning to get the impression of a personality not only dictatorial but forceful—two things that do not always go together. Mr Weston was plainly a man who not only gave orders but whose orders were obeyed. The butler said: "It is clearly understood that no one is to enter the room until Mr Weston has finished work. No one could possibly be here in the absence of Mr Weston and the secretary young lady."

"Is that Miss Rowe?" Bobby asked. "She sits there, I suppose?" He glanced at the smaller desk in the corner. "Might not Miss Rowe have been leaving as we came in?"

"Oh, no, sir, quite impossible," the butler assured him. "Miss Rowe leaves at six as a rule, and this evening it was soon after five. She happened to mention, sir, she had asked permission, as she was going to the cinema with a friend."

"Oh, yes," said Bobby. "Yes."

A trifling incident, not in the least curious this time. No doubt dozens of secretaries and typists all over England had made the same request that same evening. None the less Bobby tucked the small incident away in his mind, more from habit than from any idea that it might be worth remembering, or indeed that there was anything to make it even remotely likely to be worth remembering. Only it was fairly certain there had been no visit to the cinema, since he had seen—or rather heard—Miss Rowe near the house not long before, and he remained convinced there had been some one in the room when the butler gave warning by his slow opening of the door, some one who had thought it wise to depart in secrecy and haste. Some one, too, who had apparently trusted to Mr Weston's dislike of any intrusion into this room during his absence for protection against interruption. Some one therefore who had knowledge of the household routine. Miss Thomasine Rowe, for instance? The butler was saying again in the same anxious voice:—

"You won't think it necessary to mention it, sir?"

"About Miss Bell?" Bobby asked. "Police never mention anything that isn't necessary. Mr Weston's instructions about Miss Bell aren't police business, are they?"

"Oh, no, sir."

"Well, then, that's all right. We don't talk about what's not our business. Where is Mr Weston?" he added, glancing again, and this time with less satisfaction, at his wrist watch.

"He is still at table, sir. With young Mr Weston Wynne."

This time Bobby was really annoyed. He had had no dinner yet, and was he to be kept waiting and hungry while another sat in calm digestion?

"Have you told him I'm here?" he demanded wrathfully.

"Oh, yes, sir, as soon as you arrived, sir."

"Then," snapped Bobby, "tell him again, and tell him I can't wait any longer."

The devout priest ordered to desecrate his own high altar could hardly have looked more aghast.

"Oh, Mr Weston wouldn't like that," he said, as if that were conclusive. "Mr Weston would not care to be reminded. As much as my place is worth."

"I shouldn't think it's worth much anyhow," retorted Bobby. "Not with any one like Mr Weston. Does he expect me to kick my heels waiting here while he finishes his dinner?"

"Oh, no, sir; it's not quite like that, sir," protested the butler. "The fact is, sir, in confidence, sir, dinner has been over some time, sir, but a very heated conversation is in progress. Between Mr Weston and young Mr Martin Weston Wynne. Very heated indeed, sir. Gave me quite a turn, sir, to see how the gentlemen looked at each other when I announced your arrival, sir. It was then I remembered about the young person and William, sir, always doing the wrong thing, sir."

Was this another curious incident, Bobby wondered, this coincidence of apparently a family quarrel with the summons here? Or was it no curious incident, but rather a normal one?

"Well, all that's nothing to do with me," he said. "They can have a rough and tumble for all I care. You can either tell Mr Weston that I am here and can't wait any longer or that I was here and couldn't wait any longer. Just as you like."

The unfortunate butler looked if possible even more aghast.

"But . . . but . . ." he stammered. "I assure you, sir, Mr Weston would be most annoyed."

"Inspector Owen is already most annoyed," retorted Bobby and made for the door.

He opened it. Behind him hovered a pale-faced butler, shocked to the marrow of his butlerian bones, and a trifle inclined to expect an immediate thunderbolt from on high. As Bobby, followed by his pale, protesting acolyte, emerged into the inner hall another door opened and out there bounced—the appropriate word—a young man, followed by another, much older.

Neither of them noticed Bobby. The younger man strode down the hall as the dawn is said to come up from Mandalay—that is, like thunder. The older man called after him. The young man turned. They faced each other, and one could almost see the mutual flame of fury pass between them. Rage itself made manifest, and yet neither spoke a word. Behind Bobby the butler scuttled away—again the appropriate word. One felt he felt he had seen something whereon no butler's eyes should rest. Bobby watched with interest. Two strong men face to face, and east or west or north or south, it's much the same when the strong and the violent are in taut, fierce opposition. The young man said softly:—

"If it's going to be like that, by God, I know what I shall do."

CHAPTER IV

BOBBY INDIGNANT

When he had said this the young man turned and went—still like thunder—along the hall and out by the front door. This he closed behind him with a careful restraint that somehow managed to seem more violent than ever could have done a mere banging.

The young man had been tall and slim and fair; good-looking, too, in the same so-called Nordic style that was also that of Bessie Bell. Physically, Bobby thought, they would have made a well-matched pair. The older man was tall, too, but of a dark complexion, and yet between the two there was a certain family resemblance, though again the elder had small, close-set, alert eyes of a curious and unusual greenish-grey tint, and the younger man's eyes were widely spaced and of a deep, dreamy blue. Both, however, had the same type of prominent nose with thin, clear-cut nostrils, and both had a small, pursed-up mouth with red, rather prominent lips. The young man, too, was clean shaven, and Mr Weston wore a small moustache, a close-cropped beard, nor was his a pleasant smile as he watched the young man go.

He turned to Bobby, and his smile became pleasant, amiable, kindly. A fascinating smile, it managed to convey the idea of establishing some-how a complete confidence and trust. Bobby felt its charm and felt himself instinctively on guard against it. It seemed to him to resemble altogether too closely the smile of one who was at the same time murmuring: "Will you walk into my parlour?" But it helped him to understand the current tales of Mr Weston's perpetual triumphs in the lists of love, tales that declared no woman could resist him for long, and that indeed few tried. Yet behind the pleasant smile seemed to lurk a steely and relentless energy that Bobby thought was apparent, too, in the alert, greenish-grey eyes. A strange dominating character, Bobby thought, and one that made of its own private individual will, its God. One, too, in whose way it would be always dangerous to stand, so that Bobby felt a challenge implicit in every atom of the other's personality. Yet there was still fascination and attraction in that smile of his as Mr Weston said:—

"Inspector Owen, isn't it? So good of you to come along. That young man was young Martin Wynne, a cousin of mine. Didn't like what I felt I ought to say to him. Oh, well, young men, you know, young men." He dismissed young men with a wave of his hand, at once authoritative, benevolent, and understanding. "Just come into my room a minute, will you, inspector?"

He led the way back into the apartment of the imposing walnut desk and the enormous safe. He motioned Bobby to one of the superb easy-chairs into which you sank as though never to rise again. He produced a cigar case and offered it.

"Help yourself, inspector," he said. "Take a couple. You won't often see any like them these days. Cost five bob each before the war. Unobtainable now. Luckily I laid in a store. Hoarding, I suppose."

He laughed pleasantly, still holding out the cigar-case, though Bobby made no attempt to accept his offer. Sitting as upright as he could in the depths of his chair, Bobby said:—

"Thank you. I don't smoke much, and never cigars."

Mr Weston gave Bobby a sharp, appraising look. He was not used to having his gifts declined, and was not quite sure what to make of the experience. From a lower drawer of the big walnut desk he produced glasses, whisky, soda water. He began to pour out the whisky.

"Say when," he invited Bobby cheerfully.

"Thank you," Bobby said, "but I am here on duty, and I never drink spirits on duty. I understand from your letter that you are in need of police advice or protection. May I ask you to explain?"

Mr Weston put down the glass he had already begun to fill. He leaned forward, staring at Bobby, and somehow there was apparent in that strong gaze all the formidable power of the man. Bobby stared back at him, meeting the other's gaze squarely. Mr Weston's prominent red lips parted in a faint smile, showing the strong, square, even teeth behind. One was reminded of a pike or a shark ready to swallow its next victim.

"I've heard of you," he said unexpectedly, "Isn't your father Lord Hirlpool?"

"No, he isn't," snapped Bobby with great indignation.

He had done his best to live down his connection with one of Britain's most impecunious peers. He hoped it had been forgotten. Intolerable to find it cropping up again. What business was it of Mr Weston's or of any one else if he had an uncle in the House of Lords—not very often actually in the House of Lords, though, for his respected relative was much too busy trying to make both ends meet to permit of his paying any marked attention to his legislative duties.

"A pretty close relative, isn't he, though?" Mr Weston persisted. "You are in the line of succession, I take it?"

Bobby squirmed. It was the secret dread of his young life that some day he might find a coronet clapped willy-nilly on his head. The thing might happen, though fortunately it wasn't likely. But in these days of bombs and sudden deaths more likely than it had been. And few know what a handicap a title can be to a man who has no money to support it. A Lord Hirlpool an inspector of police. Appalling thought! Bobby said stiffly:—

"My family affairs need not be discussed. I will ask you to be good enough to explain why you sent us the message we received this morning. I understood from it that you had something to communicate requiring police attention. What is it, please?"

"Well, I had something I thought I might want to tell you, but I'm not so sure now," Mr Weston answered slowly. "I've rather changed my mind. You know," he added suddenly, "I've heard of you. May be a peer some day and talk at times like an extreme socialist. Some of the County Watch Committee are a bit—well, worried."

Bobby nearly fell out of even that enormous chair, so surprised he was. He forgot even to be indignant. He said a little wildly:—

"Me? Me? Good lord, who told you that? I'm a policeman, that's all. Nothing to do with politics or social standing or anything else, only with the plain human values of the every-day man." He got to his feet. He said: "If you have anything to tell me affecting the King's peace or public security, kindly do so."

"Oh, it's not so simple as all that," retorted Mr Weston. "Sit down, my good man, and don't make a fool of yourself. I've a good many friends—some on the Watch Committee—and you might be wise to remember who you are speaking to."

"I am speaking," Bobby retorted, "to a citizen who has the same right, and no more, as has any other citizen, dustman or duke, to claim the help or the protection of the police. And that's all."

"I'm not much used to asking for help or protection," Mr Weston answered quietly, and Bobby felt that was probably true enough. "For my own reasons I wished for the presence here this evening of an officer of police. As things have turned out, your presence was not required. Which is not to say that it hasn't been useful—even very useful. If you feel your time has been wasted, I'm quite willing to pay for it." He peeled off a pound note from a fat roll he took from his breast pocket. "That makes it all right, I suppose?"

"If you mean," Bobby said, ignoring this, "that you have knowledge of a breach or threatened breach of the law and do not give information, you become an accessory before the fact. If you have no such knowledge and have simply brought an officer of police here for your own private ends, you have been guilty of something like a public mischief, for which, if it were worth while, you could be prosecuted. I will ask you to remember that for the future."

He began to move towards the door. Mr Weston, who by now was nearly as angry as was Bobby, called after him:—

"Young man, you'll hear more of this."

Bobby stopped and glared at him over his shoulder.

"I shouldn't be surprised," he said. "I think there is something decidedly queer going on here this evening."

"What's that? What do you mean?" demanded Weston.

Bobby hesitated, already a little sorry for what he had said. If he refused to answer, Mr Weston would probably question the butler, and most likely find out from that easily frightened individual, by life-long training prone to obey, about the meeting with Bessie Bell. If he did hear of it, Mr Weston would not improbably vent his anger on the unlucky butler for what had been apparently a breach of orders. Bobby had no wish to get the old man into trouble and so he said:—

"Well, it's nothing to do with me, but when your man showed me in here before, I think there was some one in the room who didn't want to be seen and who left by the window in a great hurry. That's all. I didn't see who it was, but it struck me as a little curious."

Mr Weston frowned. Bobby pursued his way towards the door. Mr. Weston said.—

"Wait a minute."

He went to the big safe, opened it and looked inside.

"You have sharp eyes," he said thoughtfully.

Bobby did not stop to ask him what he meant. He opened the door and went out. Mr Weston was apparently too interested in the safe and its contents to take any further notice of him. Bobby knew the way, though, and let himself out. His car was standing in the drive where he had left it. He got in and drove off, hungry and bad-tempered. He did not feel he had shone in the recent interview, and he had an uneasy feeling that it would have been wiser if he had stayed longer and tried to get a clearer understanding of what was going on. Trouble brewing, he thought, and even bad trouble. It seemed likely it was private ends Mr Weston had sought to serve by securing in the house the presence of an officer of police. What private ends, Bobby wondered? Private ends that needed the unexplained presence of police might easily become of public interest. Only at present there was nothing on which to take action. That of course was the classic difficulty the police were always faced with. Impossible to take action until there was something to take action on, and then it was too late.

He drove on. At a turn in the drive he saw some one come out from among the trees and wave to him to stop. He obeyed. A woman came quickly towards the car, and then paused and looked startled.

"Oh, I'm so sorry," she said. "I thought it was some one I know. It's getting so dark. I am sorry."

"Not at all," Bobby answered politely. A pleasant low voice, he thought. He could not see her plainly, for here under the trees the shadows were already heavy. But he had the impression of some one young; and, though he could not distinguish her features he none the less had the impression, too, that she was also attractive. Certainly her voice was pleasing, and she held herself and moved with a kind of lovely grace not even these dark shadows could conceal. Young and attractive, he told himself, and he remembered that Mr Martin Wynne had been young and handsome. At a venture he said:—

"Was it Mr Martin Wynne you were expecting? I think he left some minutes ago."

The girl drew back, plainly startled and a little confused as well. His had been a good guess, Bobby told himself.

"Oh, has he?" she said. "Oh, thank you. I'm so sorry I stopped you."

Bobby said it was of no consequence at all. The girl slipped away into the gloom. Bobby continued on his way. He caught sight of another figure slipping through the trees—a woman, too, he thought. Something secretive and furtive in her movements made him think vaguely that perhaps she had been following the girl who had spoken to him, perhaps watching her. He wondered why? He was aware of an impulse to stop, but did not and drove on. He had to call at headquarters again before going home, and already it was late. Besides, there was nothing he could do, nothing that warranted his interference. Yet stronger than ever in his mind was the conviction that there was mischief afoot.

Four women concerned in it, he thought. Bessie Bell, who had once been almost beautiful. Thomasine Rowe, of the strange, compelling voice. The unknown of the graceful bearing who had stopped him in error. This other he had just seen going silently on her secretive way.

He was aware of an impression that he was destined to know more of each of them.

His uneasiness translated itself into a rate of speed that out in the open road bright moonlight permitted, though behind him a thick bank of clouds was piling up that later broke into gusts of rain. Luckily for him these did not break over the city itself till much later—between three and four, when there was a deluge that lasted for a little less than an hour.

At last he was able to get home, where he found Olive engaged in what she always described as the normal job of a policeman's wife—that of watching her best endeavour in the cookery line slowly spoil because there was no one there at the proper time to eat it.

Very severely she asked him what new excuse he had to put forward; and he told her he had met three interesting young women, seen another he thought might prove more interesting still, and made an influential enemy. So Olive said it served him right if the influential enemy was a result of meeting three interesting young women, not to mention another who might prove more interesting still, because that seemed an excessive allowance for one day; and, anyway, why had he made an influential enemy?

Bobby explained it was a policeman's job to make enemies of crooks, and he rather thought he had that evening met an outsize in crookery—one of the formidable sort who keep within the law. Olive pointed out that crooks who keep within the law are no business of the police, but indeed often the stuff wherefrom are hewn the great and powerful. On which sage reflection they went to bed, to be awakened early next morning by the clamour of the telephone bell.

Bobby answered it and turned to Olive, who, anticipating the worst and no time for a decent breakfast, was already beginning to dress.

"I've got to hurry," he said. "Mr Weston has been found dead from a knife-wound in his study at Weston Lodge Cottage."

CHAPTER V
FAMILY PAPERS

BOBBY WAS not the first to arrive at Weston Lodge Cottage. He had been delayed on the road, and in any case had farther to go by a more circuitous route than those of his staff at headquarters whom he had summoned by 'phone.

Sergeant Payne, his most capable assistant, was already busy, measuring, examining, questioning. Finger-print and photographic experts were hard at work. A doctor was making a preliminary examination of the dead man's body. Constables were on guard. In fact, all the usual routine of an important investigation was in full progress.

In the household itself there was complete chaos, as was perhaps only natural. The women servants were having hysterics by turns in the kitchen. William, the footman so cuttingly described as a mere boot-and-knife boy having no right to call himself footman except as a war-emergency measure, hovered in the background, torn between excitement and fear and frequently saying "Coo" in shrill, subdued tones. Hargreaves, the white-haired butler, after a brief but stormy session with Payne, had locked himself in his pantry, which he seemed to regard as his sole protection against immediate arrest and execution.

Payne was very bitter, and expressed the most heartfelt wish that the butler could in fact be so dealt with.

He deserved it several times over, declared Payne fiercely.

"You wouldn't have thought it possible," he said to Bobby, who knew, however, that in this world no degree of stupidity is beyond possibility, or even probability. "The very first thing they did after the maid who found the body had had hysterics in the hall was to pull the knife out of the wound. After that they proceeded to carry the dead body into the next room. That white-haired old fool of a butler said it didn't seem right to leave the poor master all huddled up on the floor. Then it occurred to them they shouldn't have, so they carried it back again. I told the whole boiling what I thought of them," he added with a touch of gloomy satisfaction in his voice, "and now the butler's shut himself up some-where and the women are throwing fresh fits somewhere else. Believe it or not, they lost their heads to such an extent they don't even know for certain whether the french windows were open or shut. The curtains were drawn; they do know that much. But one of the maids says she thinks the butler opened the windows to let air in, and the butler thinks he didn't, and neither of them certain."

"Not too good," Bobby said. "Finger-prints all messed up, I suppose, on the knife?"

"I think every one in the house had a go at it, picking it up and handling it," Payne answered moodily. "It's on the desk there."

Bobby went to look. A Japanese weapon with a handle of carved bone or ivory. Bobby was not sure which. A deadly, business-like thing, admirably adapted for that work of killing for which it had been designed. Bobby found himself reflecting how different it was in its murderous efficiency from most Oriental weapons. Other Eastern peoples were apt to overload their weapons with ornament and fantasy, as though thinking as much of display as of war. Not so the Japanese. They thought only of killing. Well indeed had the weapon served its purpose this time.

Bobby tried the edge and then the point, examining them closely.

"Recently sharpened," he said. "Looks to me rather an amateur sort of job, too. You noticed? Only the point and a few inches above it have been seen to. All the rest blunt. Where's the body?"

"Next room," Payne said. "The doctor's there," and therewith he returned to his present task of measuring, comparing and recording the bloodstains near the safe.

Bobby went into the next room where the doctor was busy. He found it strange thus to meet in death the man he had seen so short a time before lusty in life and strength. The doctor told him death must have been nearly instantaneous. The blow had been dealt downwards, through the throat, behind the collar-bone, towards the heart. It had been delivered with great force. There had been a comparatively small issue of blood, and though the murderer's clothing would probably show stains, that might not be so to any marked extent. Death had almost certainly occurred about eleven or a little later, with a margin of error of about a quarter of an hour each way. He added a few more medical details, of little value to the investigation. Bobby asked if the blow could have been delivered by a woman, and the doctor looked startled, but said it was quite possible. Women, he said, in a moment of terror or excitement could strike with great force. And of course there were some women of very considerable muscular strength.

Bobby went back into the study, as the room Mr Weston had used was generally called, though business and not study was its purpose. He began to examine the objects arranged with the knife on the huge walnut desk. The ordinary contents of a man's pockets. Nothing at first sight to rouse special interest. Bobby noticed that the fat roll of notes he remembered was still there, still looking as fat as ever. Gold watch and gold cigar-case were there, too, so apparently robbery had not been the motive. For the rest, keys, a handkerchief, fountain pen, silver, copper, and so on, a wallet with letters which would have to be examined with other papers, and a small book, of a size to slip easily into a coat pocket. It was entitled "What It will Be Like", and Bobby picked it up to glance at it. Payne said:—

"Political, seemingly. By some one called Acland or something. Do you know who he is?"

"Member of Parliament, I think," answered Bobby, who had heard vague talk about a political movement called "Common Wealth"—one of many formed by those who search so eagerly for that new world which can come only from a new heart. Bobby knew nothing about it, whether it was "right", "left" or "centre". He had been far too busy since the outbreak of the war to have time to spare for any of the new movements of the day. He noticed that on the title-page was scribbled: "Please read and let me know what you think. Dan Edwardes." Turning over the pages, Bobby found many such pencilled ejaculations as "Rubbish." "Pestilent." "Rot." "Fiddlesticks." "Drivel." Occasionally the comments were even fiercer. In one place language seemed to have failed the commentator, and was replaced by thick underlining and a row of notes of interjection. This was against a suggestion that workers in a factory should be allowed to choose their own foremen from among themselves.

Bobby put the book down. "Mr Weston wasn't much impressed, evidently," he remarked. "Mr Dan Edwardes wasn't going to get a very favourable reply. I wonder who he is?"

Payne had no information to give. He was looking at that fat roll of notes, the gold watch and cigar-case. He remarked:—

"Did things in style, didn't he? I've an old aunt. She had a nice little business, and when she sold it she put what she got for it and all her savings into Weston West shares. Never had a penny of dividend, for years, and all she's got now is the old-age pension with what the rest of us can stump up."

Bobby hardly listened to a story too common in Midwych for it to attract much attention. He was looking at a tray on which stood glasses, whisky and soda.

"Been tested for dabs?" he asked.

"Oh, yes, sir," Payne answered. "Both glasses used. Dabs on both of them. On the glass to the left unidentified as yet, but apparently a man's, from the size. On the right those of Weston."

For in the compelling democracy of death, the victim had lost already even the common title of "Mr".

The telephone rang—the one on the desk, a private number not listed in the telephone directory and known only to Mr Weston's intimate friends and business associates. Bobby picked up the receiver and answered. A voice asked for Mr Weston. Bobby asked who was speaking, and was told that it was Mr Dan Edwardes and why didn't Mr Weston answer? Wasn't he there? Bobby, remembering the name on the title-page of the little book "What It Will Be Like", was interested. He answered cautiously—for he had no desire that the news of the murder should be spread too far too soon—that Mr Weston was not available, and was it anything important Mr Edwardes wished to say? In return he got a tart demand to know who he was and what business that was of his? He wasn't Hargreaves, was he? Who the dickens was he? And why, if he was neither Mr Weston's secretary or butler, was he answering on Mr Weston's private 'phone? Bobby asked for Mr Edwardes's number, received it, promised to ring again as soon as possible, and rang off while the other end of the line was still spluttering indignation and surprise.

"Short-tempered gentleman," Bobby remarked; and a constable came in to say that a young woman was there—a Miss Rowe. The women servants had apparently seen her arrive and had intercepted her. For some time she had been with them, hearing full details of the tragedy. Bobby, vexed, wanted to know why orders had not been obeyed and all newcomers brought to him immediately. He was told that Miss Rowe's approach had not been noticed. It seemed she had come by a private gate and path that—for pedestrians or cyclists—provided a short cut from the road to the rear of the house.

As this private way had not been known to Sergeant Payne or any one else—or to Bobby himself—it had not been under observation. A natural and excusable oversight, no doubt, but unfortunate all the same. Bobby had wished to observe for himself Miss Thomasine Rowe's reaction to the news and to hear what she had to tell him before she had had time or opportunity for reflection. Now she would have been able to consider well what to say. Her first impression, too, all blunted by chatter with the maids. All that might not matter, but then, again, it might. Bobby told himself that the inquiry was not beginning very well.

He went across to the busy finger-print expert, still working away with his gadgets in all likely and unlikely spots. He had secured a good many impressions, since the discovery of the murder had been made before the usual morning sweeping and dusting. Bobby thought probably his own would be among them. He asked about the safe. The finger-print expert shook his head sadly. The handle was covered with dabs, but so confused and so superimposed one on another that nothing of any use could be hoped for. Bobby tried the handle of the safe. It opened. So it had not been locked. Payne, still busy with his primary task of measuring and recording all bloodstains, looked up with a gasp, much taken aback.

"I never thought of trying it, sir," he said apologetically.

"Forgotten to lock it, perhaps," Bobby said. "I wonder. There's a gadget to hold the tongue of the lock back when required. Look at that," he added.

"That" was a small pile of bank-notes. Ten of them, and each for fifty pounds. With them was an empty envelope marked "Family papers re Aggie and child". Bobby looked at them with considerable interest and at the envelope with an interest even greater.

"Five hundred pounds is a nice little sum," he remarked, "but why had Mr Weston got it in his safe in notes almost as easily traced as a cheque, and why is the envelope endorsed 'Family papers'? Bank-notes aren't family papers. Is it a case of theft, only for family papers and not for cash? And, anyway, who is 'Aggie'?"

CHAPTER VI
LINES OF APPROACH

SINCE SERGEANT PAYNE had no answer to give to these questions, he proceeded with his general task of examining and reporting on the condition of the room. Since Bobby also had no idea even of the answers he expected, he went to the pantry, where Hargreaves had taken refuge from the hail of Payne's reproaches, and managed to coax the butler from that retreat.

Not that Hargreaves had much to tell. It was apparently the routine of the house that the domestic staff was expected to stop in its own quarters after about half-past ten, the hour when Hargreaves was accustomed to lock up. From this making secure for the night, however, the front door was always omitted, as were also, not unnaturally, the french windows of Mr Weston's study.

"But why the front door?" Bobby asked. "I can understand Mr Weston would see to the windows where he was sitting, but suppose there was a late caller? Did Mr Weston answer the door himself?"

Hargreaves looked discreet in that manner which implies that only the least encouragement is needed to make discretion change to the extreme of indiscretion. Bobby provided that encouragement by a sharp reminder that this was a case of murder and nothing must be kept back. So Hargreaves coughed and said it was the general gossip that Mr Weston occasionally received late at night visitors of whom he did not wish the staff to be aware. Bobby asked what sort of visitors, and after more hesitation and protestations of ignorance Hargeaves said he supposed sometimes it might be gentlemen on business and sometimes ladies on pleasure. But he didn't know. All he could say for certain was that on occasions there had been found in the study traces of powder, cigarette ends marked with lipstick, once a lace handkerchief, glasses to prove liquid refreshment had been partaken of, and so on. Naturally he had never allowed such matters either to be referred to by the other servants or to be mentioned by himself, knowing as he did that it was as much as his place—

"Quite so," interrupted Bobby. "Do you know the name of any of these visitors? Did any of them come last night?"

Hargreaves said he knew no names. It would have been as much as his place was worth, etc. The previous night he had gone up to bed immediately after half-past ten, as soon as he had seen to as much of the locking up for the night as he was responsible for. He had stayed up a short time, reading the evening paper, and he admitted that he had heard sounds which might have been Mr Weston moving about or might have indicated the arrival of a visitor. He had paid them no attention. Why should he? Then, just as he was getting into bed, about a quarter past eleven, he thought he had heard a cry or call. He was not sure. He went to the head of the stairs to listen. As it was not repeated and all seemed quiet, he went back to bed again. He had asked Mrs Parham, the cook, and she, too, fancied she had heard some one cry out about that time, but she had taken no notice and had gone to sleep again. Nothing to do with her, and Mr Weston not a gentleman to encourage any display of curiosity. None of the others had heard anything. Did Inspector Owen think this cry they had heard or thought they heard could have come from Mr Weston at the moment when he was stabbed?

Inspector Owen thought it possible, or even probable. Further questioning revealed that during the day the front door was never locked, and remained, in fact, unlocked and unbolted until Mr Weston fastened it before retiring. Hargreaves hinted that if Mr Weston was awaiting one of his late visitors, he would know exactly when to expect them and would be waiting at the front door, thus saving the necessity for any bell-ringing or use of the knocker.

Not much help in all this, Bobby thought gloomily, though it did seem to confirm the doctor's belief that death had occurred soon after eleven. It meant that ingress and egress were both equally easy until Mr Weston went to bed, which had not happened the previous night. There had been a late visitor, but nothing to show who it was. Payne's statement that nobody knew for certain whether the french windows of the study had been bolted or not, Bobby found to be correct. In the general excitement no one could be sure. After Hargreaves and William had carefully carried the dead man's body into an adjoining room—"as a mark of respect"—one of the maids had opened the window to "let out the smell of the blood". But whether she had had to unbolt it first she simply could not remember. Not that, Bobby supposed, the point was of much importance. Admittance might as easily as not have been obtained by the unlocked front door, and the murderer could have left that way with perfect ease.

Bobby went on to ask questions about Bessie Bell. It appeared that after Bobby's departure she had had an interview with Mr Weston, who himself had let her out of the house on its termination. Hargreaves had seen them cross the hall about nine, had heard Mr Weston say good night, and had seen him return alone. Becoming discreet again, Hargreaves admitted to an impression in the household that ladies who were thus seen out by the front door, sometimes went round to the study and were there admitted by the french window. Not that he knew for certain. It would have been as much as his place—

"Quite so," interrupted Bobby. "Did she come by car, or was she cycling or walking, or what?"

Hargreaves said she had come on a cycle, and he supposed she had so departed. But he did not know. Nor did he know whether she had used the front way by the drive or the private way passing the rear of the house.

Bobby reflected gloomily that it was wonderful how little people knew, especially when they didn't want to know too much. He was not sure that Hargreaves's innocent ignorance was not a little too complete to be true. Of course, the man might be a bigger fool than he seemed. But butlers are not generally fools—men, indeed, as a rule of a vast and varied experience.

Nor did Hargreaves know of any one named "Aggie". At least, not of any "Aggie" in any way connected with Mr Weston. But he did know Mr Dan Edwardes. Mr Edwardes had been at one time a frequent visitor to the house. Recently he had come less frequently. He was a large shareholder in, and a director of, the Weston West Mills Company. Recently certain differences had arisen between them regarding the management of the mill company. How serious, Hargreaves did not know. Until the outbreak of the war, Mr Edwardes had more or less retired. He had been content merely to attend occasionally the meetings of the board. Since the war became serious with France's sad acceptance of defeat, he had been more active. The war had brought him great suffering. He had lost three sons. One in France during the great retreat. One in Libya. The third and last had been shot down over Germany during an attack on Bremen.

"A changed man, they say," Hargreaves remarked. "I did hear say he had quite lost his mind. The poor master used to say he had gone crazy."

Bobby wondered whether the gift to Mr Weston of the little book "What It Will Be Like", which from the brief glance he had given it seemed to put forward some novel and even revolutionary ideas, was a sign of this change and a cause of the accusation of insanity. Anyhow, Mr Weston did not seem to have shared in his fellow-director's interest, to judge from the violent scribblings on the margin of "What It Will Be Like".

He told Hargreaves that during the time he and his assistants might be forced to remain in the house, he would like to make use of the small garden room in which he had seen Bessie Bell the day before. Hargreaves promised to see that that was arranged, and Bobby asked him also to request Miss Rowe to meet him there. Then a constable arrived to say that a Mr Martin Weston Wynne had just arrived and said he was Mr Weston's nearest relative in England. Bobby said he would like to see him at once and asked Hargreaves to explain to Miss Rowe. Then there appeared Payne, looking hot and excited. Closer examination of the study had revealed traces suggesting that some one had been hiding under the great walnut desk. Bobby asked what traces, and was told "Dabs".

It appeared that the finger-print expert, continuing his explorations and anxious to add to his bag, had tested the knee-hole of the desk. There he had found, with both pleasure and surprise, very clear and distinct "dabs" on the under-surface. Their position seemed to make it clear that some one had been crouching there, supporting him or herself in that cramped and awkward position—probably herself, though, since the space provided for the knees of a sitting person was only small—by pressing one hand against the panelling. Also the dabs, though not yet developed, were certainly small, and probably a woman's.

Bobby rubbed his nose and thought things were getting complicated. No simple case this. Apparently three lines of approach. First, some kind of family feud or quarrel, as indicated by the odd endorsement on the envelope that had presumably held the ten fifty-pound notes and possibly other papers as well, though the presence of bank-notes of such high value with "family papers" seemed hard to understand. Did it mean, Bobby wondered, some kind of blackmail that had taken an unexpected turn? Again, the terms on which Mr Weston and his young cousin, Martin Wynne, had parted might be another result of some family dispute.

Secondly, a second line of approach, might it be not a family but a business feud or quarrel, as suggested by Mr Edwardes's choice of so odd a gift to his chairman as the book "What It Will Be Like", that little handbook of revolution by consent, and possibly, too, by the quarrel with Martin, if Martin, now holder by Mrs Weston's legacy of a fairly large block of shares in the business, was inclined to back Mr Edwardes's new and disturbing ideas.

Finally, the third line of approach, Hargreaves's hints of discreditable intrigues, hints apparently confirmed to some extent by the unexplained presence of Bessie Bell the previous night and now by this odd tale of a possible hidden witness, who might be a woman, crouching beneath the great walnut desk. Possibly confirmed, too, by Miss Thomasine Rowe's early departure on pretext of a visit to the cinema that had apparently not taken place, since Bobby had his own ears to tell him she had still been in the vicinity of Weston Lodge Cottage at a much later hour. Could it be, Bobby wondered, that these were her finger-prints so curiously discovered in so odd a place? A very good bit of work, anyhow, Bobby decided, to the credit of the finger-print expert. Not every one would have thought of searching in so unlikely a spot.

All very puzzling, though; and now the next thing indicated was a talk with Mr Martin Weston Wynne, at present waiting in the garden room and simmering with only partially suppressed indignation because hitherto he had been refused all information, and even access to the room where the murder had been committed.

CHAPTER VII

BALANCE OF POWER

To THE garden room, accordingly, Bobby made his way, and found waiting there the same young man he had seen depart so much like thunder the previous night. Again he received an impression of a family likeness that resided more in a general resemblance than in any marked similarity of feature, and again he noted eyes that seemed in their softer, almost dreamy expression as though in some way withdrawn from those immediate surroundings on which the older man had seemed always so fiercely intent. A clever face, Bobby thought, with that broad forehead, and he asked himself what lay behind the dream eyes that flashed now as it were into sudden awareness and quick combat as their owner began to demand explanations and to be told what had happened and what right Bobby or any one else had to refuse him information.

A formidable young man in some ways, Bobby decided, as he parried these demands by explaining that as yet no one knew much to tell any one, and how had Mr Martin Weston Wynne heard so soon of what had happened? Martin retorted sharply that every one had heard of it. Why not? Was it to be kept secret? The news was all over the place. Twice he had been rung up to know if it was true. At his boardinghouse the milkman had told the servants, who had told all the guests, who had again all in succession told Martin.

Bobby sighed. Only to be expected, of course. Talk about the mysterious way in which news spreads through savage lands. Nothing, nothing at all, to the way news spreads through the English countryside. Fortunately he had taken his precautions, and the flood of newspaper men—already he could hear the trampling of the feet of the coming multitude—would be at least held up for the time.

"I understand," Bobby went on to Martin, "you are a near relative?"

"Not near exactly, though I believe I'm the nearest in England," Martin answered. "There are other cousins in Australia. I don't know much about them. I don't think Mr Weston kept in touch at all."

Martin went on to explain that he himself had never seen much of the dead man. Mr Weston was very much the rich man of the family, and riches divide. There had never been any disagreements to speak of, merely a drifting apart natural between incomes in five figures and incomes in three—and not very high in the three-figure column either.

Martin himself had managed to pay for much of his own education by winning various scholarships. Mr Weston, hearing of this, had given not ungenerous help.

"I know it sounds ungrateful," Martin went on, "but I think he looked on me as an investment, a promising investment. His idea was to train me to carry on the business. Only I didn't see much fun in running the Weston West Mills. I upset him pretty badly once by talking about Blake's satanic mills. Besides, I got interested in aero-dynamics." Martin's spare, lean face lighted up, so that for the moment it was almost as though he became a different man—"now, that is something for a chap to work at. I've ideas. Need time and money, though—lots of both." His expression changed again. "Uncle Weston didn't like it. I used to call him uncle though we are only cousins. He called me an ungrateful cub. I suppose perhaps it did look a bit like that. Anyhow, he got another chap in to train for the Weston West stakes—Jack Wilkie. I'm afraid that didn't work either. I heard the other day that he had quit, too. So I haven't seen much of Mr Weston for some years. I wrote once or twice, but he didn't answer, so I dropped it. Then I got my present job—I'm with the Wych General Aircraft people, in their research department. The stratosphere. I wrote to uncle again to tell him, and he wasn't too pleased. I heard he had made inquiries about my salary, and when he found it was only £400 a year he was rather disgusted and thought it a bit of a slur on the family. Some of the family would be jolly glad to have as much. Then aunt—Mrs Weston, you know: that's what I always called her—died and left me a big block of shares in the Weston West Mills Company. That rather brought uncle and me together again. Uncle was upset about it, though. He didn't at all like it. I mean, about the shares being left to me. I rather think he asked his solicitors if the will could be upset or the legacy cancelled somehow. No go, of course. Her property, and she could leave it where she liked. Besides, he got everything else."

"Was that what the quarrel was about last night?" Bobby asked. "You remember? I heard you say something about knowing what you would do, wasn't it?"

"I thought you were coming to that," Martin said gloomily. "I suppose it doesn't look too good if you have a flaming row with a man who is found murdered next day. Uncle wanted to buy those shares, and I wasn't parting. No reason why I should stick a knife into him because of that, though."

"Was that all?" Bobby asked, not quite seeing why a refusal to sell a block of shares—especially shares on which a dividend seemed a somewhat remote prospect—should engender so much heat. "Why did you say you would know what to do?"

"Well, he was making all sorts of threats," Martin answered slowly. "I don't know how far he meant them, but I got rather mad. Of course, he has a good deal of influence. I daresay he is in with some of our bosses, though I don't know. These big financial johnnies do rather hang together, you know, for fear of hanging separately, I suppose. Not that all that bothers us much on the science side. But I daresay he had thought up some scheme. He was always great on schemes."

"Are you sure there was nothing else?" Bobby asked, for he thought Martin was trying to evade giving a direct answer, that he was talking just a little too much, as if he had something he wished to hide beneath many words.

And now he saw Martin give him that swift, fierce look that brought out so strongly his otherwise not very noticeable resemblance to his dead cousin.

A young man of hidden strength of feeling, Bobby told himself again, of restrained passions of the force of which he himself might not be fully aware. Only what were they? Bobby wondered, and so far felt he had no answer. Martin was speaking again, slowly and carefully.

"What do you mean? What else?" he asked. "What else should there be?"

"Well, you see, that's what I was wondering," Bobby answered amiably, but did not press the point. Instead he asked: "Do you know a Mr Dan Edwardes?"

"Mr Edwardes is one of the directors of the Weston West Company," Martin answered, a little relieved, Bobby thought, at the change of subject. "I suppose he's the man you mean. What about him?"

"Did he and Mr Weston get on well together, do you know?"

"Well, just recently," Martin answered slowly, "Mr Edwardes has been taking more interest in the business. Before, he never bothered much. Only attended board meetings occasionally, and let uncle run the show his own way. Mr Edwardes has only two interests in life—cooking and Greek grammar. Bit of a mixture. If he shows in a London restaurant the whole place goes into a huddle to see he's satisfied. Generally he isn't. He is chairman of the kitchen committee of the Classic Club, and I believe their food makes the best French stuff look like coffee-stall provender. And he has written a pamphlet on the use of the past preterite—if I've got that right—in Greek drama, without which no scholar's library is complete. I did hear uncle Weston didn't half like it when he began to take an interest in the business, and I know he was a good deal upset over some of Mr Edwardes's new ideas. I think you should ask him himself for details if you want them."

"I'm told Mr Weston described Mr Edwardes as having gone out of his mind—being crazy, in fact," Bobby said. "Do you know anything about that?"

Martin smiled.

"Oh, that was only uncle's little way," he explained. "He always thought you were crazy if you disagreed with him. He called me crazy when I went in for aero-dynamics instead of business. I expect he called Wilkie crazy when he quit."

"You mentioned him before," Bobby asked. "Who is he?"

"Wilkie? Oh, he's a cousin, too. Only on the other side. Aunt's side. I knew him at Oxford. Clever chap. I don't think he was very keen on the Weston West Mills either, but he took it on when I quit. I suppose he couldn't stick it. I know he is out now, anyhow."

"Can you give me his address?"

Martin shook his head.

"We don't keep in touch," he said. "I expect he'll turn up when he hears about this. Sure to."

"You don't seem a very united family," Bobby remarked.

"As much as most, I suppose," Martin answered, frowning a little, as if he did not much like this remark. "It's not a very close connection anyhow. Rather distant cousins. That's all. I told you. Wilkie's on Aunt's side. I don't know what sort of relations that makes us. He and I never hit it off very well. We're not interested in the same things, and we never saw very much of each other, even at Oxford. He called me a prig and I called him—other things. I don't see why you want to know all this," he concluded resentfully.

"I have to know as much as possible about Mr Weston," Bobby explained. "I work in the dark till I have some knowledge of his life, his background, his habits. For example, have you any knowledge of personal enemies?"

"None likely to murder him," Martin answered. "Why should they? He wasn't popular, exactly, but you don't murder people because you don't happen to like them."

"Sometimes you do," Bobby observed thoughtfully.

"Oh, well," Martin muttered. He said uneasily: "I can't somehow realize it even now. Murder—well, it's incredible."

"Yes. I know. So it is," Bobby agreed. "Till it happens. Then it isn't any longer. Has Mr Weston ever said anything to you about a will?"

"Lord, no," Martin answered. "He wouldn't. If you are wondering if my name's in it you may be pretty sure it isn't. I should say very likely he never made one. He hated the idea of dying. Some people do. Wouldn't think of it. Some people won't. Odd, when we all know it's the one thing that's bound to happen. Now it has."

"If he died intestate," Bobby remarked, "you would be one of the heirs?"

"Well, yes, I suppose so," Martin agreed. "Doesn't take you long to think things up, does it?"

"It's what I'm here for," Bobby said mildly.

"Well, his solicitors will know," Martin said. "I don't. May have left it all to charity for all I can tell."

"Can you tell me anything about his personal habits?" Bobby asked next.

"Nothing," came the prompt answer. "I've been entirely out of touch with him for long enough. It's only because of getting a job near here that I've seen anything of him lately."

"You came to dinner last night?"

"He asked me. He wanted to talk about those shares I told you of. He wanted to buy, and I meant to hang on."

"Was there any special reason why you wouldn't sell?" Bobby asked. "I believe they don't pay any dividend—are they quoted on the Stock Exchange?"

"Oh, yes, about a penny each, I believe—no, it's more than that really, but not much more," Martin answered. He hesitated, and then went on: "Aunt asked me not to part. She left me a letter saying so. She thought it would be a check on uncle's doing quite what he wanted to. You see, they are ordinary shares, and carry voting power. That's all. Not much check, I'm afraid. But that was her idea."

"Couldn't you explain further?" Bobby asked. "I don't quite follow. Why did Mrs Weston wish a check on her husband? That number of shares wouldn't give control, would they?"

Martin gave Bobby another of those glances of deep, smouldering wrath that seemed to tell so plainly of strong passions held strongly in reserve.

"I don't see why you want to dig all this up," he said. "I don't see what it has to do with you. I suppose you could find out anyhow. It's a long story. Aunt got bitten one time with the Hitler bug. Thought it was wonderful how he cured unemployment, and why couldn't some one do the same here? So she tacked on to the Blackshirt crew, but of course, no decent-minded person could stand that lot for long. But she still worried a lot about unemployment. There was plenty of it round about here. Uncle told her it was part of the order of things. Good times, bad times, and one had to be balanced against the other. Sometimes a man made money and sometimes he lost it. Sometimes a man had a job and sometimes he hadn't. We all had to take it as it came, rich and poor alike. Aunt still thought it was worse for a man to go hungry than for a man to have to give up a Rolls-Royce for an Austin Seven. Then she got bitten with one of these new political fads. Some one she knew there told her about some new political movement—Common Good or Common Wealth or something. I don't know anything about it myself. Politics are mostly bunk. Anyhow, just before her death she sent a book about it to old Dan Edwardes, and he fell for it rather heavily."

"Was it a book called 'What It Will Be Like'?" Bobby asked.

"Oh, you're on that, too, are you?" Martin asked, frowning. "Know it all, don't you?"

"No," said Bobby. "There's a copy, though, in the study. Apparently Mr Edwardes sent it to Mr Weston."

"Oh, did he, though?" exclaimed Martin, surprised. "I expect that's what uncle meant when he called Edwardes crazy. I daresay the book is crazy, for that matter. I don't know. But I doubt if uncle would be impressed."

"He wasn't," Bobby agreed. "Not if the marginal comments in it are his. Do you think Mr Edwardes wanted to put the ideas in the book, whatever they are, into practice?"

"That's about it."

"But surely he couldn't without Mr Weston's full consent?"

"Well, you see," Martin explained, though with some hesitation, "that's where my block of shares comes in. The total ordinary share capital is £50,000 in one-pound shares. And it is only the ordinary shares that have voting powers. Uncle held twenty thousand. Old Dan Edwardes holds the same. Now I have five thousand. The odd five thousand are held in small lots by various people. That means, you see, that Mr Edwardes and I hold exactly half the votes. To balance us, if we came in together—I don't know that that'll happen: I shall have to know more about it—but if we did uncle would have had to get control of every single other share outstanding to stop us. Impossible, of course."

"I think I see," Bobby said. "Your holding gave you the balance of power in any dispute between your uncle and Mr Edwardes?"

"That's about what it came to," Martin agreed.

"What was at stake, then," Bobby said, "was the control of the Weston West Mills concern with all that that implies?"

"That's about it," Martin agreed reluctantly.

CHAPTER VIII

HIGH STAKES

IT WAS Bobby who broke first the heavy silence that followed on Martin's last remark. He said slowly:—

"High stakes."

"Money had nothing to do with it," Martin declared abruptly. "If that's what you're thinking, you're wrong. It wasn't money at all."

"What was it, then?"

"Power," Martin said. He got up and went to stand before the fire-place, his hands in his pockets, his eyes heavy and angry. "What uncle liked was running things his own way and seeing every one else did what he said. That's all."

"And Mr Edwardes?" Bobby asked.

"He hardly knows what money is," Martin answered. "He's always had plenty; it seems to him something that just happens, like a fine day. All he really wants is a library full of Greek grammars and a kitchen to play about in."

"He might miss money if he lost it, though."

"Not if you left him his Greek grammars and his pots and pans."

"They, too, depend on money," Bobby said.

"Oh, well," Martin said.

"What made the difference of opinion, then," Bobby asked, "between him and Mr Weston? Did he want power, too?"

"Lord, no. The last thing on earth he wants. Only he's changed lately. The war, I suppose. Woke him up a bit. He's lost three sons. None left. Enough to wake up any one, I suppose."

"A heavy loss," Bobby agreed. "But I don't see the connection. Why should it make him want to take over control of the Weston West Mills?"

"Oh, he doesn't."

"But you said—"

"What he wanted was to take the control away from uncle and hand it over to the workpeople."

"Oh, well," Bobby said in his turn. He added: "Pretty drastic."

"I've not read that book myself," Martin said. "'What It Will Be Like', I mean. But that's where Mr Edwardes got the notion. Common ownership, or something. I don't know. But I can't imagine anything more likely to upset uncle. Like asking a bishop to turn atheist. If uncle had murdered Mr Edwardes, you could understand it. Nearly. But not the other way round."

Bobby was still looking puzzled.

"If you mean some sort of profit-sharing scheme—" he began, but Martin interrupted.

"Oh, no," he said. "That wouldn't have bothered uncle a lot. There was something of the sort already. Bonuses. Rather complicated, I believe. Uncle was working out a scheme to extend it. Why not? It didn't matter to him. I expect he would just as soon have seen money going to his workpeople as to his shareholders. This cut much deeper. Mr Edwardes wanted the workpeople to have the right to choose directors among themselves by themselves. A majority on the board. The workers would have been giving orders to uncle then, not uncle to the workers. I don't know if it would pan out all right. Probably not. I don't know. I've never gone into it properly. I hadn't made up my mind which to back—uncle or Mr Edwardes. I told Mr Edwardes: 'Can you trust working-class directors?' He said: 'Can you trust capitalist directors?' I said: 'Well, we have to,' and he said 'Why?' and I shut up because I didn't know. But to give up control of his own mills—well, it meant death to uncle."

"So it seems," Bobby said.

"I didn't mean that," Martin exclaimed angrily and uneasily. "You've no right to catch me up like that. I only meant—"

"Yes, I know," Bobby said.

"What I'm trying to get at," Martin said, "is that you're all wrong if you think money had anything to do with it. I know it may sound a bit funny, but money never counted with uncle. He spent all his life plotting for it and scheming for it and working for it—getting it, too—and he didn't care a damn for it. What he liked was bossing people—and things. Making things happen the way he wanted. He wasn't the acquisitive type. He was the dominating sort."

Bobby nodded, for indeed this was the impression he himself had received. An arrogant man, who believed that others should be puppets to dance at his will.

"Nothing in all that to cause murder," Martin asserted. "A difference of ideas, that's all."

"I think," Bobby said, "more men have killed and been killed for ideas than for money."

"Oh, I don't know," Martin said, but looked rather taken aback.

"Ideology," Bobby went on. "Like this war. Ideological war—the boss idea, the Hitler idea, against the right of Tom, Dick and Harry to have a say. Mr Weston, the boss—for the good of Tom, Dick and Harry, no doubt—on one side, and on the other Mr Edwardes, not so much for the good of Tom, Dick and Harry, as for their rights. Reproduction of the Axis against the United Nations."

Martin left his stand before the fireplace and sat down. He looked troubled and somehow smaller. He said:—

"I was trying to show the Weston West Mills business couldn't have anything to do with what's happened. I only seem to have made it worse."

"You have opened up new possibilities, certainly," Bobby agreed, "but only possibilities."

"You had better see old Dan Edwardes for yourself," Martin told him. "Then you'll see how ridiculous it is to suspect him for even one moment."

"Oh, I daresay," Bobby agreed. "Only—well, murder is a crime apart. The motive for theft is always—theft. Simple. The motive for murder may be—ridiculous. When one man was asked once why he had poisoned his sister-in-law he explained that it was because she had such thick ankles. Why did Lizzie Burden kill her father and mother? Because she didn't like them? A ridiculous reason. You don't murder people because you don't like them. Or maybe it is love of—power. The murderer likes to feel himself a kind of god— able to kill or to spare."

"Does all that mean you think old Dan Edwardes murdered uncle?" Martin demanded.

Bobby sighed.

"I don't think," he complained, "I've ever had a case without it's being concluded that because I ask questions about some one, therefore I've made up my mind he or she's the murderer. I ask questions because I want to know the answers, not because I know them already. When a murder happens, every person who could physically be guilty has to be considered—including yourself and Mr Edwardes. Unless an alibi can be proved. And a good sound al- ibi is often highly suspicious. By the way, talking of ideas, you have ideas, too. About the stratosphere. Take a lot of time and money to work out?"

"A lot," Martin agreed steadily. "More even than the five thou- sand uncle offered for those shares of mine—cash down. Waved the cheque at me. I could have done with it. Not much, of course, but I would have taken it like a shot. Why not? Par offer, and the things quoted at a bob or two on the Exchange—when they are quoted at all."

"Well, then, why did you refuse?"

"Oh, I don't know. Well, you see, aunt asked me not to part. All the same, I was pretty badly tempted. That's why I lost my temper, I expect. I told uncle to go to hell, and he laughed like anything and said bad temper was a good sign of common sense returning. He thought it meant I was giving in, and he said I could have another week to think it over. That made me really mad. Five thousand pounds is a lot of money to turn down. Especially when you want it as badly as I do."

"But you still refused?"

"It's queer up there in the stratosphere," Martin said slowly. "Damn queer. At least, I mean you think it is. Once I thought I saw a great green land there, trees and people and little running streams, all bright and shining. You get light-headed. Lack of oxygen. Or too much. The queer thing is the pilot thought he saw it, too. Why did we both think we saw the same thing? Thought transference, I expect. Or else I started babbling and he heard and that started him off, thinking he saw the same. Another time I thought aunt was there—Mrs Weston, I mean. It's down in my notes. That's what I go up for. Notes, I mean. Atmosphere. Temperature. Resistance. All that. Another chap pilots, and I take notes. The odd thing is, I don't remember a thing about aunt. It's only that it's written down there, among my notes. Precise coherent details, and then a note 'Aunt here', and then more instrument readings, all quite clear and in order, and then 'Don't sell shares', and her signature. Shook me up when I saw it—shook me up good and proper. Couldn't believe it. In her own writing, or else a damn good copy. What do you make of that?"

"I suppose it could be said your sub-conscious mind was at work," Bobby remarked. "The shares would be a good deal in your thoughts, to sell or not. Your aunt's prohibition, too."

"Yes, I told myself all that," Martin agreed. "Only there's aunt's own writing. Her signature as well. If my sub-conscious mind did that, my sub-conscious mind is a good deal better forger than I am. I took the trouble to show it to a handwriting expert. He said it was undoubtedly genuine. Only it can't be, can it? I told uncle last night, and you ought to have heard him laugh. I expect you want to."

"No," said Bobby. "Very interesting. Outside my line at present."

"I suppose you don't believe a word of it?"

"Oh, I always believe what I'm told," Bobby answered. "Until I find reason not to. Do you know a Miss Bessie Bell?"

The abrupt question plainly disconcerted Martin. His expression changed. He hesitated, stared again, and did not speak.

"Do you?" Bobby repeated.

"If you mean the girl at the Wych Arms in town," Martin said, "I've been there sometimes."

"Did Mr Weston mention her last night?"

"No," Martin answered. He looked puzzled and uneasy. "No. Why on earth should he?"

"I believe Mr Weston's reputation in that way wasn't too good," Bobby said. "Wasn't there some sort of scandal that made Mrs Weston leave him?"

"I don't know," Martin answered. "I know there was a lot of talk and gossip. She never said anything and I didn't ask. So far as I know there's never been any talk about uncle and Miss Bell. I've always heard she has a very good idea of how to look after herself. Jollies you along so far and not an inch farther."

"So I believe," Bobby agreed. "It makes me wonder all the more why she was here last night?"

"Nonsense, she wasn't," Martin told him. "Rot! What gave you that idea?"

"Well, I saw her and spoke to her," Bobby answered.

"Oh, I didn't know," Martin muttered, and looked more worried and troubled than occasion demanded, or so Bobby thought. "Is that why you were here? Why were you here? I thought it was A.R.P., or something like that. Uncle's district warden or something, isn't he? Why were you here?"

"I don't know," Bobby answered. "Mr Weston gave up A.R.P. a long time ago. He asked me to call. Apparently there was something he wanted to tell us and then he changed his mind. I wasn't pleased."

"I don't know what that means," Martin said. "I don't understand. You aren't going to worry her, are you? You can't think she did it?"

"Well, it doesn't seem likely," Bobby agreed. "But you never know. The most unlikely person sometimes. You can't make any suggestion as to why Mr Weston wanted Miss Bell here last night?"

"No," Martin answered. "No more than I can guess why he got you along. Up to something, I expect," he added moodily.

"All the same, I should like you to think it over," Bobby said.

"Meaning you don't believe me?"

"Meaning that often when people try, they remember things they had quite forgotten till then. You see, your uncle asks you to dinner. The same night he gets Miss Bell here—and myself. There must have been some reason, and it does seem, doesn't it? as if that reason had some sort of connection with all three of us."

"Well, I don't know anything about it," Martin answered sullenly. "I daresay uncle had some scheme on. He was great on schemes. But I've no idea what he was up to this time."

"Well, think it over and see if anything strikes you," Bobby said.

He thought it as well to end their talk there, for he did not suppose Martin was in any mood to say more, and he knew by long experience that second thoughts often bring more readiness to be communicative. For he could not help feeling that Martin knew more than he had told. Nor did Martin succeed very well in hiding his relief in being thus dismissed. When he had gone Bobby sent for Payne.

"I've got a job for you," he said as soon as the sergeant appeared. "You'll hate it. A pub job."

Payne tried to look depressed and failed.

"You know the Wych Arms in town?" Bobby asked.

"I've heard of it," admitted Payne cautiously.

"The head barmaid there is a Miss Bessie Bell. I want you to find out all you can about her. And if she's on her job, I want you to notice if any one tries to talk to her privately—especially if it's Mr Martin Weston Wynne."

"Yes, sir," answered Payne. "There's always the 'phone," he added.

"I know," Bobby said. "Can't help that. Notice if she's called away to take a call. If she is and she goes out, follow her. What I want to know is if either young Martin Wynne or any one else tries to get in touch with her."

"Very good, sir," Payne said. "Miss Rowe is asking what she's to do and can she see you."

"I'll see her next," Bobby said. "Send her in, will you?"

"Very good, sir," Payne said again. "I've just finished looking through the safe, sir. I found this." He produced a document. "It seems a confession of forgery—forgery and embezzlement. £500. Signed by some one called Wilkie—John Weston Wilkie."

CHAPTER IX
SOMETHING WRONG

BEFORE BOBBY had time fully to take this in, before he had time to consider its import and significance, there came impetuously into the room a tall young woman of such dark, rich, passionate beauty as for the moment quite to take his breath away.

She was young, not far advanced in the twenties, with hair and eyes each of a depth of utter blackness to match the other, with clear-cut, well-formed features and a small red mouth, parted to show white even teeth behind the crimson lips. She seemed, by exception, to use no make up, even the rich crimson of her lips was evidently natural, and when she moved it was with a swift, untrammelled ease. The moment she spoke Bobby recognized the distinctive voice, low and slightly husky, in it an odd mingling of the compelling and the caressing, he had heard over the 'phone the day before. So he knew this was Miss Thomasine Rowe, Mr Weston's secretary, and Payne's startled and remonstrant "Miss Rowe" was not needed to identify her. Ignoring Payne, she swept as it were upon Bobby, intent and determined.

"I must know what it means," she told him passionately. "I can wait no longer, I can stand it no longer. Who killed Mr Weston? Why? Is it true? Is it—murder?"

She paused the fraction of a second before she uttered this last word. When she did speak it, she flung it out like some fierce challenge. When neither Bobby nor Payne answered, she said again:—

"If it's murder—is it murder? Then who is the murderer? Who?"

Again she flung the last word at Bobby like a challenge, or indeed like a defiance, and Bobby said mildly:—

"Oh, yes. Miss Rowe, isn't it? Won't you sit down?"

She took no notice. She stood there waiting, as it were dominating them both by the fierce intensity of her emotion. Bobby found himself remembering Bessie Bell, an odd contrast in her gold-and-white magnificence to this dark beauty. There was something about them, dissimilar as they were in their looks, yet something in their manner, in their being, in the atmosphere they made around them, that gave them, he thought, an odd mutual resemblance.

"Is it true?" she asked once more, "is it true he was murdered?"

"I am afraid so," Bobby answered. "Do you think there is anything you can tell us to help us to find the murderer? Won't you sit down, though?"

Payne had already pushed forward a chair for her, and now she accepted it and seated herself. More quietly she said:—

"It's so hard to believe. Why should any one kill him?"

"There again perhaps you can help us," Bobby said. "You were his secretary?"

"His private secretary," she explained. "There was Miss Kitson at the Mills. I never went to the Mills. I worked here. Mr Weston used to attend to most of his business here. I think it was only routine work that he saw to at the Mills."

"Yes, I see," Bobby said. "You would know more of his private affairs, then?"

"I knew what he chose to let me know," she answered, leaning forward in the eager, emphatic attitude that seemed characteristic of her, as if somehow she filled every passing moment with her own intense vitality. Bobby noticed now that she wore an engagement ring, a valuable-looking diamond on her left hand. She saw the direction of his glance, as she seemed to see most things, and she moved her hand and touched the ring with another finger as if to make it more noticeable. She went on: "Yesterday when I left he was alive and now he is dead—murdered. That's a word to get accustomed to—murder."

"More than a word," Bobby said gravely. "A deed. A fact. Can you suggest any reason? For instance, had Mr Weston any enemies?"

She answered at first by a long, sweeping gesture with one arm. It was as though she swept his enemies together and disdained them, but held them there for Bobby's inspection. Then she said:—

"He was a hard man, a strong man. Relentless. Nothing soft or flabby about him. He knew what he wanted and he took it as his right, and if you got in his way you got hurt, and if you didn't, you didn't."

"Well, it's he who got hurt this time," Bobby remarked, and she turned and stared at him with a kind of obscure menace, but did not speak. Bobby went on: "Is there any one in your mind? I mean, any one likely to go as far as murder? Have you ever heard any threats made against him, for instance?"

"I could give you a list as long as my arm," she said, lifting a long white arm in a gesture that suggested such a list would be indeed interminable.

"As for threats—" With another gesture she seemed to dismiss threats as idle, not worth notice. "But there's not one of them of all I know would have the guts. Murder," she said again, dark and sombre. "It's a word. Just a word. But it would make many afraid."

"So it would," Bobby agreed drily. "You can't help us, then? Do you know of any recent quarrel, for instance?"

"Oh, yes," she answered. "Quarrels. That's one thing. But murder—" the word seemed to have a fascination for her. "Isn't murder more likely to come from an old grudge than from a new offence? I should think murder's a thing needs time to work up to." She seemed to expect an answer to this, but Bobby did not reply. She went on: "Recently he has been furious with Mr Martin Wynne. That's a cousin. He's been here this morning, hasn't he? You've seen him. I take it you don't suspect him? Mr Wynne's head is always in the clouds. Literally. Above the clouds. He came to dinner last night, and I think they had it out. It was because of Mr Dan Edwardes. Now if Mr Weston had murdered them—the two of them—you could understand it."

"Oh. Why?"

"They were trying to get control of the Mill. At least, Mr Edwardes was. All Mr Wynne cares about is money to build aeroplanes to go higher than any one has ever been before. But Mr Edwardes had some scheme for turning the Mills over to the hands to run for themselves. Well, of course, that wouldn't have done. Chaos in a week or two and bankruptcy next. You couldn't expect Mr Weston to agree, could you?"

"Could he have stopped them?" Bobby asked. "I gather that with Mr Wynne's help, Mr Edwardes would have a voting majority."

"I'm sure," she answered, with her red lips parting in a disdainful smile, "Mr Weston would have been more than a match for the two of them—even if they did hold a majority of the shares. A boy who can't think of anything but what's up in the clouds and an old man who doesn't know anything about business or anything else." Again that scornful smile parted Miss Rowe's red lips and showed the white even teeth behind. "He wouldn't have needed to murder either of them," she went on, "though I think he might have done, perhaps, if there had been no other way. I don't know that I should have blamed him either. Self-defence, wouldn't it have been? Is it murder if it's self-defence? I don't think so. Haven't you a right to defend your own? The Mill, it was like his child. If any one tried to take away from you what you valued most—your wife, your child, if you have them—wouldn't you be ready to kill? Only, of course, that has nothing to do with it, because it is Mr Weston who has been— murdered." Once again she seemed to bring out the last word with difficulty, as if she found it hard to pronounce, as if it needed an effort, and yet forced herself to say it loudly and clearly. "So all that's beside the point," she said.

"Who is John Weston Wilkie?" Bobby asked.

"Mr Wilkie? Have you heard about him? He is a cousin, too. He had a good position in the business—at the Mills. Then Mr Weston hoofed him out. I think it was something about money, but I don't know. There was a scene between them and he went. He can't have anything to do with it either, because he lives in London now."

"We shall have to get in touch with him," Bobby remarked. "Perhaps we shall hear from him when he knows what has happened. Do you know what he does now?"

"I think he is on the stage—music-hall, rather. It is what they call a song-and-dance act with some trick conjuring thrown in. Something like that."

"Probably he travels about the country, then?"

"I don't know," she answered indifferently. "But I do know Mr Weston made him a small allowance, and I think he had to promise to stay in London or the south."

"Do you know if Mr Weston made a will?"

"I never heard of his doing so," she answered. "I don't think he would. You seem to think a private secretary knows it all. She doesn't. If there is a will, Mr Wilkie won't be mentioned, I expect. Or Mr Wynne either."

"If Mr Weston died intestate, they would both be likely to come in for a share, wouldn't they?"

"Mr Wynne might. Not Mr Wilkie. He is only a very distant cousin of Mr Weston's wife. She's dead, you know. There may be a will leaving everything to him, and that may be why Mr Wilkie murdered him. Or Mr Wynne. I suppose that's what you are thinking about them both. I don't think it's likely."

"I don't either," Bobby agreed, "but we have to consider everything. I'm afraid, Miss Rowe, I must ask you a somewhat intimate question. There seems to have been a good deal of gossip about Mr Weston's private life. Have you any knowledge of his relations with women other than his wife?"

Miss Rowe shrugged her shoulders.

"No," she said. "Of course, I know there was a lot of talk. Some one told me once there were illegitimate children of his in the cottages near here and in Midwych, too. He left me alone. He knew I was engaged." She showed her left hand where shone that valuable-looking diamond Bobby had already noticed; and for the moment her whole expression changed, softened, there came a new look into those darkly brooding eyes of hers, she glowed, as it were, with a kind of inner warmth, her whole body seemed to offer itself, yield itself to a deep, concealed emotion. "If he hadn't behaved," she went on "he would soon have needed a new secretary—and a little arnica and sticking-plaster, too, perhaps." She flashed a look at Bobby, and half lifted that white, strong, shapely hand of hers, as if to intimate she could have used it with effect, nor was Bobby much inclined to doubt the fact. Then she laughed. "Just now," she said, "it is the employer who is afraid of getting the sack, not the secretary."

"I suppose so," Bobby agreed. "Do you know a Miss Bessie Bell?"

"No," she said. "I never heard of any one of that name. Why? Is she some one who was here last night?"

"Why do you ask that?"

"I'm not a school-girl," she retorted. "I know very well Mr Weston had women visitors. The servants were never allowed in this part of the house after dinner. Sometimes women came to dinner, and after they left by the front door he let them in again by the study windows. At least, that's the story. Nothing to do with me. He didn't tell me about that sort of thing."

"You left rather earlier than usual, didn't you, last night?" Bobby asked.

"Yes. Mr Weston told me I could. I wanted to go to the cinema. To see—" and she named a popular picture running at the time in Midwych.

"Did you go to it?"

"Yes, certainly."

"Did you go alone or with a friend?"

"Is this to see if I have an alibi?" she asked, looking amused. "Well, I have, fortunately. I went with Mr Franks. My fiancé." And again her whole being seemed suffused with a kind of soft, inner glow. "You can ask him if you like. He works for the Midwych Central Iron and Steel Company—that's why he is not in the army. He's not allowed—thank goodness," she added below her breath.

"I'll get in touch with him," Bobby said. "A matter of form. I'm sure he will confirm what you say. If any one suggests there is evidence you were back near here last night, what would you say?"

"That they were liars, and rather silly liars, too," she retorted promptly. "Why should any one say anything so stupid? How could I? I was with Mr Franks at the Super-Superb." She looked straight at Bobby, those dark, strange eyes of hers open to their widest, her red lips parted. "You don't think I came back here to kill Mr Weston, do you?" she asked, a little catch in her breath.

"We have to put all kinds of questions to all sorts of people," Bobby explained smilingly. "You remember I was saying just now we can't even take your visit to the cinema for granted. So we shall have to ask Mr Franks, and even then we have to remember that often a man will feel himself bound to back up a lady's story. Did you happen to see or speak to any one else, by any chance? Or is there any other confirmation you can think of?"

"Well, I suppose Mr Franks might have the ticket stubs still, if that's any good. And I told my landlady where I was going, and she heard me come in. It was rather late—midnight. Is that enough? Oh, and I remember Mr Franks saw a friend of his and went to speak to him. I kept out of the way. Mr Franks said they went the same way home, so we dodged into a covered doorway opposite to get out of the rain, and waited a bit till they had gone. You see," she added with that kind of warmth and inner glow which seemed to come at once to her when she spoke of her fiancé. "I don't think we were very anxious to talk to any one else. We don't get much time together. Ronald is often working late and Sundays, too. We just walked home together rather slowly after the rain stopped."

Bobby said he quite understood that with working hours so long meetings must necessarily be rare. He asked a few more questions on routine matters, and then let her go with the understanding that she was to remain in the house for the day in case her services were required.

"Mr Weston's solicitors have been informed," Bobby explained. "I'm expecting them any minute. They'll have to take charge till we know if there's a will and, if so, who are the executors. Most likely they will be glad of your help for a time."

She went away then, and when she had gone Bobby turned to Payne.

"Something wrong there," he said. "I can swear I heard her talking to some one—a man, I think—in the grounds when I got here last night."

CHAPTER X
STAFF UNDERSTANDINGS

At this Payne gaped, open-mouthed.

"Well, then," he said, repeated: "Well, then", and paused, uncertain how to proceed.

"Long before the murder," Bobby pointed out, looking worried. "When I got here first, as I was driving up the avenue."

"Still—" Payne said and paused again.

"Not evidence, anyhow," Bobby said. "She has a distinctive voice, and I am sure I recognized it. But then I had only heard it once before and that was over the 'phone. Good enough for me, but other people could say I might be mistaken. All the same, I'm putting her down in my own mind as a liar. But that's a long way from proving her guilty of murder."

"I suppose," Payne admitted reluctantly, "she may possibly have been hanging about for her own reasons and not wanted to say. Could she be one of Weston's fancy women on the prowl to see if he was carrying on with some one else?"

"Well, there's that," agreed Bobby. "Though she did strike me as being very much in love with her young man—Franks, didn't she call him?"

"Well, yes," admitted Payne. "I forgot that. Sort of all lighted up inside, she was, when she spoke of him. You know, sir," Payne went on reflectively, "I don't think I should much like to be that young woman's best boy."

"Why not?" Bobby asked, a trifle amused. "I can imagine any youngster as proud as a peacock to walk down Market Street with her and watch all the other men turn and stare. The women, too. I've not often seen a more striking-looking girl."

"Yes, I know. That part of it would be all right," Payne admitted. "I was thinking of the way she sort of lit up inside. Her life for his all right, but his for her. Give all and ask all and more. Totalitarian, if you see what I mean. Rather frightening, somehow."

"A fire not so much to warm as to burn, to consume," Bobby said thoughtfully. "Perhaps you're right. You're getting quite a psychologist, Payne."

Payne looked as if he were not sure whether this was a compliment or the reverse.

"Dangerous, that's what I should call her," he said. "Dangerous. Definitely. I wouldn't put it past her to stick a knife into any one who tried any funny work with her."

"Nothing to suggest any one ever did—Weston or another," Bobby remarked. "Besides, she's clearly all gone on her Ronald Franks young man. No one could sham the way in which she sort of glowed at his name. Must be a bit out of the way himself to make a girl like her feel like that. Even if Weston had tried it on, she would never have let it get far enough to make knifing necessary—a smack across the face, perhaps; and she looked hefty enough to give a good one, too. Still, I think it might be a good idea to look up Mr Franks, see what sort of a young man he is and if he confirms her story. Of course he will. After you've finished with Miss Bessie Bell. I very much want to know what she was really doing here and who it was spoke to her at the window while she was waiting in this room. Bad luck the heavy rain last night washed out the footmarks in the flower-bed outside. Better go ahead with all that at once."

"Very good, sir," Payne answered. "There's just one thing more. Constable Clerke has sent in a report."

"Clerke?" repeated Bobby. "Oh, yes. Old pensioner, isn't he? Called back for war service. Oldish man, rheumaticy, not very fit, a bit deaf, too. Isn't he down for discharge again?"

"That's the man, sir," agreed Payne. "No good at all, and isn't trying, either. He was on this beat last night, and his report is that there was some one in the lane that runs behind the grounds here. Nothing in that, of course. It's a short cut for a good many people—especially after closing time at the 'Green Lion'. Clerke says it was somewhere about eleven. He remembers hearing the church clock strike. So apparently nothing to do with the murder. He didn't see the chap clearly. Says seemingly the chap had dropped a torch and was groping about for it in the hedge and ditch by the side of the lane. He said something to Clerke about having hurt his eye, but Clerke didn't take any notice. My own idea is Clerke was afraid the chap was drunk and he might have trouble. Which there isn't if Clerke can help it. He's all for a quiet life and his discharge as quick as can be."

"Not much meat there," grunted Bobby. "When you get back see if you can get any confirmation. Not very likely you will. Oh, and warn Clerke not to say anything."

"No fear of his doing that, sir," Payne assured him. "I'll warn him all the same. All he wants is to keep out of anything that might delay his discharge."

Therewith Payne departed, on his way out pausing to send in to Bobby the old butler to be questioned afresh.

"Let's see, your name is Hargreaves, isn't it?" Bobby asked when the butler appeared. "First names?"

Hargreaves hesitated, coughed, and did not answer at once. When Bobby looked up in some surprise, he noticed, too, that this morning the man's hair seemed changed somehow—slightly muddied in tint, it now seemed, and less venerably white than before. He wondered what the cause might be, and Hargreaves said, still hesitatingly:—

"Well, sir, when applying for a situation, I generally give it as Thomas. Ladies seem to consider it more suitable."

"Do you mean it's not your real name?" Bobby asked.

"Well, sir," Hargreaves said again, looking a trifle red and embarrassed, "you see, sir, I was christened Lancelot Galahad. My father, sir, was a great admirer of the late Lord Tennyson. Ladies do not seem to consider it suitable for service."

"I don't see why," Bobby said gravely. "Two jolly good names if you ask me. Anyhow, if those are your right names—on your identity card, are they?—they had better go down. I wanted to ask you if you know the address of Mr John Weston Wilkie?"

Hargreaves shook his head.

"No, sir," he answered. "He's been left fully a year."

"Has he been back?"

"No, sir," Hargreaves said again and coughed. "I don't know if I ought to mention it, sir," he began hesitatingly, "but it was generally understood by the staff, sir, if I may say so, that the late Mr Weston made Mr Wilkie an allowance on condition that he remained in London."

"Why was that?" Bobby asked.

"Well, sir, it was generally understood by the staff, sir, if I may say so, that there had been a somewhat violent scene between the two gentlemen. It was generally understood by the staff, sir, if I may say so, that Mr Weston addressed extremely violent reproaches to Mr Wilkie and that in return Mr Wilkie threatened the late master with personal violence."

"Oh, yes," said Bobby interested. "What made the staff think that?"

"The assumption, sir, was based on a statement made by the under-housemaid, a not too trustworthy witness. I am inclined to doubt if it would be wise to attach too much credence to her declaration."

"Perhaps not," agreed Bobby. "What did she say?"

"Well, sir, if I may say so, I always make it a point to discourage gossip among the staff. It did, however, come to my knowledge that the under-housemaid informed others of the staff that Mr Wilkie had threatened—er—to repeat verbatim what the under-housemaid reported—threatened to slit the old geezer's gizzard. The exact significance of the words used escaped me at the time, but I have since gathered that they conveyed a menace of violence pushed to an extreme against Mr Weston's personal security."

"I think," Bobby agreed, "that's about what it came to. Is the young woman still here?"

"No, sir, she quitted our employment shortly afterwards in order to better herself. I am unaware of her present address. Possibly Mrs Parham, our cook, may be acquainted with it. But I don't think so. But if I may say so, sir, Mr Wilkie was a gentleman of somewhat theatrical tendencies. It is understood by the staff that he now occupies a leading position in a London theatre. I must say," added Hargreaves, suddenly becoming more human, "he and Miss Olga Severn could give a most amusing show—with him dancing fair wonderful and her taking you off a marvel and Mr Weston to his face like." Hargreaves paused and coughed. "It was generally understood by the staff that though the late master laughed a lot, he wasn't so pleased as all that, and it led to words between him and Miss Florence Severn, the young lady's aunt, she is, as he thought did ought to have taken measures against such."

"Did the young lady take you off, Hargreaves?" Bobby could not help asking.

"Most amusing in a way, sir," Hargreaves admitted, "but it was generally agreed by the staff, sir, if I may say so, that though certainly laughable, there was not the least resemblance. I can assure you, sir, much as I was entertained, I had not the least knowledge who the young lady was supposed to be taking off."

"Do you think Mr Weston took seriously Mr Wilkie's threats?"

"It was generally considered by the staff, I believe, that the late master was to some extent disturbed by Mr Wilkie's observations. It was thought probable that that accounted for the suggestion that Mr Wilkie should not come north of the Thames if he desired to continue to receive a small remuneration sent to him at regular intervals. But the late master was of a somewhat nervous disposition. As you are probably aware, sir, he resigned his position as chief warden. It was generally understood by the staff, sir, if I may say so, that no opposition was offered to the acceptance of his resignation, as it had not been found easy to get in touch with him pending the cessation of the first air raid in our vicinity. You are probably better aware of the facts, however, than I am, as I always consider it my duty to discourage most severely any tendency to gossip among the staff."

"Very wise of you," approved Bobby, and Hargreaves looked gratified. "Er—if you should chance to remember anything else the staff understood, you won't forget to tell me?"

"Certainly, sir, I will be most punctilious in doing so," Hargreaves assured him, and, as Bobby said he thought that was all, he moved towards the door. With one hand on the door-knob, he paused and said: "I fancy, sir, I have observed that you have occasionally directed your attention towards my hair?"

"Well," Bobby admitted, "on our job one does get to notice things almost automatically, even when it's no concern of ours. I did think it looked a bit different somehow."

"I have regrettably omitted, sir," Hargreaves confessed, "owing to the general disturbance caused by recent events, to give it my accustomed attention. Ladies, sir, frequently display a preference for white hair in those holding a position as butler. It seems to be a general belief among ladies that a sense of responsibility and discretion is thus indicated. So it has been my habit, sir, to rub in each morning a certain—er—bleaching preparation, so to say, of my own invention. In my profession, sir, if I may say so, it is often necessary to play up to the gentry's most fatheaded ideas."

"I expect it is," agreed Bobby, quite fascinated by this glimpse into the technical secrets of a profession of which outsiders know so little. "Oh, by the way," he went on, "there's something else I wanted to ask. When I was leaving here last night a young lady stopped me in the drive. I couldn't see her very well, it was dark under the trees, so I can't describe her. She took me for Mr Martin Wynne, and when she found I wasn't, she faded away. Have you any idea who she could be? Probably some one living near here, as it was fairly late."

"I couldn't say, sir," Hargreaves answered cautiously, "but it is generally understood by the staff, sir, if I may say so, that Mr Martin Wynne has displayed marked signs of being attracted by Miss Olga Severn."

"The young lady who is a good mimic?" Bobby asked. "Who is she? Does she live near here?"

"She lives with her aunt, Miss Florence Severn, at Mayside, the house two or three hundred yards down the road from the entrance to our grounds. Miss Olga occupies the position of welfare officer at the Weston West Mills."

"I just wanted to ask her," Bobby explained, for he had no wish to have the staff "understanding" too much, "if she happened to notice any one else about here last night. Is she a friend or relative of the family, or how did she happen to get the welfare job?"

"It is generally understood among the staff," Hargreaves explained, "that Miss Florence wangled—begging your pardon, sir, the expression slipped out—I mean—"

"That's all right," Bobby interposed, "I get the idea. Is it generally understood among the staff how Miss Florence managed to wangle it?"

"Well, sir, if there's one thing I set my face against like—like flint," said Hargreaves, a little pleased to have hit on so admirable a metaphor. "Like flint," he repeated firmly, "it's gossip among the staff. But it does seem to be the general impression that Miss Florence was trying to get her hook into the old boy, and thought she had, too, but then he wriggled free, using the incident already referred to as an excuse. Great on dodges like that was the late master, sir."

"Did Miss Severn seem resentful or disappointed?" Bobby asked.

"Well, sir," Hargreaves answered, "I have no knowledge myself, and I make a great point of discouraging gossip, but I did hear that it was generally understood among the staff that she took it bitter hard—having made sure. Very hard indeed, sir, she took it. Yes, sir, very hard, and you may have heard it said, sir, hell hath no fury like a woman scorned."

Bobby put a hand to a puckered forehead.

"Yes, now you mention it," he said, "I believe I have heard that before. I can't think where."

"It's a quotation, sir," Hargreaves assured him. "From poetry, sir, and very true, too."

CHAPTER XI
REMINISCENCES

BOBBY WAS still sitting staring at the ceiling, asking himself what he had so far learned and what importance it had, and whether it, or rather some of it, was as significant and illuminating as it seemed, when one of his constables appeared to say that Mr Dan Edwardes had arrived and was asking if he could see the officer in charge.

So Bobby said certainly, he would be very pleased indeed to see Mr Edwardes, and thereon Mr Edwardes was shown in—a red-faced, bullet-headed, comfortable-looking man of about sixty or more, of benevolent appearance, dressed with a certain untidiness, wearing gold-rimmed spectacles with thick round lenses behind which two pale blue eyes blinked amiably. He reminded Bobby of a country clergyman whom no doubts ever troubled, who had no money troubles, who spent most of his time in the open air, probably tending roses in the vicarage garden.

"A terrible affair, inspector," he said as he came in. "Most distressing. Have you been able to throw any light on it?"

"There is very little we know as yet," Bobby answered.

"A burglar?" Mr Edwardes suggested.

"There is nothing to suggest that at present," Bobby told him; and was going on to ask one or two routine questions when the other interrupted him by saying:—

"Your name is Owen, isn't it? Inspector Bobby Owen? I've heard of you."

"Oh, indeed," said Bobby, slightly surprised, for though there were quarters in which he knew his name was familiar—and unpopular—he had not thought such knowledge likely to have spread into circles frequented by Greek scholars or by gourmets whose appearance in a London restaurant set the staff upon its mettle.

"Yes," said Mr Edwardes. "Yes. Of somewhat extreme socialistic views, I believe?"

Bobby fairly bounded in his chair.

"Good God," he spluttered, almost incoherent in his surprise and indignation. "Who told you that?"

"Bill Weston," answered Mr Edwardes, blinking behind his thick glasses.

"Well, I'm not," declared Bobby belligerently. "Nothing of the sort. I'm a police officer. A policeman has no politics."

"Don't you vote?" asked Mr Edwardes, blinking more mildly than ever.

"Of course I do. Why not?" snapped Bobby. "I suppose I've got a right to my private opinions. No police officer can take any open part in politics, and I haven't been to a political meeting since—since I was a uniform man and sent to one to keep fascists and communists from fighting each other. Though why fools and knaves shouldn't knock each other's heads off, I never knew. I can't imagine," said Bobby crossly "what put such a silly idea into Mr Weston's head."

"Possibly," observed Mr Edwardes, so mildly he might have been talking to a small and shy child, "it wasn't that so much as putting it into other people's heads."

"What on earth—?" began Bobby, bewildered now. "Well, why should he?" he asked.

"I've no idea," answered Mr Edwardes. "But I expect he had. An idea, I mean. A scheme. I don't think he ever felt quite comfortable unless he had a scheme to work out."

"But how in the name of all that's ridiculous," demanded Bobby, growing wrathful again, "could I come into any scheme he might have on hand, and what have my political opinions got to do with it? If I had any, which I haven't."

"Oh, I think you have," Mr Edwardes told him. "In fact, I'm sure you have. Every one has. Every one is born either a little conservative or else a little liberal. Isn't that how it goes? Too narrow a classification, of course. All the same, either you think things ought to be left alone, and then you belong to the right. Or else you think they ought to be changed, and then you're left. Or else you don't think at all, and then you're centre. Law of the human mind."

Bobby received this political analysis with a grunt and decided that he must pull himself together. He was beginning to perceive that this mild little man, blinking amiably behind those thick glasses of his, was managing somehow to lead the talk, whereas that was what Bobby himself was there to do.

"If you don't very much mind," he said with icy politeness, "we won't discuss political theory any longer. I believe you and Mr Weston were close friends and business associates?"

"No," answered Mr Edwardes. "Anything but. I've known him almost all my life. I've sat with him on the board of the Weston West Company for a good many years. I've never known a man less."

"How is that?"

"We had different interests. He despised mine. I cared nothing for his. He liked managing—things and people too. Running things. He ran them very well. In his own fashion. A remarkable man. Almost a great man. These have been difficult years in business, in textiles especially. I believe it was his intention to re-enter politics once he had Weston West and its subsidiaries firmly established. When he was in Parliament before he was not a great success. Too much the boss, too little time to give to it. If he had got in again he would have been a force—on the right."

"Is that why he was interested in my political views?" Bobby could not help asking, even though aware that once again Mr Edwardes was directing the conversation.

"I think perhaps it was because he had a use for you," came the unexpected answer.

"What?" gasped Bobby, even more utterly bewildered and also inwardly furious at the mere idea of any, one planning to make use of—him. Intolerable. "What use?" he asked feebly.

"I do not know," Mr Edwardes answered, "but I think if I did know I should know who killed him and why."

Bobby made an effort to recover himself.

"Look here, Mr Edwardes," he said, leaning forward and trying to speak with an impressiveness that he felt had no effect whatever on the mild little man before him. "I don't know what you mean, but I warn you if you know anything and keep it hidden, the consequences may be extremely serious. I must remind you that murder has been committed, and I must ask you to be more explicit."

"Inspector Owen," Mr Edwardes retorted, with just the faintest suspicion in his voice of an ironic reproduction of Bobby's warning tone, "I know no more than I have told you. Which is that Bill Weston loved to plot and scheme and that he had some reason for wishing it to be believed that you had socialistic views. I believe there is a general idea that when the present Chief Constable dies or re-signs, you will succeed him. If it was put into the heads of the Watch Committee that you hold extremist views—well, they may hesitate. In fact, it might then have depended on whether Mr Weston sup-ported or pooh-poohed the idea, whether you got the appointment or not."

"Mr Weston wasn't a member of the Watch Committee," Bobby said crossly.

"Mr Weston," Mr Edwardes said gently, "was seldom a member of the committees or other bodies which did what he wanted done."

"Wasn't he?" Bobby growled. "I'm beginning to think I had a motive for murdering him myself."

"Many had," said Mr Edwardes. "Myself, for example." He beamed on Bobby as he spoke, looking more than ever like a benev-olent vicar chatting to one of his more influential parishioners. "He tried hard to secure a hold on me. He thought he had succeeded. He was wrong."

"What sort of hold?" Bobby asked suspiciously.

"When I was young," Mr Edwardes said, and sighed. "A long time ago. It is pleasant to be young. At least, one thinks it is when one is old. A delusion, no doubt, but there it is. I was at Oxford. I became one of a somewhat—er—rowdy set." He sat upright, looked prim and yet regretful, too. "A very rowdy set," he said firmly. "On one occasion some of us became involved in an argument in a pub-lic-house, during which it appears a man was killed. Stabbed. My own recollections were and are extremely confused. Extremely so. I trust and believe the incident referred to occurred after I and my friend—or at any rate myself—had left. Efforts were made to trace us. They failed. Appeals were made to us to come forward. They were not answered. There was an inquest and an open verdict. The matter dropped, the more easily perhaps as the unfortunate man was of an extremely violent disposition and such evidence as there was showed that he had himself been using threats. He had been convicted of assault two or three times, he was known to have ex-pressed a willingness to 'swing for a copper', and I imagine the po-lice were not sorry to be rid of him. Bill Weston ferreted it all out and tried to use it to bring pressure on me. I pointed out that if at the time it had been impossible to trace any connection with me, it would be even more impossible after all these years. I reminded him of the laws of libel and scandal. The incident did not improve our relations. If you like, you will find full reports in the local paper of the time, together with some severe remarks on the conduct of young men believed to be Oxford undergraduates and present at the killing. I hope that is not true. I hope we had all left first. I don't know, none of us were at all clear next day about what had really happened. Myself least of all. It seems certain, though, that the knife with which the stabbing was done was one I had been using to cut bread and cheese for myself."

Bobby wondered what to make of this story and why it had been told. He said:—

"What use did Mr Weston want to make of it?"

"Well, you see, we had a serious difference of opinion. Mr Weston tried to use it as a threat to make me agree to his wishes. There was a deadlock. Solved now by his death. It seems almost providential."

"What was the difference of opinion about?"

"Business. The future of the Weston West Mills."

"But I understood you interfered very little in the business?"

"Hardly at all," agreed Mr Edwardes. "My interests were quite different. The study of Greek, for instance."

"I heard you have written a treatise on the use of the preterite, is it?" Bobby asked.

Mr Edwardes smiled with mingled tolerance and pleasure.

"Martin told you that, I expect," he said. "Martin, I fear, does not appreciate the interest, or indeed the importance, of my studies. The use of the preterite tense is of course extremely interesting, but it is the employment of the particle—but I shall only bore you if I talk about that. Martin thinks it important that men should fly ten or twenty miles above the earth. A singularly pointless proceeding, it seems to me. But Martin would give all he has—and all you have, for that matter, if he could get hold of it—to be able to do that. Now, the Greek use of the preterite, the employment of the particle, have their significance in grasping Greek thought, that is to say on all thought, for all thought comes from the Greeks, and thought is all that really counts in life—not flying a few miles higher or lower."

"Was Mr Weston interested?" Bobby asked.

"He thought us both fools. That made him angrier still when differences of opinion arose and when it seemed that Martin had the deciding voice."

"What caused this difference of opinion?" Bobby asked. "You had been on the board for a good long time, hadn't you?"

"Ever since my father's death," Mr Edwardes answered. "I had more than once wanted to resign. Bill Weston persuaded me to stay on. I was useful. I always agreed to everything, let him have his own way. Until recently. My father was one of the founders of the Japanese textile industry. I was born in Japan. My father used to call himself the Frankenstein of the textile trade. When the Japanese got rid of him when they thought they had learned all he had to teach, he came home. He had made a good deal of money. He brought back with him a good many curios of one sort or another. The attics at home are full of them. Including Japanese swords and knives."

Bobby looked at him thoughtfully and doubtfully.

"I suppose you know," he said, "that Mr Weston was killed with a Japanese knife?"

"It is why," Mr Edwardes answered tranquilly, "I thought it best to tell you."

CHAPTER XII
MISSING KNIFE

FOR A MOMENT or two they remained thus, Bobby and Mr Edwardes, looking at each other across the table, watching each other, Bobby puzzled and uneasy, Mr Edwardes blinking benevolently as ever behind those gold-rimmed glasses of his with the thick round lenses, and yet still with that faint underlying hint of an ironic detached amusement.

Bobby said presently:—

"Is one of these knives missing?"

"I don't know," Mr Edwardes answered. "After my father's death I cleared out a good many of his Japanese souvenirs. Then, a few years back, when the Japanese began to make themselves unpleasant, I had the rest packed away. In boxes in the attics."

"Hadn't you an inventory of some sort? Possibly for fire insurance." Mr Edwardes shook his head.

"Not in detail," he said. "So far as I know, there's nothing of any great value. Father was never a collector. He lived in Japan for thirty years, and things accumulated. That's all. I know there were swords and daggers. A suit of Japanese armour, too. Moth-eaten now."

"Is there any way in which you could identify your Japanese property? If I showed you the knife used in the murder, could you tell if it was yours?"

Again Mr Edwardes shook his head.

"I never took much interest in the things," he said. "Since they were packed away in the attics, I have never looked at them."

"I suppose you could tell if they had been disturbed?" Another shake of the head answered this. "Were the boxes or attics secured in any way? The boxes locked or nailed up or anything like that?"

"I'm not sure," Mr Edwardes answered this time. "I should think it unlikely. I never bothered. I just told the servants to clear the stuff out of the way upstairs."

"Apparently, then," Bobby said, "any one in the house could have helped themselves? Servants? Visitors? Any one?"

"Any one," agreed Mr Edwardes. "Including, of course, myself."

"Including, too," Bobby suggested, "Mr Martin Wynne?"

For once Mr Edwardes ceased to blink benevolently.

"Well, I don't know. Well, yes, I daresay," he answered. "Martin has been to see me several times recently. Once or twice he stayed to dinner. I suppose he could have slipped up to the attics some time and helped himself. I don't think it likely. Probably one or other of the servants would have seen or heard him."

"They might not have thought it their place to question the doings of their master's guest," Bobby remarked. "You agree it is possible?"

"Everything's possible," retorted Mr Edwardes. "I thought I might as well mention these Japanese belongings of mine. You would probably have found out in any case. I didn't know you were going to turn it against young Martin Wynne."

"Have I turned it?" Bobby asked. "I didn't know I had turned anything. I have to consider everything. By the way, who told you a Japanese knife had been used?"

"It was Martin," explained Mr Edwardes. "I met him on the way here. He was coming away from Mayfield. I suppose he had been to call there. I stopped, and we talked for a few minutes."

"Mayfield?" Bobby repeated. "Where the Misses Severn live? I understand there was some talk of a likely marriage between the elder Miss Severn and Mr Weston. Is that true, do you know?"

This time Mr Edwardes shrugged his shoulders impatiently.

"I don't know," he said. "How should I? No business of mine, and I don't go about collecting gossip. Bill Weston was an extremely wealthy widower and very likely there were various ladies in the neighbourhood ready to console him. I've told you before, we were not intimate. We had practically nothing to do with each other outside our business relations—and very little in business. To be quite honest, I wasn't much more than his rubber stamp. Until recently."

"Recently that changed?"

"It changed," Mr Edwardes agreed. "I had changed. A complete deadlock resulted."

"Now solved by his death?"

"Now solved by his death," Mr Edwardes repeated steadily. "By his murder you should have said, I think. I regard it as providential. Can a murder be providential? The deadlock was complete. Neither of us intended to give way." He paused for a moment and blinked at Bobby, no longer benevolently, now with such a hard resolve as seemed to reveal strange unsuspected depths, as though beneath the easy-going dilettante, indifferent to the outer world, absorbed in ancient questions of grammar, dabbling amusedly in the deeper mysteries of tastes and flavours, proud of the trivial recognition of waiters and *maîtres-d'hôtel,* there had always existed, there had now come to the surface, a steely and relentless will, one that would draw back before no obstacle, hesitate at nothing, know perhaps no scruple in reaching its determined end. While Bobby still wondered at this revelation of a new personality come suddenly into the light, wondered, too, at the unknown depths which may lie hidden in each one of us, Mr Edwardes went on: "I do not know what the issue would have been. I think it might have been disastrous for every one. Now it has been most happily solved. By this—murder."

He paused. As it were by magic that new self of his vanished, disappeared, was as if it had never existed. Once more there sat there, no strong-willed aggressor fiercely set on his own way in defiance of all obstacles, but the mildly blinking, elderly gentleman so much resembling the easy-going country vicar chatting amiably to an influential parishioner. Bobby said presently:—

"I wish you would explain exactly what caused this change, this difference of opinion? It was concerned with the control of the Weston West Company, wasn't it?"

"Yes. Quite correct. Bill Weston and I had equal voting power. Martin held the balance."

"High stakes," Bobby mused. "I mean, the control of a company like the Weston West. Is it true you wished to give the mill-workers a share in the control?"

"No," said Mr Edwardes.

"But—" began Bobby.

"I wished them to have complete control," Mr Edwardes explained.

"That was going to extremes, wasn't it?"

"So Bill Weston thought," agreed Mr Edwardes grimly. "So he was prepared to go to any extremes to stop it. Literally. I was prepared to go to any extremes to put it through. Literally. He didn't take me seriously at first. Thought I was a little cracked. Inclined to pooh-pooh the whole thing. Then he found that Martin had more than half decided to back me up. That made him take it more seriously. He tried to get Martin to sell. He offered a big price. I couldn't match him there. At the moment I am very short of cash. My father got rid of all his Japanese interests when he left the country, but he left a good deal of his capital in Singapore and in Malaya. That will be all right again when the Japanese have been thrown out, but in the interval, things are difficult."

"Mr Wynne refused to sell, didn't he?"

"Yes. It was a big temptation. You see, it would have given him the money for some private experiments of his own, in the stratosphere. He is very excited about them. I don't know why, but he is. I think he would have accepted only for some experience he seems to have had up there."

"He told me about that," Bobby said. "It seems to have made a great impression on him."

"Quite easy to explain," Mr Edwardes said. "The sub-conscious mind. A magic formulae. Deep internal conflict between his wanting so desperately the money Bill Weston offered and his memory of his aunt's request not to sell. So up there, normal control weakened by lack of oxygen, his sub-conscious mind hit on the device of strengthening his resolution by giving him a message from his dead aunt, making it more realistic by forging her writing, with which he would be familiar. The sub-conscious mind seems to be capable of queer doings. I think that is a convincing explanation. Is it?" he concluded abruptly.

"Fortunately that's outside my province," Bobby said. "All I have to note is that for some reason, or none, Mr Wynne refused his uncle's offer and that Mr Weston was greatly angered by that refusal. You say it made the deadlock complete. I don't quite understand why. You and Mr Wynne had between you a majority of the voting power given by your holding of ordinary shares. Why a deadlock, then?"

"It wasn't so simple as all that," Mr Edwardes answered. "Weston was chairman for life by the articles of association, and the articles could only be changed by a three-fifths majority. Martin and I held only an exact half, and were only sure of a majority because it was impossible Bill Weston would be able to get all the other shareholders, without exception, every one of them, on his side, and get proxies from them all, again without exception. But it was equally out of the question for us to muster the three-fifths majority necessary. So he was secure in his position as chairman, and he could have used it, and would have used it, to wreck our plans. We might have forced through our idea of having the workers themselves elect a majority of the board. He told me he would at once sack any such directors. I said we would reinstate them by direct resolution. You can see the issue was clear-cut, battle joined."

"An awkward situation," Bobby agreed. "Now it has been resolved."

"By murder," Mr Edwardes said starkly; and took off those thick, gold-rimmed spectacles of his with their thick round lenses. Mildly he blinked at Bobby, whom now he could see only indistinctly. "Murder," he repeated as the door opened and Hargreaves appeared on the threshold.

He must have heard that word, so darkly ominous, but he gave no sign. Impressive, dignified, aloof, he stood there, and in that tense atmosphere both Mr Edwardes and Bobby turned on him startled, expectant, apprehensive looks. He said slowly as they held their breath to listen:—

"Luncheon is served."

CHAPTER XIII
THREE SONS

IT WAS AN announcement evidently welcome to Mr Edwardes, who rose briskly from his chair. Bobby, too, remembered vividly that his breakfast had been hurried. But he felt it would be wise to finish now this interview with Mr Edwardes, aware as he was of, and troubled as he was by, the impression the other gave him of a faint, sardonic irony that seemed to lie only half concealed in the mild blinking of eyes half hidden by those round, thick lenses. Suspicious was Bobby, too, that so much apparent candour might well hide many things not yet evident.

"That's very good of you, Hargreaves," he said quickly. "We shall both be glad of something to eat the moment we have finished our talk."

Mr Edwardes, who had already moved towards the door, turned back to his chair and sat down quietly.

"I forgot I was a man under authority," he said. "I might say under suspicion."

At this Hargreaves, already in the act of withdrawing, gave him a startled look. Bobby frowned. He thought the remark frivolous. Mr Edwardes saw both start and frown, and indeed Bobby was beginning to think those mild, blinking eyes saw most things. Mr Edwardes bestowed on Bobby one of his faintly mocking smiles, and to Hargreaves he said:—

"Don't look so surprised. I expect you are, too. Even more so. I imagine every butler's favourite dream is murdering his master."

"I trust, sir, I know my place too well," Hargreaves answered, cold and dignified rebuke in every tone of his voice. He said to Bobby: "Very good, sir. Fortunately it is a cold collation. Sandwiches and—er—beer or tea as preferred have been provided for your assistants. I have Mr Anderson's authority. I believe Mr Anderson is already in the dining-room."

"Give Mr Anderson my compliments," said Bobby, recognizing the name of Mr Weston's solicitor, "and say we hope to join him soon. Say in any case I hope to see him before he leaves."

"Very good, sir," said Hargreaves, and withdrew, and Bobby said to Mr Edwardes with some vexation:—

"He will go off and tell every one you have been arrested. What's the idea of starting talk like that?"

"I hope it will remain talk," Mr Edwardes retorted. "Will it?"

"Not one moment after there's sufficient evidence to justify arrest," Bobby snapped. "You know perfectly well there's none at present. You have given me a good deal of information, though. I wonder if you can give me some more. Do you know anything about Mr Weston's relations with women?"

"Only that they were scandalous."

"Do you know a Miss Bessie Bell?"

"No. I have already told you we were not intimate. I couldn't help hearing some of the talk that went on. There was a lad in one of the cottages about here who was said to be a bastard of his. Others, I believe. He never took any notice of any of them. There were stories that sometimes he took a girl to Scotland and she thought they were married because he registered at the hotel as Mr and Mrs, and then afterwards she found they weren't. That kind of marriage by repute for visitors to Scotland, has been done away with long ago. A period of residence is necessary now."

"Yes, I know," Bobby said thoughtfully.

"The woman you spoke of just now—what was her name? Bell, was it? Was she one of his mistresses?"

"I have no reason to think so," Bobby answered. "She was here last night. I should like to know why."

"If Bill Weston has a woman here at night," Mr Edwardes retorted, "there's only one probable reason."

"Probabilities are often so deceptive," Bobby remarked. "Mr Weston got me here, too. I don't know why. Was there any connection? Mr Martin Wynne was here, as well. Three of us. For different reasons or for one reason? And had the different reasons, or the one reason, any bearing on what happened later?"

"I am afraid I can't help you there," Mr Edwardes said, "but I can assure you of one thing—Sill Weston never did anything without a reason, and that reason had always to do with some secret purpose of his own." He took off his glasses and polished them, looking absently at Bobby, whom now he saw as in a mist. "Is that all?" he asked. "Luncheon is waiting, you know, and you may be sure that even in present conditions, it will not be unworthy. I can picture the admirable Hargreaves appearing on the Day of Judgment to announce 'Dinner is served'."

"Well, there is one thing more," Bobby admitted. "I don't want to press you for an answer. But I do wonder why you seem to have gone out of your way to—well, almost to draw suspicion on yourself."

"Have I?" Mr Edwardes asked. "I didn't know. You were sure to find out. That's all. Everything I've said. Isn't it less suspicious to tell all at once than to let it be discovered piecemeal? I'm fairly certain you will find all details of that old undergraduate affair I told you about in Weston's papers. Otherwise most likely I should never have mentioned it. Isn't it wiser to tell what is sure to be discovered?"

"I suppose it is," agreed Bobby, but doubtfully, for he did not find this explanation too convincing. "I think I was wondering a little if you were trying to shelter some one else?"

"Good gracious, no," the other retorted, with again that gleam of sardonic amusement. "You credit me with too much chivalry, inspector, and I fear I find you too imaginative. Surely a policeman should keep both feet firm upon the earth?"

"Imagination is useful sometimes," Bobby said. "It may lead you to the wrong guess, but it may lead you to the right one, too."

"I suppose sympathy is useful as well," Mr Edwardes said. "I think sympathy is the trump card in your technique, isn't it? I wonder how much is genuine, how much is technique to make a suspect weep on your shoulder and weep out as well what you want to know. I think your sympathy is dangerous. But I'll tell you something. I didn't kill Bill Weston. I'm not sure I don't think killing him a case of 'killing no murder'. And if I felt sure that you would hang me, why then, I would confess to it here and now."

Bobby looked up, startled. Once again there had come on Mr Edwardes yet another strange and sudden change. But now it was a change from the comfortable and disillusioned, slightly cynical dilettante to the sad and aged man for whom no longer had life savour or meaning. Difficult to say, nor could Bobby ever tell, what made this change in manner or appearance, and yet at once it was as though sat there the very type and image of all the suffering of this tragic world of to-day, where evil things and grief walk hand in hand in all the places of the earth and where are many to whom indeed nothing has been left but their eyes to weep with.

"Only, you see," Mr Edwardes went on abruptly, "I know that I should never hang. Not a man who has lost three sons in the war. Broadmoor, perhaps, or prison for life. I dislike the idea. So I don't confess. Especially as I don't happen to have done it." He put on his glasses again and became his usual plump, cool, detached, ironic self once more. He observed thoughtfully: "I can't imagine why I never thought of it. I suppose murder is too far outside the range of one's ordinary ideas."

"I heard you had lost three sons," Bobby said, a little awkwardly, for he felt he had been given a glimpse into depths no other should have seen.

"Thank you," Mr Edwardes said, responding to Bobby's tone, not to his words. "I suppose it is what changed my ideas and brought me into conflict with poor Weston—one of us bound to give way, and each of us determined it must be the other. Well, that's settled now." He seemed to fall again into his brooding mood. "Weston couldn't understand. I mean, why it made me see things differently. Well, it did. Tony, he was my youngest boy. Why is a youngest boy so often one's favourite? The other two knew, but they didn't mind, because he was their favourite, too. He joined under the Militia Act—you remember? Just before the war began. Most of the other lads with him were from the East End of London. He used to tell me how ready they always were to help him out. You see, they knew all the things he had never heard of. All the same, he said they never gave themselves airs—treated him just like one of themselves. He made one special friend. It was a surprise to Tony to find this lad had hardly ever had enough to eat till he joined the army. His mother was dead, his father unemployed, so the children generally went hungry. When Tony came home on leave he told me he hadn't known kids in England could go hungry. I said I hadn't known either. Tony seemed to think I should have. He asked me to promise to do something about it. He and his friend were killed together in France, and the machine-gun bullets that killed them didn't notice that one had been to a public school and the other not much to any school because instead he had spent his time hunting through the garbage tins of cook-shops for scraps to eat. Their officer told me they were buried in the same grave. Wally, he was the eldest, had a commission. Most of the men in his platoon were from the Rhondda. Some of them had never done any work in all their lives—unemployed from leaving school. But they were quite ready to die for the country that had never let them work. So they did, all of them, and Wally with them, cut off in Libya covering a retreat. Wally's last letter said, didn't I think something ought to be done about it? Vivian, my second boy, was in the R.A.F. Shot down over Bremen. He used to tell me how the ground men nursed his machine. Like a young mother with her first born, he said. He said it was the ground crews won the Battle of Britain. He told me about the factories after Dunkirk, when men and women worked at their machines till they dropped and slept where they lay, and then rose up to work again. He said, oughtn't they to have a say in running the show who saved the country? Wouldn't I see to it? That was in his last letter. But I didn't know what to do or how. Then I came across a book some one had written. Very persuasive."

"You mean 'What It Will Be Like'? You sent a copy to Mr Weston, didn't you?"

"Yes. Do you know it?"

"I never heard of it till now."

"Very persuasive," Mr Edwardes repeated. "It came to me almost like an answer to what my boys had been thinking. Poor Weston was very annoyed. Said it was all humbug. Vote-catching. Impracticable. Worse. Anyhow, it would never work. I said: Let's try. I said you couldn't tell a thing wouldn't work till you tried. Weston couldn't understand it when I said profit-sharing schemes weren't enough. You see, it's not only a question of more wages, better housing. What matters is control, responsibility. God made man a responsible being, and Big Business has got to do the same. So that every last little worker can feel he's not only a means, but has a hand in shaping the end as well. But Weston wanted the end to be his end. He didn't mind working-men directors so much. We could have compromised there. He felt he could always handle them. Besides, he was always more than willing to give the exceptional man a chance to show his ability and use it for the good of the business. We wanted to put the ultimate power in the hands of the common man. As in politics. We've got that far in politics. Churchill has to answer to the dustman; and if the dustman isn't satisfied, Churchill has got to go. We wanted the managing director to have to answer to the man at the bench, and if the man at the bench isn't satisfied, then for the managing director to go. Control from below. That's the point. Economic freedom. Political freedom. One no good without the other. Together there's a chance. No, more. An opportunity. A hope. That's all. Well, there it was. A deadlock. If he gave way, he wasn't boss any longer. A fate worse than death. He said that. 'I would rather be dead,' he said. Now he is. If I gave way, it meant I let down my three dead sons. I didn't intend to. There it is. Irresistible force and immovable object. Well, it's settled now. How about lunch?"

"I think it would be a good idea," agreed Bobby, feeling he needed time to think over all the implications of this strange and not unmoving narrative.

They went out together to cross the large, spacious, pleasant, well-lighted inner hall. Looking round absently, Mr Edwardes said:—

"I used to think of myself as a looker on at life. A spectator. Addison's spectator. Now life has caught me up. A trick it has, I think."

Bobby hardly heard. One of his men, the finger-print expert, had come up to him.

"Beg pardon, sir," he asked. "Could I speak to you?"

Mr Edwardes went on towards the dining-room. Bobby said:—

"What is it? Anything important?"

The finger-print specialist was a little excited. He said:—

"You remember those two used glasses on a tray, as if Weston had been having a drink with some one last night? The dabs on one of them are identical with the dabs of—him," and he nodded as he spoke towards the retreating figure of Mr Edwardes, at the moment disappearing through the dining-room door.

CHAPTER XIV
HONEY AND STEEL

Forgetting stern domestic injunctions that this was a habit of which he must break himself, Bobby rubbed thoughtfully—and hard—the tip of his nose.

"How did you get his dabs to compare?" he asked, vaguely hoping, though he knew his "F.-P." man, that perhaps there might be a mistake.

"Door-knob, sir," came the prompt response. "I treated it. The room where you were sitting. I tipped off the chap at the door to make sure any one going in opened the door themselves."

"I see," said Bobby. "Good work." He said: "Means Edwardes was here late last night."

"Yes, sir, looks like it."

"Probably the last man to see Weston alive," said Bobby, "except the murderer."

"Except?" repeated the finger-print man, lifting doubtful eyebrows as he glanced towards the still half-open dining-room door.

"Can't take it as proved," Bobby said. "We'll keep it to ourselves for the present. Carry on."

Confident that all the required steps would be taken to preserve this evidence until it was needed, Bobby went into the dining-room, where Mr Edwardes was shaking hands with Mr Anderson, the lawyer. At the table, too, was seated Miss Thomasine Rowe by Mr Anderson's invitation, for Mr Anderson, sedate and elderly family lawyer, dry in manner as his own parchments, was none the less a bit of a rip at heart, and was aware, that if he were not a sedate and elderly family lawyer, dry as his own parchments, then it would have been exciting to go places side by side with Thomasine's dark and sombre beauty. All the same it was purely for reasons of business and convenience that he had asked her to stay on for a time to give him her assistance in clearing up the estate. He had also arranged for her to take up her residence for the time in the house, since it was desirable to have a responsible person in charge. So she was leaving her lodgings in a Midwych suburb, in the house of a jobbing carpenter where she had been well liked and had made herself popular by helping not only sometimes with the cooking, in which she was something of an expert, but also the carpenter himself in some of the small repair jobs with which he was overwhelmed. As in these days of war are most competent tradesmen not caught up in the huge machinery of total war.

Thomasine herself seemed as usual aloof from her surroundings, arrogant in a kind of spiritual loneliness, though a note-book by her side, open at a page covered with recent shorthand, suggested that till Mr Edwardes entered she had been interrupting her lunch to take down fresh instructions from the lawyer.

Opposite her was seated a pale, thin little man with a thin, long face and mobile, expressive features, at the moment displaying much satisfaction as their owner contemplated the well-filled plate Hargreaves had just placed before him.

Mr Edwardes introduced Bobby to the lawyer. A few appropriate platitudes were exchanged. Miss Rowe, without moving, without speaking, contrived to make it plain that none of these had any meaning, and that all their expressions of horror and of sympathy were purely conventional. She had an air of despising them for it as much as she despised the food on her plate, though this somehow was slowly and as it were indifferently vanishing.

The small, thin-faced stranger was introduced to Bobby as Mr John Weston Wilkie. He got up to shake hands, said in a hurried and uneasy voice he was pleased to meet him, and then resumed his lunch with vigour.

"A man must eat," he said apologetically, "even if poor old cousin Weston has got his. Shocking affair. I had breakfast somewhere about seven this morning. At a coffee-stall outside the Central Station. Only place open. Shocking affair," he repeated, though it was not quite clear whether he referred to the murder or to the breakfast.

Bobby took his place at the table. Hargreaves served him with decorous attention. Mr Anderson asked if he had made any progress towards the elucidation of this most tragic event, and Bobby could almost see Hargreaves making mental note of such an admirable phrase. Mr Edwardes, always with that same undertone of sardonic irony in his voice, said that Inspector Bobby Owen had already certain suspicions as well as a reputation to sustain. Thomasine withdrew herself for a moment from her secret thoughts to throw a glance of challenge and disdain, as much as to say that here was a problem such as he would never solve. Mr Wilkie handed his plate to Hargreaves for a fresh helping of cold beef and salad and looked dismayed when it came back with a minute portion of beef.

"I suppose there's a war on," he admitted grudgingly.

"Yes, sir, most regrettable, sir," Hargreaves said. "Dinner to-night will consist for all of fish cakes. Salt cod," he added to make it plain, and went on: "The salad, however, sir, is of a substantial nature, being composed in great part of cold potato."

"Cold potato," repeated Mr Wilkie and shuddered, but none the less addressed himself with renewed vigour to his plate.

Bobby, busy with his own lunch, asked Mr Anderson if there was a will, and Mr Anderson shook his head.

"I believe not," he said. "There is always the possibility, of course. My unfortunate client may have asked another firm to act for him in the matter, but I think it unlikely. I believe I may say we had the late Mr Weston's entire confidence. Or he might conceivably have attempted to draw up himself his testamentary dispositions. One has known one's clients to do the most extraordinary things. Extremely improbable, however, in my considered opinion. I have little hesitation in saying that I consider it so unlikely that I shall hold myself justified in acting on the contrary assumption. I often urged upon the late Mr Weston the advisability of considering the matter, but he procrastinated. He found, I gathered, the idea somewhat distasteful."

Thomasine returned to consciousness of her present surroundings to look coldly contemptuous of such weakness. Mr Wilkie said:—

"He hated to think he was ever going to die."

"To die is to lose all power," Mr Edwardes said. "That is what he feared."

Thomasine gave the speaker one of those swift, searching glances of hers, in which she seemed no longer aloof from, but most keenly aware of, her surroundings, as if in some queer way she gathered the moment to herself and held it so before again letting it escape. Below her breath, she said: "Yes, power," and then seemed to regret having spoken. Mr Anderson looked puzzled and said "Well, now then", twice over, as if desiring to point out that against death there is no court of appeal; and Hargreaves, lunch being now nearly at an end, appeared with coffee and apologies that saccharine tablets had to take the place of sugar.

An unsatisfactory substitute he pronounced it, and retired, and Bobby, glancing round the table at these people so peacefully drinking their coffee, found himself wondering afresh if he had eaten in company with a murderer.

More than probable, he thought, though as yet he only suspected, and did not know. He reflected that though his career had been varied, he did not think he had ever before sat at table, one of a company of whom one had as it were come straight from murder.

But then he reflected that very likely his suspicions were quite wrong and none of them had anything to do with it.

"Better coffee than the muck I got this morning," Wilkie said abruptly. "Glad of it, though. Soaked I was with that heavy rain. What I want to know is why Cousin Weston sent for me. Anderson says he doesn't know."

"You only got to Midwych this morning?" Bobby asked. "Is that so? When did you hear what had happened?"

"Anderson told me. He wrote to say Cousin Weston wanted to see me, so I came along. I went to his office first to know what was up."

"My late client," explained Mr Anderson, "was not aware of Mr Wilkie's present address. A small quarterly payment was due to Mr Wilkie, and was made by my firm on Mr Weston's account through the Chelsea branch of the Midwych and District bank. Mr Wilkie was accustomed to collect it therefrom, but otherwise there had been no direct communication for some time. Fortunately we were able to ascertain that Mr Wilkie was in Bristol."

"Cardiff," corrected Wilkie. "I had been in Bristol all right, but I had gone on to Cardiff—about a show. 'Miss and Death'."

"Miss—who?" Bobby asked, thinking he had not heard correctly.

"Not Miss who," Wilkie said. "'Miss and Death.' An act. Very well known. Tops the bill as often as not. Knife-throwing act. Ned Jones. He's the artiste, I mean. Calls himself Ivan Jonovitch now the Russians are so popular. Used to be Signor Jonselli till the Italians came in. There's his wife, too—if she is his wife. She's the target. It hadn't been going all that well just lately, so Ned wanted a partner to put up a song and dance and do patter to pull it together. Lend a hand with the knife-throwing, too."

"Are you good at knife-throwing?" Mr Edwardes asked.

"Not like Ned. His speciality. Only a side line with me. But I'm pretty good. Keep it up with darts. Make 'em open their eyes at the local sometimes." He smiled complacently. The smile vanished. He looked sulky as he added: "Anderson said I had better mention it. I don't see why. No one threw a knife at Cousin, did they?"

"I hadn't thought of it," Bobby said. "Hard to tell, I suppose. Does Mr Jones use a Japanese knife in his act?"

"He uses all sorts," Wilkie answered, looking sulkier still. "I don't know about Japanese. If he does, why shouldn't he? Anyhow, nothing to do with me. Only got here this morning. Train got in at four fifty. Hours late. I did a grumble to the guard and got ticked off. Told me perhaps I hadn't heard there was a war on, and I told him to cut out the smart stuff. I took a return ticket," he added, and produced it from his waistcoat pocket. "Because I didn't think Cousin Weston meant anything much."

"I had received," observed Mr Anderson, "a telegram from Mr Wilkie telling me to expect him this-morning."

"Waiting there when the office-boy arrived to open up," Wilkie grumbled.

"Mr Young, to whom I presume you refer," said Mr Anderson severely, "is not an office-boy. He is one of the senior members of our staff. He has been with us nearly fifty years."

"I half thought Anderson was ragging when he told me he had been rung up to say Cousin Weston had been done in," Wilkie continued. "Lots of people must have wanted to do it, but I never thought any one would. Murder. That's a bit stiff. After all, why should they? What about finger prints? That's how you track 'em down, isn't it?"

"Well, they are certainly useful," Bobby admitted. "But then, so are gloves, unfortunately. Besides, not every surface takes dabs readily, and some people have very dry skins and don't make dabs easily either. May I look at your finger-tips?" As he spoke he took one of Wilkie's hands and looked at it. "Normal," he decided, "but a bit on the greasy skin side. You would leave your prints all right on any suitable surface." He looked next at Mr Anderson's fingers.

"Yours, too," he said. "Rather more, if anything." Then he looked at Mr Edwardes's and hesitated. "I should say," he remarked, "yours is rather an unusually dry skin. In the ordinary way you wouldn't be likely to leave good prints—except, of course, on any specially suitable surface, smooth, polished, or anything similar."

Mr Edwardes made no comment. Lunch was over now and the party broke up. Mr Anderson took Thomasine into an adjoining room to dictate to her more letters. Bobby asked Wilkie to come to the garden room, as he would like a little further chat with him. Wilkie looked sulky, tried to make excuses, only yielded when Bobby made it plain he intended to insist. Mr Edwardes remarked that for his part, if the inspector had no objection, he would like to return home, and Bobby said that was all right as far as he was concerned. Mr Edwardes thanked him and said:—

"You know, I am wondering a good deal what was behind all that talk of yours about dry skins and greasy skins and looking at our fingertips?"

"Why should there be anything behind it?" Bobby asked, and Mr Edwardes twinkled at him from behind those heavy, gold-rimmed glasses of his and said it was his impression that there was generally something behind everything done by Inspector Bobby Owen.

"Oh. I don't know," Bobby retorted. "Why? Isn't it rather interesting that some people don't leave dabs very easily, at any rate in normal conditions?"

"Is it?" Mr Edwardes asked. "Do you know, I think you are a very formidable young man? Honey and steel," he mused. "A rare combination. A strong combination. I wish I knew what was in your mind. I think you don't give up very easily, do you?"

"Not when I am on the track of a murderer," Bobby answered, looking at him steadily.

CHAPTER XV

MOTIVE

WILKIE, WHO had overheard, though he had not seemed to pay it any attention, this brief exchange of question and reply between Bobby and Mr Edwardes, was looking very excited as he followed Bobby into the garden room.

"You think it's him?" he began, not even giving Bobby time to seat himself. "I shouldn't wonder. I expect you're right. I know Cousin Weston was pretty badly frightened of him."

"Oh. Why?" Bobby asked.

"Bats in the belfry," explained Wilkie, touching his forehead to make his meaning plain. "The poor old mucker has had all his three sons killed in the war. Hard luck. Pushed him over the border. Definitely."

"I didn't notice that he showed any signs of insanity," Bobby remarked.

"Loonies don't as often as not," Wilkie told him. "Have a gasper?" Bobby politely declined. "Don't mind if I do?" Bobby said not in the least. "Not gaspers at all," Wilkie explained, hovering on the verge of a wink. "Poor old Cousin Weston's special. Box in the dining-room. Helped myself. Why not? Poor old blighter hasn't any use for them now, and I have. I can tell you for a fact he was dead scared of old Dan Edwardes."

"What makes you say so?" Bobby asked.

"Oh, things I've heard," Wilkie answered, airily waving his cigarette. "Edwardes wanted to hand over the Weston West Mills to the workpeople. The whole shebang. Lock, stock, and barrel. Sort of monomania. Got it into his head he had to because of all his sons being killed. Plumb crazy. No connection. Cousin Weston wasn't going to stand for that, of course. How could he? But, if you ask me, old Dan let the idea work on him till he took this way out. At least, that's how it looks to me. Definitely. When I got Anderson's letter to say I was wanted again, I rather guessed that was the trouble. Cousin was scared of what old Dan might be up to next and wanted protection." The little man straddled before the fireplace and looked fierce and important. "If I had only come along at once I might have saved him."

"Do you mean," Bobby asked, "you think Mr Weston was actually anticipating that Mr Edwardes might attempt to murder him?"

"I expect so. Definitely."

"What I mean," Bobby said, "is: Is that just a general idea of yours or do you know any facts to support it, anything said or done?"

"Oh, well," Wilkie said, slightly disconcerted. "Pretty plain, if you ask me. Definitely. Look at the set-up. Cousin couldn't give way. Simply couldn't. Look what it would have meant. Whole she-bang messed up. Absolute ruin. Total. And old Dan gone off the rails with this idea of what his dead sons wanted done. Three sons killed, and killing in his mind. Definitely. Of course, he's looney. They won't hang him."

"You are going a little fast, Mr Wilkie, aren't you?" Bobby asked smilingly.

"Putting two and two together and making four, that's all," retorted Wilkie. "Definitely. Isn't that what you detective john-nies do?"

"Well, yes," Bobby admitted. "But we have to make sure that it really is a two we are adding to another two. If the two we thought was a two turns out to be another figure, the addition will be all wrong. I wonder how you know all this. I understood you and Mr Weston haven't been in touch lately?"

"Oh, well," Wilkie said. He threw away what was left of the cig-arette he was smoking and lighted another. "Oh, well, one hears things, you know."

"How?" asked Bobby in a tone that showed he expected a more precise reply.

"Oh, well, pal of mine," Wilkie explained, a trifle unwillingly. "We wrote sometimes. Not so often, but we did. He knew I had had a job at the Mills. Couldn't stick it, though. I'm an artist, not a busi-ness man. So I quit. Cousin Weston was mad, but I'm an artist, and I told him you couldn't make silk purses out of sows' ears, and off I went."

"I see," said Bobby. "Naturally, after telling him that. Who is this friend of yours?"

"I don't see what that has to do with it," Wilkie grumbled, but when Bobby still waited, looking very much as if he meant to know, Wilkie said sulkily: "Oh, well, if you must know, he's the Rowe girl's best boy. High stepper, that girl, isn't she?"

"You mean Mr Ronald Franks?" Bobby asked, expressing no opinion on Miss Rowe as a "high stepper" or otherwise, and in-wardly both surprised and interested by this fresh appearance of Mr Franks in the sequence of events.

"Know about him, do, you?" Wilkie asked. "Straight from him to me, straight from her to him. Good enough?"

"Are you an old friend of Mr Franks?" Bobby asked. "Was there any special reason why you and he wrote to each other?"

"No, no, just good pals," Wilkie answered airily.

"Nothing more? an old friendship?"

"You want to know it all, don't you?" Wilkie grumbled, and something in the tone in which Bobby said "Yes" made the other look a trifle less self-satisfied as he straddled there before the fireplace. "Oh, well," he said as Bobby still waited, "I asked him to tip me off how things were looking here. After all, I'm one of the family. I'm the only relative in this country, except Martin Wynne. Martin and him parted brass rags, but you never know. Martin was dead keen on getting money. Some wild-cat scheme or another he had on hand. Flying aeroplanes higher than they ever flew before. That sort of thing. Nothing in it, naturally. I just asked Franks to drop me a line from time to time to let me know how things were developing."

"Developing in what way?"

"In any way. If Martin was going back to a job at the Mill. If they were patching things up between them. Why not? Perfectly natural." "Oh, yes," agreed Bobby. "Perfectly."

"Martin wanted him to stand the racket for his aeroplane scheme," Wilkie went on. "Cousin wasn't having any. Definitely not. If old Anderson's right, and there's no will, Martin will get a cut. I shan't. Nothing in it for me. I'm family but not blood kin. But Martin will be on velvet." He paused and looked at Bobby. "There's a motive," he said, "if that's what you're trying for. You keep an eye on Mr Martin Wynne. No pal of mine. I could never stand him. Awful prig. Do anything for cash, though, to get his aeroplane scheme tried out. Inventors are like that. Definitely. I wouldn't forget that."

"I won't," Bobby promised. "Did Mr Franks, in his letters to you, say anything about Mr Wynne?"

"I don't think so. No. Martin's a deep one. Definitely. He was here last night. Did you know that?"

Bobby was about to say "Definitely", but checked himself in time.

"I did," he admitted; "but how did you know if you only got to Midwych this morning?"

"Oh, that was Hargreaves," Wilkie explained. "The world's No. 1 gossip. Has the wireless beaten to a frazzle when it comes to broadcasting the latest. You can't blow your nose in this house without Hargreaves knowing."

As if to emphasize his words he blew his own nose loudly, and Bobby expressed concern and hoped Mr Wilkie hadn't got a cold as a result of being caught in the rain that morning.

"Woke me up, it was so heavy," Bobby remarked. "Thank goodness, it wasn't time to turn out, so I could snooze off again. There's another thing I wanted to ask you. Do you know Miss Bessie Bell?"

"The girl at the Wych and Wych Arms? Yes. Why? Fine girl. What's she got to do with it?"

"Have you ever heard there was anything between her and Mr Weston?"

"Definitely, no," Wilkie replied, looking surprised. "Cousin Weston knew his onions O.K. when there was a bit of skirt in it. Deep as you like. But Bessie Bell, you had to mind your step with her. As jolly as you like, but just one inch too far and you got it in the neck. As like as not, you would be warned off the premises. Why, I've known a bloke who tried to get a bit too fresh—bloke in a big way, too, city councillor and all that—told not to show his face in her bar again for a month. He didn't either. Knew better. You can take it from me, nothing between her and Cousin Weston. He got 'em all right and plenty, but he didn't pick 'em up in pubs. No need to."

"Do you know Miss Severn?" Bobby asked.

"The old girl, do you mean? Set her cap at Cousin and made good running, too, till he turned her down. She won't be shedding any tears, if you ask me." He paused, frowned, lighted a fresh cigarette, said: "I wonder if that's it. I mean, did he turn her down because he had had all he wanted and then sweet good-bye? She's not the sort to take that lying down. Definitely. With that temper of hers, I wouldn't put it past her to slip a knife into any bloke who did her wrong, You find out what she was doing last night and if she was out late and why. There's a tip for you, inspector. Definitely."

"Well, now," Bobby said, "that's three tips you've given me. Mr Edwardes as out of his mind. Mr Martin Wynne as wanting his share of the estate for his aero-dynamic inquiries. Miss Florence Severn as the woman scorned."

Wilkie looked at him sulkily, not quite liking Bobby's tone.

"Well, why not?" he said. "Dan Edwardes has bats in the belfry. That's definite. Martin's next of kin or near and wants money the way inventors always do, and that's the way a mother wants her baby saved when the house catches fire. Of course, there may be a will and he may be out, and there are illegitimate kids, too, several of them if you ask me, but they don't count, do they? Not unless there's been a marriage he never let on about, and he was much too wary a bird to be caught like that."

"I'll have a search made," Bobby said. "Just on the chance. And Miss Severn?"

"Oh, well, that's only an idea. But it fits. You wait till you've seen her. Fine woman and hard as nails."

"There's a Miss Olga Severn, too, isn't there?" Bobby asked.

"Nice little thing, not much to look at, but she grows on you," answered Wilkie. "I thought Martin was keen on her at one time, but he has cooled off lately. Very likely she wasn't so keen on a boy with his head always in the clouds."

"I daresay not." agreed Bobby. "Oh, there's one thing more. I wonder if you would mind giving me a complete time-table of your movements from the time you left Bristol to visit Mr Jones of the 'Miss and Death' act in Cardiff till you reached Midwych this morning. A pure formality, of course."

"I don't see why I should," Wilkie said, flushing angrily. "I call that a bit thick. I'm not a suspect, am I?"

"If you were I certainly shouldn't say so," Bobby answered. "All I want is facts I can verify so that I can clear those not concerned. Definitely," he could not help adding, and wondered if he would ever get the word out of his mind again.

But Wilkie looked no whit appeased, looked indeed angrier and sulkier than ever.

"I don't think you've any right to ask any such thing," he declared. "I've my alibi all right. I was in the train all last night. You ask the guard. I expect he'll remember. Bit sharp I was with him. I've my return ticket, too. Date on it. There it is. Look for yourself." He flung it on the table before Bobby. "I don't see why I should bother with time-tables to please you, and I damn well won't. It's an insult."

"Sorry you take it like that," Bobby said equably. "Of course, you are within your rights in refusing. No one can be forced to answer questions they think might incriminate them."

"You've no right—" began Wilkie furiously. "It's not that—" but Bobby checked him with a gesture.

"One thing more," he said. "In going through the papers in the safe, we came across a confession of forgery and misappropriation of funds signed by you."

Mr Wilkie's mouth dropped open. He looked very disconcerted. He came away from the fireplace and sat down in one of those enormous chairs in which he seemed forlorn and lost.

"It's not true," he said weakly. "I mean, I never did. I mean, the old blackguard bullied me into signing it. Not a word of truth in the whole thing." His voice, so shaken at first, began to recover confidence. "There was money missing, but I never had it. A bit careless I may have been. I don't deny it. Trusting others. I hadn't had a penny. I swear that." He lifted a hand as if prepared then and there to take any oath Bobby might propose. He went on: "What could I do? He wouldn't believe me. I knew he was going to kick me out, anyhow. He made that plain enough. Brutal about it. A brute all through. He said he would allow me twenty-five quid a quarter if I signed. So I did. I thought a hundred a year was worth a signature. What about it?"

"Well, it did just cross my mind," Bobby admitted, "that the recovery of that confession might be a motive, don't you think?"

CHAPTER XVI
VANITY CASE

IT WAS a disturbed little man, a pallid little man, his forehead suddenly damp, his mobile features eloquently proclaiming sudden dismay, who now stood and stared at Bobby across the table in the garden room. He stammered something incoherently. Bobby said:—

"I wish you would change your mind about that time-table I asked you for."

"Look here," Wilkie muttered. "Now then. You don't . . . you can't ... I mean . . ."

He paused, he looked nervously, imploringly at Bobby. Bobby said:—

"Yes? Well? Don't? Can't? What?" Wilkie did not answer. More and more plainly his expressive features showed his alarm, his anger, his dismay. Bobby continued: "Well, about that time-table. It would help us a lot."

"All right," Wilkie muttered gloomily. "I don't see why." He began to sidle towards the door. "I'll do my best. You can't expect me to remember what I was doing every minute."

"Oh, no, no need," Bobby assured him. "Just the broad outline, as near as you can get it. If you don't mind letting me have it as soon as possible."

Looking gloomier and sulkier than ever, Wilkie withdrew. Entered at once, for he had been waiting his opportunity, the finger-print expert.

"Miss Florence Severn has just been here," he said. "You know, sir, the Miss Severn."

"I'm afraid I don't know," Bobby answered. "Why 'the'?"

"She's the lady golfer," explained the other; and Bobby, who had never indulged in that odd pursuit of little balls into little holes, tried to look impressed. "Won," continued the finger-print man, who, when he was not finger-printing, regarded golf as man's highest interest here below, "won the Wychshire Open Amateur in 1931, the only lady who ever has won it—at the nineteenth hole. Jolly good at tennis, too."

"The complete athlete," Bobby said. "What did she want?"

"It was about a vanity case a niece of hers had lost. She thought she might have left it here, and if we came across it, would we send it back to Mayfield, where she lives, close by. I asked the old butler bloke, and he said there was a vanity case in a drawer of the dressing-table in the little cloak room off the hall, though he didn't know how it got there. I thought I might as well test it for dabs." He paused dramatically. Bobby said: "Jolly good idea," and waited. The finger-print man said: "The dabs on the vanity case are the same as those on the inside of the kneehole of the study writing-table."

Bobby, startled this time, sat upright.

"Are they, though?" he said thoughtfully.

"Means," said the finger-print man, "means the young woman was hiding there, and what for? if it wasn't to slip out—and slip her knife in. That's how it looks to me."

"So it does, doesn't it?" Bobby agreed. "It's a complication," he said, half to himself.

"Dabs," said the finger-print man, awe and reverence in his voice. "Dabs—they tell you things, do dabs."

"So they do," agreed Bobby, even more thoughtfully. "They told us things about Edwardes, too, didn't they? I'll have to have a chat with Miss Severn."

There was still a certain amount of routine work to be attended to, but, as soon as that was finished for the time, Bobby walked down the road to Mayfield. He found it a small, pleasant-looking house, standing back from the road in a garden still devoted more to flowers and less to carrots, cabbages and turnips, than the really austere patriot could approve. A cardinal rule of police work—one that sad experience has bitten deep into every police force—is that no woman should ever be interviewed save in the presence of a witness. Too dangerous, otherwise. But Bobby felt he could pass off this particular call as one of ordinary routine rather than as an official inquiry. He knocked, and, when a maid opened the door, he explained he had merely called about a missing vanity case he understood one of the Misses Severn had lost.

He was shown into the drawing-room, a comfortable-looking, conventionally furnished room that at first sight seemed to offer none of those small clues to the characters of those using it for which it was his custom to look. He noticed, indeed, that the furniture, carpets, curtains', all had a well-worn and even shabby air, but then we are often told that in war-time it is our duty to be shabby. That duty had apparently here been well performed. He had not much time for such reflections. Almost immediately Miss Florence Severn came in.

She was a small woman, but of strong, compact build, and, though in these days it is often difficult to distinguish between the maiden of sixteen and the grandmother of sixty, Bobby guessed that she was most likely ten or fifteen years older than the thirty she seemed to wish to appear. Probably she had never been a pretty woman, for her features were large and irregular; and her too elaborate make-up deprived her, as it deprives so many women to-day, of all individuality and expression save for that indicated in the quick, eager, heavy-lidded eyes and the large, firm mouth.

No, Bobby decided, never a pretty woman, even in the first flush of youth, but a woman of will and determination. She showed, too, a well-balanced ease of movement that pleased, as it pleases to watch a leopard's sinuous walk, and that bore witness to those past athletic triumphs of the links and the tennis-courts. He was not quite sure why, beneath that heavy mask of make-up, in spite of the light and easy poise of her bearing, he sensed a profound unease, even a hidden terror, that only a strong will prevented from showing itself in panic. He thought possibly it was because of the impression she gave of an inner tension, of every faculty and power she possessed all summoned to her need. But what need, he wondered, and he wished that he could see more plainly her eyes so well veiled beneath such swollen, heavy lids. Recent tears, he thought, and all this make-up in part designed to hide them. But why should they be hidden? What more natural than that such a tragedy so near at hand, to a close neighbour, should produce the tribute of a few tears? He found himself thinking that perhaps she had worn this same tense air in the hour when she had won the Wychshire Open Amateur at the nineteenth hole. An absurd comparison, no doubt, for more was here at stake than any athletic triumph or defeat. He wondered, as these thoughts raced through his mind, what were her thoughts, for she had not spoken yet, and as she stood there in the doorway, his card in her hand, he knew very well that the eyes beneath those swollen, heavy lids were forming their own impression of him.

"Inspector Owen?" she said, coming forward from the door, where she had seemed to linger for the moment. "Is it about this awful thing that's happened?"

"A terrible affair, isn't it?" he said conventionally, still doing his best to co-ordinate impressions that he found in many ways contradictory.

"I can't tell you," she began and paused. He could see that she was trembling slightly. "Such a shock," she murmured. "You must excuse ... a neighbour ... a dear friend ..."

Again she paused. It seemed she was finding it difficult to control her emotions. Bobby uttered a few commonplaces. She said abruptly:—

"I think perhaps I ought to tell you. Mr Weston and I saw much of each other. Only two days ago, he suggested marriage. I asked him to let me have a little time before I answered."

"That must have made the shock of what has happened still greater," Bobby said with grave formality.

She sat down. She did not ask him to be seated. She seemed for the moment to have forgotten his presence as he stood watching her with grave attention. She put up one hand before her eyes as if to shut out some vision or some memory. Her lips moved, but what she said was inaudible. Bobby remained standing and waiting. He noticed her hand; a little large, well-shaped and strong, with strong, firm wrists. A hand that could, he felt, wield well a golf-club or a tennis-racquet—or even a knife, he thought. She looked up and said:—

"Please excuse me. Please sit down. This awful thing—I hardly know what I am doing—or saying. Have you found out anything? It's so difficult to understand. Or oughtn't I to ask?"

"It is early yet to be sure of anything," Bobby answered. "I really came about a vanity case."

"Oh, yes. Olga's; she's my niece. She had lost it. I thought perhaps she might have left it—there." She shuddered slightly, as if even this faint reference to the scene of the tragedy brought its memory back more vividly. "I thought I would ask. I think it wasn't only that. It was partly because I wanted ... I don't know what. I wanted to be near, I didn't want to stay away as if it all meant nothing to me." She seemed more composed now. She clasped those strong, shapely hands of hers across her knees and leaned forward. "I wonder if you can understand. He was so near to me, so very near, so dear. Yet I have no rights, no standing. None. For all any one knows we were just ordinary friends and neighbours. I wanted to ask if I might see him again, just once, the last time. I didn't dare. I asked about Olga's vanity case instead." Till now she had not used gesture and the profound emotion she so evidently felt she had been bringing more and more under control. But now her nervous agitation seemed to overcome her; and she began making quick, vague movements with her hands, shaking them oddly, so that a ring she was wearing, and that must have fitted loosely on her finger, fell to the floor and rolled away. Bobby recovered it for her. Valuable, he thought. Diamond and rubies. She thanked him and put it back on her finger. "I must have it altered," she said. "To fit. It's always doing that. I shall be losing it. He saw it and admired it, that's why I've begun to wear it lately. You know, I can't believe it's really true. I feel as if I shall never sleep again." She repeated: "I think I shall never sleep again. Have you found Olga's vanity case? They're hard to get now, and dreadfully dear. Like everything else."

"There is a lady's vanity case we've found," Bobby said. "Possibly Miss Olga Severn could identify it as her property. I hope she won't mind if we ask permission to keep it for a time."

"Keep it? Why?" Miss Severn looked puzzled. "It's nothing to do with what's happened, surely?"

"I shouldn't think so," Bobby assured her. "Most unlikely. Red tape, I suppose. Police have to work so much by official regulation. Do you know a Miss Bessie Bell?"

The question evidently surprised and startled her, puzzled her as well. She flung at him almost the first direct look he had received from those swollen, heavy-lidded eyes of hers; and he saw those strong hands of hers close tightly on each other in a grip that showed the knuckles white. She answered by another question.

"Who is she?" she said, and her voice was hoarse and thick.

"Well, you see," Bobby explained, "it appears she was present last night. I wondered if you could give me any information about her. If you had ever heard Mr Weston mention her. There's a suggestion that he had sent for her. If he did, I should like to know why."

"I have never heard the name," Miss Severn said then. "I don't think Mr Weston ever mentioned it. Business, I suppose. Why do you ask me?" Her voice was still hoarse and indistinct. She moistened dry lips. "I don't know," she repeated. "Who is she?"

To this question, shot out abruptly—fiercely, indeed—Bobby did not reply. He thought to himself that though Miss Severn might not know, she clearly suspected. Jealousy, he decided—a hot and angry jealousy. He wondered if in jealousy lay the cause and motive of the crime. But jealousy is a direct and simple motive, and in all this there seemed much else. It seemed to him too tangled a mixture of motive, doubt, and suspicion, for so simple and primitive an emotion as jealousy to be the explanation. Yet it might be.

"Bell? You said Bell? Bessie Bell?" Miss Severn was repeating, and once more she asked: "Who is she?"

"You see, what I want to know," Bobby explained, "is why she was there. Apparently she left early in the evening. Do you think there is anything else you can tell me that might help?"

He went on to ask some more questions. From her answers he learnt nothing that he had not known before. She had certainly been on close and familiar terms with the dead man, but there were things she was ignorant of. She knew little, for instance, of the threat that had apparently developed to his control of the Weston West Company. Bobby asked when Miss Olga Severn would be back from her office, and was told she had already returned.

"She is packing," Miss Severn explained. "She finds it too far here from the Mill. She is welfare officer at the Weston West Mills. I asked Mr Weston to let her have the post for a trial, and he did. Now she says she must be nearer, and she is going to lodge with one of the workpeople quite close. I think her idea is that then any of the girls who like can come and talk to her after hours, and of course it will save a lot of running to and fro."

Bobby asked if he could see her. Miss Severn rang for the maid and told her to tell Miss Olga the police inspector would like to see her. The girl looked very wide-eyed and excited and alarmed, and withdrew. A few moments later Olga Severn came into the room, and it needed but the first glance aunt and niece exchanged to tell Bobby that between them enmity ran like fire.

CHAPTER XVII
OYSTER

LIKE HER aunt, Olga Severn was small in stature, graceful and easy in all her movements, but rounder and less square in build. Like her aunt again, she had small claim to beauty; for her features were irregular in shape and too large for her small face, but she had the advantage of a clear, fresh complexion unspoiled by any excessive use of make-up, and there was about her a certain bright eagerness of expression, as of one who held out always open hands to life. She was dressed very quietly, and gave at first the impression of a demure, retiring, even insignificant personality, though closer acquaintance showed a firmness latent in the strong lines of the mouth and chin, in the direct and steady eyes, in the clear and even tones of the voice. Even-tempered and sensible, Bobby thought, and he wondered what deep cause made her seem now towards her aunt as one prepared both to parry and to strike.

Miss Florence explained who Bobby was. Bobby explained he had called about a vanity case understood to be Miss Olga's property. She agreed she had lost one, but looked both puzzled and suspicious when she was told where it had been found.

"I don't know how it could possibly have got there," she said.

"You must have forgotten it yesterday when you went to talk to Mr Weston about the works concert," her aunt told her shortly. "One of the servants saw it and put it out of the way till it was claimed."

"It wasn't yesterday, it was the day before when I called about the works concert," Olga said, still looking puzzled. "I know I've had it since."

"Well, that's where it was found," the elder Miss Severn insisted. "Some one picked it up. You know you are always leaving it about."

Olga did not answer this, but the look she gave her aunt was hard and challenging, and the look she received in return was like it. Bobby, who had risen when Olga entered, felt he was standing between two enemies, prevented perhaps only by his presence from displaying a more open hostility. He tried to relieve the tension by asking a few vague questions of small importance and then went on:—

"I'm wondering if I might venture to ask you two ladies to help us?"

"Yes, of course, if there's anything we can do," Miss Florence answered at once, but Olga was silent, looking distrustfully at Bobby.

"Well, it's like this," Bobby said. "I expect you know about finger-prints. Every one does. It's important for us to be able to sort them out and make sure which belongs to who. I wonder if you would very much mind if we asked to be allowed to take your impressions, so as to be able to classify and identify any we come across."

He looked amiably from one to the other, nor was it difficult to see that neither welcomed the suggestion. Not surprising, perhaps. A good many people seem to have an idea that the recording of finger-prints is much the same as conviction and sentence. Was it only fancy made him feel that this time for such objection there was a deeper cause? Olga was the first to answer.

"No," she said simply. "I would rather not."

A simple plain denial. No explanation or excuse offered. In harmony, Bobby thought, with a stronger will, a more clear-cut decisiveness of character, than was apparent at first in her quiet, reserved demeanour. A bit of a psychological problem, Miss Olga Severn, he told himself. Miss Florence broke in on his thoughts with a sharp refusal couched in the form of an attack.

"I think that's a most improper proposal," she declared; and now it was a little odd to see how these two, aunt and niece, so plainly hostile, ranged themselves on the same side, on the defensive. "I don't think you have any right whatever to ask such a thing."

"I asked a favour," Bobby protested, "I didn't claim a right."

"Well, I think it gross impertinence," Miss Severn told him. "I shall most certainly consent to nothing of the kind."

"Oh, in that case—" said Bobby and left the sentence unfinished. "Please let me say how sorry I am you take it like that." He looked at Olga as if inviting her to change her mind. She shook her head without speaking. Bobby made no attempt to press the point. He knew it was wiser not to insist too strongly at first. Better, having made a suggestion, to leave it to grow and fructify if it would. If it failed to do so, then, if necessary, pressure could be applied. He went on, still speaking directly to Olga: "Well, at any rate, I hope you won't mind coming with me now to see if you can identify the vanity case as yours."

"Is that necessary?" Olga asked.

"Well, you see, if it turned out not to be yours at all, that might be important, mightn't it?"

"Very well," she said then. "I will come if you wish it."

"Better put on your gloves," her aunt interposed. "They can get your prints from anything you touch."

"Oh, well, hardly anything," Bobby said smilingly. "In fact, not anything by any means."

"I shan't be a moment," Olga said.

She left the room and came back almost at once. She had provided herself with a wrap and was wearing one of those gay scarfs which seem of late in the feminine wardrobe to have replaced the hat. With some amusement Bobby noticed that she had taken her aunt's advice and had put on gloves, though he fancied somehow these were articles she often dispensed with. They left the house together, and Bobby had the idea that the older woman's gaze followed them with a kind of sombre triumph, as though in some way what was happening was happening as she desired, or even as she had planned. As they walked along, Bobby said:—

"I wonder if there is any chance that you will change your mind about letting us have your finger-prints." She shook her head. Bobby went on: "Well, I hope at any rate you won't mind my asking you a few questions."

"I suppose that depends on what they are," she answered stiffly. "Not if they are impertinent. I'm glad I'm not a policeman," she flashed with sudden emphasis that revealed again how much of will and of decision was hidden behind that quiet, almost demure exterior.

"You are a welfare officer, aren't you?" Bobby asked. "Isn't a policeman a kind of welfare officer, too?"

"Welfare officers don't go about prying and poking and questioning," she snapped, evidently indignant at the comparison.

"Don't you?" he asked mildly. "Well, then, I wish you would tell me how you get to the bottom of things? If one of your mill-girls is unhappy at her work, if there is malicious gossip going on, if things aren't running smoothly, how do you find out how to put them right, if you don't pry and poke and ask questions?"

"That's quite different," she told him still more indignantly.

"I wonder why?" he mused. "Much the same idea, I should have said. Something wrong and how to put it right. Except that this is murder," he said with a sudden sternness in his voice, "and murder is—well, murder. If murder goes undetected and unpunished, who is safe?"

"Oh, well," she said.

"Don't you think, then, I have a right to ask for your help?"

"But I can't help you; I don't know anything."

"People sometimes say that quite honestly when really they know a great deal," Bobby told her. "It was you who stopped my car last night?"

"Well?"

"You thought I was Mr Martin Wynne, didn't you? Did you want to know what had been arranged with Mr Weston about the shares in the Weston West Company? Or was it something else?"

"You must ask Mr Wynne. I'm not going to say anything about it."

"Saying nothing is sometimes saying a good deal," he remarked smilingly.

"I don't know what you mean," she answered, and did not smile.

"There's another thing," he continued. "I am wondering why you and your aunt have quarrelled so bitterly."

She stood still then, staring at him in great surprise.

"What do you mean? How do you know?" she demanded.

"Oh, my dear young lady," he answered. "I'm not blind."

"No, I think you see a lot," she said. "Well, suppose we have? People do quarrel, don't they? About nothing sometimes. It has nothing to do with—with what's happened. How could it? I'm going away. She'll miss what I used to pay. She has lost a lot of money through the war. I expect she'll be able to get some one else if she tries."

"You don't tell me much, do you?" Bobby remarked. "I still don't know why it happens that your quarrel with your aunt happens just at this moment. It seems, you see, as if there might be some connection." She shook her head once more. "That's what I should like to judge for myself," he went on. "If I don't know, then I have to guess. And when a policeman starts guessing, no telling where he'll stop." She remained silent. He continued: "Miss Severn tells me Mr Weston had proposed marriage."

"Told you—what? That he had proposed? Are you sure?"

"I am quite sure that is what your aunt said," Bobby replied. "She has not told you?"

"No," Olga said. "Did she say if she had accepted him?"

"I understood she asked for time to think it over."

Olga walked on, looking puzzled and thoughtful, evidently turning over in her mind a piece of news that a good deal surprised her.

"I knew they had been seeing a great deal of each other," she said presently. "My aunt has said nothing to me."

"Do you think it's true?"

"I suppose it must be, if she says so. Why not? It doesn't matter what I think, does it?"

"Do you know Miss Bessie Bell?"

"No. Why? Who is she?"

"She was here last night."

At that she gave him a quick look.

"I'm not a child," she said. "A welfare officer gets to know plenty. Is she one of Mr Weston's mistresses?"

"I don't think so. I have no reason to. Rather the contrary. Mr Weston's reputation seems well known."

"There's one girl at the Mill who is said to be his daughter. I don't know if it's true. The story is that her mother thought she was married because they went to Scotland together and then found it didn't count, somehow. Perhaps it's all a story. If it's true, it's beastly of him to pretend she isn't. I never saw anything like that myself. I expect I'm not pretty enough."

"He seems to have chosen a pretty secretary," Bobby remarked.

"Miss Rowe? Yes, she's lovely, isn't she? Have you been hearing gossip about her? You needn't believe it if you have. Thomasine's lovely, of course, and—well, Mr Weston is dead and I don't want to say anything about him, but that may be why he engaged her. But Thomasine is most awfully in love with the man she's engaged to, and I am absolutely perfectly sure she would soon settle any man who tried to be a nuisance. If Mr Weston did try, he soon found it was no good and gave it up. Even aunt was never jealous of her."

They had reached the house now. She identified the vanity case as her property at once, and insisted afresh that she could in no way account for its getting into the drawer where it had been found.

"I am sure I had it yesterday, and I wasn't near here yesterday," she said.

"Can't you make any suggestion where you might have left it?" Bobby asked once more.

She shook her head, but Bobby had a strong suspicion that if she had wished she could have made a good guess.

"I never did like oysters," he told her as she was going, "and from now on I shall like them less than ever."

"If you mean me," she retorted, "they used to call me a chatterbox at school, but no one has ever called me an oyster before to-day."

"Sometimes a chatterbox can be turned into an oyster," Bobby told her. "By fear, for instance—fear for itself or even by fear for another."

CHAPTER XVIII

PERFECT SECRETARY

Bobby, who had come to the door of the house with Olga to see her out, stood for a moment or two, watching as she walked away down the long drive. He noted that her shoulders drooped, that she walked slowly, that her air of brisk vitality had gone. He told himself that his questions had troubled her, and he wondered if presently she would think it wise to tell him why. A voice by his side said with a mingling of question and reproach:—

"You've let her go then, sir? Not good enough for a pinch?"

It was the finger-print man who was speaking, and he looked disappointed. Bobby said:—

"She knows a lot, but she won't speak."

"If you ask me," said the finger-print man, "she knows it all. Or why was she hiding in the knee-hole under the writing-table?"

"The set up is not complete," Bobby answered. "In fact, it's full of holes. You don't think a crossword puzzle finished when you've done one corner. Don't forget the dabs you found on the second glass. Mr Edwardes's."

"Oh, well," the finger-print man said doubtfully, "if you ask me, a man might easily drop in for a drink and then be scared to admit it when he heard there had been a murder; but why should a girl go hide under a writing-table? That's what I say. She slipped out, her knife slipped in, and there you are."

"It may have been like that," Bobby conceded.

The hour was late. Much had been done, much remained to be done. The rattle of the typewriter in a room nearby showed that Miss Rowe was still busy on the tasks the lawyer had left her. He was going, Bobby understood, to apply for letters of administration, as it seemed certain there was no will, and the only relative at hand, Martin Wynne, was more than willing for Mr Anderson to assume all responsibility.

Bobby went in to ask Miss Rowe if Mr Anderson had said anything about the probable value of the estate or how much Martin's own share was likely to amount to. Miss Rowe did not know exactly, but was certain that both the estate and Martin's share of it would be substantial.

"Mr Anderson thinks it will be divided among six of them," she said, "unless, of course, there is a will and it turns up in time, or unless he hears of some one with a better claim."

"Why? Who could that be?" Bobby asked.

She seemed to consider. Her fingers hovered over her machine. Then she said:—

"Mr Weston said something once that made me think perhaps he had been married before. It was when he was very upset when Mrs Weston left him before the war. It was something he said about a man being a fool to get married, and he ought to have known better, because once bit was twice shy. I wasn't paying much attention, and I'm not sure of the exact words. It wasn't anything to do with me how many times he had been married. But I did hear afterwards that he had gone to Scotland with some one and it was what they call an irregular marriage, and so it had never been acknowledged."

"Well, that's interesting," Bobby said. "It might be as well to have a search made just in case."

"Would that be any good if it was one of those irregular marriages?" Thomasine asked, looking interested.

"Makes it more difficult," Bobby admitted. "There's no necessary registration, of course. But a woman generally likes to have something to show. They can go before a sheriff or get themselves convicted in a police court—an irregular marriage is a civil offence and there's a small fine. Something like that. Or else the man might repudiate it. There must be some sort of proof of acknowledgement on both sides."

"Suppose she had letters mentioning their marriage and speaking of Mr Weston as her husband?"

"If they were written by him and accepted as genuine, that might do," Bobby said. "Or they might give confirmatory detail—time, place and so on. What matters is proof of consent on both sides."

"Suppose a woman wrote to a man calling him her husband and signing 'your loving wife' or something like that, would that be enough?" "I hardly know," Bobby answered. "Legal question. I should think it might do, provided there was proof the letters were answered without protest. Or even if the man kept them by him. But if Mr Weston were married before, then he committed bigamy when he married a second time, and I don't think that's likely."

"No," Thomasine agreed; "but the first wife, the Scots wife, might have died—in childbirth, perhaps."

"Yes, there's that," admitted Bobby thoughtfully. "Have you said anything to Mr Anderson?"

"He didn't seem to pay it much attention," she answered. "He said it didn't amount to anything more than a lot of talk and gossip, and he would wait for a claimant to turn up, and if he did he would want very satisfactory evidence," and as she said this there was a slight accent of contempt in her voice, as if she felt that evidence was but a small thing and that the truth should be enough by itself.

"Lawyers are taught to be cautious," Bobby said. "By the way, I'm told that Mr Weston and Miss Florence Severn were contemplating marriage. Do you know if that is true?"

"She may have been," Thomasine answered briefly. "He wasn't."

"I take it," Bobby went on, "Mr Anderson has taken charge of the ten fifty-pound notes we found in the safe?"

"He hasn't mentioned them to me," Thomasine answered; and her hands, hovering over the machine, seemed to hint that there had been enough of this aimless questioning and that they would like to be free to resume their work.

"You can't make any suggestion what the money was for? Or why it was in an envelope marked 'Family papers'?"

She shook her head.

"No," she said. "I've no idea. He told me to make a note of the numbers, and I did and I gave it him. I don't know what he did with it. I daresay it was in his pocket or one of the drawers."

"I don't think so," Bobby said. "No."

"I saw him put the notes in an envelope," she continued. "He gave it me to put in the safe. I didn't notice what was on the envelope. I didn't look. That is all I know."

"Did Mr Weston often make payment by notes?"

"Not that I know of. Generally he paid by cheque, like most people. I remember I wondered a little about the notes. I don't think I had ever seen a fifty-pound note before. I didn't say anything. Mr Weston didn't encourage questions. It was nothing to do with me."

"The perfect secretary," Bobby said with a smile and went away; and the rattle of the typewriter pursued him into the outer hall.

Mr Anderson had instructed the domestic staff to continue their usual routine. Thomasine, too, was now staying at the house. Bobby arranged for a constable to remain on duty to see that nothing was interfered with. Then he drove off to the county police headquarters in Midwych, where Sergeant Payne was waiting for him.

Payne had found out a good deal about Miss Bessie Bell, but nothing to her discredit and nothing to explain the summons by Mr Weston she had apparently received. Her reputation was without stain. She might, indeed, be described as almost on kissing terms with every customer; but she preserved strict discipline in the saloon bar over which she presided both for customers and for her assistants. One of her girls, indeed, had been known to hand in her notice in a temper, declaring that one might as well work in a nunnery, but that perhaps could be thought exaggeration—especially by nuns. It was, however, a fact that on at least one occasion Bessie had intervened with tact and effect to prevent another of her girls from making a bigger fool of herself than seemed necessary. By a coincidence this girl was now maid at Mayfield, Bobby had seen her when he called there. As for the landlord of the Wych and Wych Arms, he described Bessie as being worth her weight in gold. As she was a buxom lass and weighed a good hundred and fifty pounds, this was a serious compliment. There was one blot on her escutcheon, however, and one that interested Bobby because it seemed out of character. She was said to be mean and never to spend a penny if she could help it, to go, indeed, to extremes to save any odd sixpence. Nor was this due to any family claims. Her parents were dead and she had no relatives requiring help. It was supposed she was "scraping and saving" to buy a business for herself.

"Anything to suggest Martin Wynne has been in touch with her?" Bobby asked.

"No," replied Payne. "He's not known at the Wych and Wych, and he's been at work all day. Can't check 'phone calls, of course. Or letters for that matter."

"We had better arrange to keep an eye on her," Bobby observed thoughtfully. "And I want to know what time Mr Wynne got home last night. Try to find out, but don't start gossip if you can help it. Anything about Mr Franks, Miss Rowe's young man?"

"He's here," Payne answered. "I got him to wait in case you wanted to question him. It seems O.K. that he and Miss Rowe were at the cinema last night. He has the ticket stubs. The serial numbers show they were bought round about the time the big picture comes on; and a friend, name of Reynolds, works at the same place, confirms seeing them leave about eleven—near the murder time. Of course Reynolds may be lying. But he is quite clear about it. Says Franks paid him half a crown he owed him. Says no one is likely to forget it when Franks pays up all on his own."

"Side-light on character?" suggested Bobby smilingly.

"Yes, sir," agreed Payne and continued: "Miss Rowe's landlady backs her up to some degree. Says she heard Miss Rowe come in at half-past eleven, and she knows the time because she heard the grandfather clock on the landing strike. Not much to go on. Clocks can be tampered with. Miss Rowe seems to be a bit more used to tools than are some women. But there it is for what it's worth."

"Yes, I see," Bobby said thoughtfully. "I think I should like a word or two with Franks if he's here. Curiosity, I'm afraid. I don't see at present where he comes into the picture at all. But I do rather wonder what sort of a glamorous youngster has made such an impression on a girl like Thomasine Rowe. If any girl could pick and choose, she could. Drop her handkerchief where she likes, so to say."

"Yes, sir," agreed Payne with a covert smile. "I'll bring him in."

Payne went off on his errand. The 'phone bell rang. Bobby answered. The message was from the city police to say that, as asked, they had made inquiries at the various shops in the city, pawnbrokers and others, likely to stock Japanese knives, and that one shop had reported the recent sale of such a knife to a customer giving the name of Thomasine Rowe.

CHAPTER XIX
ENIGMA

BOBBY HAD no time to digest this piece of information, for the door opened and there appeared Payne, in company with a scrubby, undersized youth, so utterly undistinguished he seemed the very quintessence of the senior office-boy, from whom had been abstracted every feature that could possibly differentiate him from any other.

Weak eyes peered from behind his spectacles, from his lips hung a bedraggled cigarette, his hair was plastered thick with brilliantine, he gave a general impression of regarding a bath as an ordeal to be avoided as long as possible, and it was plainly some time since he had remembered to provide himself with a clean handkerchief.

Bobby fairly gasped. Payne so far forgot himself and discipline as to bestow a wink on his superior officer. The newcomer looked both frightened and sulky. Bobby found himself reflecting that if this young man did not suffer from what Plautus called the mail's misfortune of being too handsome, at any rate his looks were those Thomasine's dark and angry beauty had found irresistible. Yet there was something about the boy's little red pouting mouth, under his only good feature, a well-shaped, prominent nose with thin, clean-cut nostrils, that made Bobby fancy that somewhere or sometime he had seen him before. Possibly he had passed him in the street and had noticed him because of his very "unnoticeability", if a word can be coined for the occasion. Recollecting himself, Bobby babbled, a little wildly, for indeed his surprise was great:—

"Oh, yes, Mr Franks, isn't it? Mr Ronald Franks? Yes. So good of you to come along. It is Mr Franks, isn't it?" he added, wondering faintly if there wasn't perhaps, after all, some mistake somewhere.

"That's right," mumbled the young gentleman in question.

"Oh, yes. Do take a seat," Bobby said. "Oh, yes, Mr Franks. Yes. Let me see, you and Miss Thomasine Rowe are engaged, aren't you?"

For Bobby still clung to the belief that there must be two Ronald Franks, and that this must be the other one.

"That's right," said Mr Franks again, and once more Bobby blinked bewilderedly, this time at the marked lack of enthusiasm noticeable in the young man's tone.

"Now, let me see," Bobby went on. "Take another cigarette, won't you?" Mr Franks seemed half reluctant to dispense with the damp, chewed fragment dangling from his lips, but finally helped himself to one from the proffered box. "Yes. You and Miss Rowe went to the Superb cinema last night, didn't you?"

"That's right," said Mr Franks once again; and Bobby wondered if perhaps these were the only two words of the language with which the young man was acquainted.

"I expect you've heard of what's happened?" Bobby went on.

Mr Franks nodded; and, a little to Bobby's relief, did not this time say "That's right", but instead:—

"Nothing to do with me."

"No, no," Bobby agreed. "No. It's only that we have to ask everybody we can get hold of if there's anything they think they can tell us. I've had the pleasure of a long chat with Miss Rowe, and if you'll allow me I should like to congratulate you on your engagement. We think you're a very lucky young man indeed."

"That's right," said Franks, falling back on his accustomed formula, and speaking so gloomily that Bobby half expected to see him burst into tears.

"A most striking young lady," Bobby said quickly, hoping to stave off any such crisis, but with the unexpected result of making Franks start violently and stare at Bobby with a swift return of that look of fear he had shown when he first came in, but that had vanished before Bobby's amiable and pleasant manner.

"Whatjer mean?" he mumbled, and gave a glance towards the door, as if he meditated flight.

"Well, Miss Rowe made a great impression on us all," Bobby said, feeling a good deal puzzled by Franks's manner. "The sergeant and I are old married men, or else I think we should both feel envious. Eh, Payne?"

"Yes, sir," said Payne, playing up gallantly, but crossing his fingers as he spoke, for to his mind Miss Thomasine Rowe was best admired at a distance—a good long distance. Personally he would as soon have married a thunderstorm.

"Ho! Would you?" said Franks bitterly.

"I'll wager," continued Bobby with a smile, "all your pals think you have carried off the prize of the year."

Franks gave a faint and watery smile in return, and looked at Bobby rather as a dog looks when called upon to perform a trick it knows beyond its powers. He did not speak, and Bobby had to drop the subject. He could not very well ask, as he so much desired to do, what on earth Mr Franks thought a girl like Thomasine Rowe saw in him. Instead he asked a few unimportant routine questions, and in the midst of them Franks blurted out:—

"I'm trying to get dereserved."

"Oh, indeed," said Bobby. "Not easy for any one in the engineering line. Want to join up?"

"That's right," said Franks. "Training takes a year, and it looks like now as if it would be over before then." He added sharply: "Mind, that's confidential, that is. Don't you go telling her."

"Oh, I quite understand," Bobby answered, thinking, however, that all he understood was to whom the pronoun referred. "Police can keep secrets, you know."

He did not detain the young man much longer, and when Franks had departed, Payne said solemnly:—

"Beats Bannagher, that does, and Bannagher beats the band."

"That's right," said Bobby mechanically.

"What does the girl see in that little bit of salvage?" demanded Payne, not so much of Bobby as of the whole wide, mysterious universe.

"What does any girl see in any of us?" countered Bobby; to which Payne returned a mumbled comment to the effect that he hoped he at least did not so strongly resemble a stray bit of chewed rag.

An odd little interview, Bobby thought, and he supposed he was letting run away with him that imagination for which old Dan Edwardes had rebuked him, if he told himself that in one remark and reply there might well lurk a strange significance. Too slender and too fanciful an idea to build upon, though, and when he got home and told his wife, Olive, about young Franks, he did not mention it, but talked instead of how queer it was that so striking a girl as Miss Rowe should have fixed her affections on so commonplace a young man. But all Olive said was that men and women loved not as they chose, but as they must.

"What struck me," Bobby went on, "is that Franks is just about plumb scared. Any mention of the girl's name made him thoroughly uncomfortable. "

Thereon Olive explained that Bobby was confusing two entirely different things. If young Franks were merely afraid, that was all right, because fear was one of the noblest of human attributes. But if he were just uncomfortable, that was bad, because being uncomfortable was merely an animal quality. So Bobby said she might know what she was talking about, but he didn't, and he didn't know either how what he had learnt from Franks fitted in. Yet he felt that it did somewhere, and might even fit in as key piece, and anyhow he was so tired and sleepy he couldn't even think.

All the same, tired though he was, Bobby's sleep that night was troubled by many dreams, through which there followed one another as in an unending solemn saraband, the figures of the strangely contrasted women who in some way or another seemed concerned in the enacted tragedy.

Bessie Bell was there in his dreams, the barmaid, tall and blonde and afraid; and why was she afraid? For even in his sleep he knew that to her challenge and defiance were more natural than fear. Why, again, had she obeyed the dead man's summons to his home; and was there some strong reason why the easy and careless generosity of her natural character had taken on so careful an economy of "scraping and saving"?

There in the procession of the long dance through his dreams was Thomasine Rowe, the tall, dark secretary, of aloof and sombre beauty, one framed as it were by nature to receive the homage of young men, but who apparently had laid all the full richness of her gifts at the feet of the most commonplace of youths. Then, too, if he were right in his belief that it was her voice he had heard as he approached Weston Lodge Cottage on the night of the murder, what had been her errand there, and why had she denied it? What, too, was the significance of her purchase of a Japanese dagger? If a coincidence, how strange! Yet could it mean what on the face of it it seemed to mean?

Then into the orbit of his dreams swung the figures of two other women: Florence Severn, the athlete, still with much of that lithe ease in movement which had won her her triumphs on the links and the tennis-court, and Olga Severn, welfare officer, who had lost a vanity case, and between whom and her aunt enmity burned like fire.

To and fro they seemed to weave in his dreams, first one and then the other to the front, and he thought that continually they passed one to the other an envelope that bore on it the inscription, "Family Papers re Aggie", and he thought that each as she received it or tossed it away again, looked at him in mockery because she knew but he did not, and he thought that always enormous finger-prints were showing on this envelope, but always fading away again into nothingness just as he was about to examine them more closely. Then in the background, not joining in the dance, but looking on, there stood, he thought, a man, a dead man, holding out a diamond and ruby ring, yet not so much in explanation as in warning.

"One's enough," this dead man seemed to say; and then it was an indignant elbow inserted with dexterity and effect in his ribs that recalled him to wakefulness.

"What is the matter with you?" Olive's voice demanded in the dark. "You keep twisting and turning and grunting."

"Sorry," Bobby said. "I think I've been thinking in my sleep."

"What have you been thinking?" Olive asked.

"I don't know," Bobby answered. "Tell me, what makes two women hate each other?"

"Jealousy," Olive answered.

"Jealousy of whom?" Bobby asked. "Of the old rich man with both feet on earth or the poor young man with his head in the clouds?"

But Olive had gone to sleep again; and following that excellent example he slept more soundly, till there broke on his slumbers the unwelcome tinkle of the alarm clock.

"The first thing to do," he remarked as he began to dress, "will be to find out if Martin Wynne was out late that night, and if he was, to look for a summer-house."

"Well, a summer-house, yes," Olive conceded, "but how will it help—even if there is one?"

"Dabs," said Bobby.

"I should say the first thing," Olive objected, "is to find out if it was really Miss Rowe who bought that Japanese dagger. Any one can give any name."

"I've great respect for that young woman's intelligence and will-power," Bobby told her, "and I shall be very much surprised if it turns out to be any one else."

"You mean, don't you?" Olive asked, "if it does turn out to be her?"

"No, I mean, if it doesn't," Bobby answered. "If I allowed my-self ten inches of water in the bath this morning, should we lose the war?"

"I expect so," Olive said; and, in a spasm of wifely devotion: "Look here, you have seven and a half, and I'll make do with two and a half."

"Oh, I say, will you?" said Bobby, deeply touched. He added as he was about to depart for the bathroom. "The real puzzle is: Why were ten fifty-pound bank-notes in an envelope marked: 'Family papers re Aggie'?"

"I can tell you a bigger puzzle than that," Olive called after him. "What are you going to have for breakfast when I've forgotten what an egg looks like and the last of the bacon ration went yesterday?"

CHAPTER XX
BETTER DEAD

ON HIS WAY to county police headquarters that morning Bobby called at the shop where his city colleagues had discovered that a Japanese knife had recently been purchased by a customer giving the name of Thomasine Rowe. Nor was it difficult for Bobby to assure himself that the Thomasine Rowe of the purchase was identical with the Thomasine Rowe who had been the dead man's secretary. She was not one to be easily forgotten, nor one whom it was difficult to identify by description.

"Very striking young lady indeed," the shop assistant said, and Bobby agreed.

"I have heard her called that before," he remarked. "I think it's true."

The shopman did not quite understand.

"You wait till you see her," he said. "Then you'll agree." He leaned across the counter. "Is it about the murder?" he asked in a low, confidential voice. "The paper says Mr Weston was stabbed and that Miss Rowe was his secretary. If he got monkeying about with a girl of spirit like her—well, I wouldn't blame her, would you?"

"If police jumped to conclusions the way some of you people do," Bobby remarked severely, "I don't know what would happen. Probably I should arrest you on the spot as a likely accomplice."

"Here, I say," protested the shopman, feeling this was going much too far.

"Jumping to conclusions," said Bobby. "Don't you do it. And remember there are such things as actions for libel. Wouldn't like to pay a few hundred pounds damages, would you?"

"Here, I say," protested the shopman again, feeling this was going very much further than going too far.

"Besides," added Bobby, more mildly, hoping that for a time at least he had scotched that love of gossip so deeply implanted in fallen human nature, "you sold the thing as a paper-knife. Paper-knife. Japanese. One," he read aloud from the ledger entry shown him.

"That's right," agreed the shopman; and so Bobby said "Definitely?" in a questioning voice, and the shopman said: "Definitely right," which Bobby decided was probably the strongest affirmative (polite) the other knew.

"All the same," added the shopman, "it was steel, and good steel. I will say that for the Japs. Steel's a thing they know about. Not much of a job to sharpen it up."

"I suppose you didn't do that?" Bobby asked; and the shopman looked alarmed again and said "Definitely, no," and Bobby went away, feeling he had at least done his best to keep the man from talking.

All the same he was not much surprised when that afternoon the *Midwych Evening Intelligence* announced that an important clue had been discovered, the county police having been informed of the provenance of the murder weapon by the active and intelligent city police—the reporter of the *Intelligence* thought it important to keep in with the city rather than with the county police and moreover had a grudge against Bobby, whom he considered much too secretive. And this statement was all the more impressive and all the more to the prestige of the city police as so few of the readers of the *Intelligence* knew what "provenance" meant.

"So now," Bobby said to himself moodily, as he proceeded on his way, "now we have traced a connection with Japanese knives to three of them—Miss Rowe, old Dan Edwardes, and the Wilkie chap."

At headquarters there were various matters needing attention, and then Sergeant Payne appeared with his report. It was a fact that Martin Wynne had returned home very late on the night of the murder. No one could say the exact time, but it was certainly well on in the small hours. Very unusual, for Martin, though he often sat up late, was seldom out after supper.

"Very cheap sort of place where he lives," Payne added. "Guinea and a half for bed, breakfast, dinner and full board on Sundays, and how they do it on present prices beats me. Looks it, though—everything on the cheap, I mean. Got to be, at that price. He has the name of being hard up, and you have to be hard up all right for it to be noticed in a place like that. Sort of doss-house, if you ask me. Only some of them seem to think it's not so much that he's hard up as that he's mean. They say he gets a good screw where he works."

"Four hundred a year, he told me," Bobby remarked.

"There you are," said Payne. "It would run to something better than a hole like that, wouldn't it?"

"Knows a better hole but won't go to it—and why?" mused Bobby. "Perhaps he is like Miss Bessie Bell—scraping and saving. To carry out this new idea of his for stratosphere flying, perhaps."

Payne looked as if he thought achieving flight in the stratosphere would be but poor compensation for the discomforts of a guinea-and-a-half boarding-house. He added that it would take a lot of "scraping and saving" on four hundred a year to get together the five thousand pounds Martin had spoken of.

"Though that'll be all right," added Payne, not without intention, "when he comes in for his whack of the old man's coin."

Bobby agreed, and presently went off to visit Miss Bessie Bell at the Wych and Wych Arms. The house was not yet open, though every one was very busy getting ready for the hour the licensing laws permitted. Bobby explained his identity, and was shown to a small, dark sitting-room at the back of the building. Thither soon came Bessie, and stood in the doorway, looking at him. She did not speak, but stood silently. He was a tall man, but she was not much below his height, and her plain black dress suited her well, toning down the full exuberance of her personality. The ill-lighted room, too, hid some of those traces that a certain rich carelessness of life had marked her with. He thought again that she looked a splendid animal as she stood there waiting in her blonde magnificence. Somehow she reminded him of a lioness at bay, with her head thrown back, her upright attitude, the steady gaze of her blue and challenging eyes fixed full upon him. He could well believe the stories told of her. Of how, for instance, when some man had offended her by a licence of speech passing beyond even her liberal standards, she had simply taken him by the scruff of the neck and had run him out into the street. Or the other story of how, when a young girl had appeared in the bar obviously the worse for drink, Bessie had administered physical correction across her knee with, it was said, good reformatory effect.

Yes, a lioness poised in defence, he thought; only what was she defending, and why? He found himself comparing her with Thomasine Rowe, as upright, as poised, almost as tall, though so much more slender and finer in build. Of her he thought as of the tigress pacing through the deep jungle, alert and seeking—only seeking what? And the memory came to him also of those other two, the aunt and niece, Florence and Olga Severn, unknown factors, with wrath about them like a cloud. If these first two were lion and tiger, the Severn women were like hovering falcons, ready to swoop and strike—only striking where?

Abruptly Bessie spoke.

"I've been expecting you," she said. "I knew you would never leave me alone."

"Oh, well, you see," Bobby explained apologetically, "you were one of the last to see Mr Weston alive."

"Suppose I was," she asked, "does that show I killed him?"

"Has any one suggested you did?" he asked.

"If that's not in your mind, why are you here?"

"For information."

"You'll get none from me," she retorted, "for I've none to give."

"Why did Mr Weston send for you to visit him that night—the night that proved to be the night of his murder?"

"Only he could tell you that, and he is dead. I don't know."

"Is it as well for you, I wonder," Bobby asked, "that he is dead and cannot tell?"

She looked at him angrily.

"Think so if you like," she said. "What do I care what you think?"

"Are you really asking me to believe," Bobby said slowly, "that Mr Weston sent for you and you did not know why and yet you went and he talked to you and you went away and still you do not know why?"

"You are clever, aren't you?" she said. "That's a question, isn't it?" She came from her position by the door where she had been standing and sat down. She looked up at him, her magnificent wide blue eyes, that in her girlhood had so emphasized her claim to more than mere prettiness, fixed full upon him. She lost her likeness to the lioness at bay. It was with a simper that suited her ill that she said:—

"Oh, well, I suppose I guessed. If you're in the hotel business you soon get to know men like Mr Weston. Well, of course, he's dead now, but every one knew. Plenty of money, and free with it if he liked you. Well, there you are. I mean, if you took his fancy, like, there wasn't hardly anything he wouldn't do for you."

"You mean Mr Weston wanted you to be his mistress?" Bobby asked.

"Well, now," Bessie simpered, "that's a way to put it. But I suppose it's what it comes to."

"Miss Bell," Bobby said, "why are you lying? I know enough of you and about you not to believe a word of that story. Besides, it doesn't stand up. If it had been like that, Weston wouldn't have gone about it that way. No need. Now, won't you tell me the real reason?"

"It's no good me telling you things if you won't believe me," she said sullenly.

"Who was the man you spoke to at the window of the garden room there?" Bobby asked abruptly.

For a moment she looked disconcerted, but recovered almost at once.

"I don't know what you mean," she said. "I didn't talk to any one at any window. Why should I?"

"That's what I want to know," Bobby answered, but did not pursue the subject, since, after all, his memory of fresh footprints in the earth under the window of the garden room was no proof that a conversation had there taken place. Instead he asked abruptly:—

"Why did Mr Martin Wynne ring you up the morning after the murder?"

For a moment she looked more disconcerted still, and this time she recovered more slowly.

"Martin Wynne?" she repeated. "He is Mr Weston's nephew or something, isn't he? How do you know he rang up? Why shouldn't he? How do you know?"

Bobby did not answer this, especially as he had not known, but only guessed. His silence won an answer, though, as silence often does, and Bessie said:—

"He wanted to ask if I had heard about the murder, and of course I had. We hear everything here, and he wanted to know if I could tell him anything, and I couldn't, and that's all."

"How did he know that you had been there that night?"

"Did he know? He didn't say so. If he did Mr Weston told him, I suppose."

"Hardly likely," Bobby said drily, "if Mr Weston had asked you to come for the reason you gave. Is Mr Wynne a friend of yours?"

"No," said Bessie, and spoke as if she meant it. She went on: "He's been in sometimes. He doesn't use the house, but he has been in. You don't think he had anything to do with it, do you?" She looked scornful. "Him," she said, "why, he wouldn't notice you enough to kill you. Flying—that's all he thinks of."

"There's nothing you can tell us would help us in any way?" Bobby asked once more, and once more she shook her head, this time without speaking. He went on: "Mr Weston let you out himself, didn't he?"

She nodded, looking at him warily, as if afraid of what this admission might be taken to imply.

"I've been told," Bobby said, "that sometimes Mr Weston let a woman visitor out by the front door and then let her in again by the french windows of his study."

"I don't know anything about that," she said sullenly. "I came straight back here, and that's all there's to it, and no more you can make of it."

"Meet any one on the way, or speak to any one when you got in?" Bobby asked.

"No," she admitted. "No. I had plenty to think of. It was a fine night then, and moonlight, and I didn't hurry. When you've been behind the bar all day a breath of fresh air isn't so bad. I've my own key, and when I got back I went straight to bed."

Bobby rose to his feet.

"I'm afraid I shall have to ask you to let me have another chat," he said. "You see, there's only one thing I'm sure of, and that is that there was something between you and Mr Weston you don't want me to know. Something you are so anxious to keep hidden you are prepared to let yourself be thought lightly of, rather than risk its disclosure. It is very foolish of you. Now I shall have to find out what it is, because it may have something to do with Mr Weston's death, and so I've got to know. If it hasn't, then it's no business of mine or of any one else, and you would never hear another word about it. Police keep many secrets. Much better tell me, because the truth is bound to come out."

"Why should it?" she retorted. "I won't tell, and he can't now he's dead. And better dead, thank God."

CHAPTER XXI
BOX OF CHOCOLATES

FROM THE Wych and Wych Arms, where Bobby felt his talk with Bessie Bell had done little more than increase the dark bewilderment in which he walked, he went on to Weston Lodge Cottage. Miss Rowe had to be asked about that Japanese dagger she had bought, sold to her as a paper-knife, but so easily provided with edge and point.

He knew she was still working at the Lodge and was likely to continue to do so for some time, since winding up the dead man's estate would be a long and complicated process, and in the present dearth of clerical help Mr Anderson would be only too glad to retain her services.

Hargreaves, looking much younger, though also less dignified, now that his hair had resumed its natural shade of reddish brown, took Bobby on his arrival to the study, where Thomasine was busy with her typewriter and a great pile of documents.

Strong nerves had Thomasine Rowe, Bobby told himself, to be sitting so quietly at her work in the room where death so short a time before had struck so swiftly and so suddenly. When he said something to this effect she gave that proud and scornful smile he was coming to think characteristic of her, but made no comment. He explained that he wanted to ask a few questions, and she left her place at the typist's table by the window where she was working and seated herself in one of the big arm-chairs.

"Shall you mind if I smoke?" she asked.

Bobby answered that he hadn't the least objection, though he hoped she would not mind if he didn't, as he was on duty. Police weren't supposed to smoke on duty, and it was bad for discipline if subordinates saw senior officers giving themselves little indulgences.

"Oh, well, discipline," said Thomasine, with again that remote and proud smile of hers. "Oh, I suppose it's good for subordinates," she agreed carelessly; and Bobby told himself that this young woman, typist or secretary or whatever she called herself, had little sense of being a subordinate.

She was lighting her cigarette now. Enormous as was the chair, slight in build as she was, she seemed to fill it entirely, and once more he noticed the easy speed she showed in every movement. Of Bessie Bell he had thought as a lioness, of this girl as a tigress; and again, and more strongly, he had the impression of a tigress, not so much at bay as crouching in readiness to spring at need.

"What I've chiefly come about," Bobby explained, "is that Japanese knife you bought in Midwych some little time ago."

"Oh, you've found that out, have you?" she asked, with a curled lip. "Thorough, aren't you?"

"We do our best," he answered. "Of course you know a Japanese knife was used in the murder. When Mr Weston was found—there"—Bobby pointed to the exact spot—"lying there, it was sticking in his body."

If he had meant these words, his gesture, as a further test of her nerves, there was no result. Her eyes followed his pointing hand, her gaze rested on the spot indicated, by not so much as the quiver of an eyelid did she show any emotion.

"Mr Weston was killed with a dagger," she said. "A good, clean blow. What I bought was a paper-knife. You could not have struck such a blow with it."

"A paper-knife, yes," Bobby agreed. "But a paper-knife that could take an edge."

"Could it?" she asked indifferently. "I suppose you want to know if I can still produce it. Suppose I can't? What then?"

"It would then become a more serious matter than you appear to realize," Bobby answered, growing impatient now with this scornful young woman who seemed as if she held herself above all natural emotion.

"Has the knife used been identified as the one I bought?" she asked; and he could see well the challenge and the mockery in her eyes.

"I have not troubled to go into that yet," he told her. "Because I felt sure you would have a perfectly satisfactory explanation."

For the first time she seemed a trifle disturbed, as if this reply had not been anticipated, was not even welcome. Up to the present she had seemed indifferent, disdainful indeed. But now she showed herself less aloof, her eyes became attentive, more than attentive, a suggestion in them of how the tigress might look the instant before the final spring.

"I've been told you are clever," she said unexpectedly. "I didn't think it likely. It's so rare. But I think you are."

"Some other time," Bobby said smilingly, "I should like to argue that most people are clever, and that it is not brains people lack, but purely and simply the will to use them. Too much trouble. But I do rather wonder why you have changed your opinion about me. For the life of me, I can't see why."

"You've a sound judgment," she said. "You judge well. You don't think I killed Mr Weston, do you?"

"I certainly don't think you killed him with that knife you bought the other day," he told her.

"Yes, you are clever," she repeated, and now her eyes, watching him, were keen and hard. "I bought that knife as a present for a friend on her birthday, and I sent it her more than a fortnight ago."

"You can give me her name and address?"

Thomasine went back to her place by the window. There she typed a name and address on a half-sheet of notepaper. She came back and gave it him. He thanked her and put it in his pocket.

"I am wondering a little," he remarked as he did so, "why you never mentioned it before?"

She had gone back to the big arm-chair. She settled herself in it, again with that air of somehow making her slim and youthful body fill it entirely. There was once more a faint disdain in her voice as she said:—

"Would not that have been what you call causing a public mischief? Sending police on a fool's errand. Giving them a red herring to follow. Or perhaps I wanted to know how effective police methods really are."

"Yes, I see," he said, smiling back at her. "That explains it perfectly. There is just one more small point. You tell us you and Mr Franks went to the cinema in Midwych that evening. The ticket stubs Mr Franks gave me shows they were purchased shortly before the big picture you went to see comes on. There is also a witness who is prepared to swear he saw you and Mr Franks leaving—at about the hour of the murder."

"Well, then," she interrupted, "doesn't that clear us if you are really suspicious of us? Isn't that what you call an alibi?"

"Oh, yes," Bobby agreed. "Most complete. All the same, there is another witness—a generally reliable and certainly truthful witness—who says he heard you here, in the Weston Lodge Cottage grounds, at a time when you would only have been able to get to the cinema in time for the big picture by hurrying—in fact, only by the use of a car or a motor-cycle, perhaps. Did that happen?"

She did not answer him for a moment or two, taking time first to provide herself with a fresh cigarette. Then she said:—

"I suppose you mean yourself. I suppose you mean you are your own reliable and certainly truthful witness?"

"Oh, well," he said, slightly disconcerted. Then he said: "Why do you think so?"

"You may be clever, but I am not an utter fool," she retorted. "There was no one else here that night you would be likely to call reliable and certainly truthful. You don't know enough about them, for one thing."

"Let me return your compliment," he said, smilingly. "About being clever, I mean."

"What makes you think whoever it was you really saw was me?" she asked. "It was getting dark, wasn't it? You couldn't see any one clearly enough to be sure. Was it that you heard some one talking and thought it was me?"

"Your voice is easily recognized," Bobby admitted.

"I suppose so," she said. She seemed deep in thought. She had put down her cigarette and allowed it to go out. She leaned forward, frowning, intent. She said: "If it is easily recognized, it is easily imitated. Have you thought of that?"

"Why should any one imitate it?" he asked doubtfully, for this did not seem to him a probable explanation.

"I don't know," she admitted. "I don't know why a good many things happened that have happened. Especially that night when Mr Weston died. But I know some one who could imitate me, imitate me marvellously."

"Miss Olga Severn?" Bobby asked.

"You know about her?" Thomasine asked, and not as if best pleased. "You know a lot already, don't you? Well, Olga Severn gave imitations at a works welfare concert. Very clever. One of me. Behind a screen. Mr Weston giving me a letter to take down—a letter to her it was supposed to be—about welfare. And me making suggestions. She took us both off exactly. When the screen was knocked over, the workpeople could hardly believe it was all her. If she didn't want you to know it was her, and yet thought you had seen some one, she might have done one of her imitations to put you off."

"Yes, I see that," Bobby said. "A little complicated. Only why should she? I can't imagine why Miss Olga should murder Mr Weston?"

"More can I. But it's not only murder that takes you out at night. Sometimes it's something quite different."

"A love affair?" Bobby suggested. "Yes. Has Miss Olga one?"

"I don't know, and if I did I wouldn't tell you," Thomasine flashed back. Then she added thoughtfully: "Mr Weston never bothered me. I think he knew better. But if half the tales you hear are true, he was a man many women have had reason to think better dead."

"Do you think it was a woman, then?" Bobby asked.

"Gracious, no, and certainly not Olga. The aunt more likely. Only it's silly to guess at random. I would as soon suspect any one— you or me or—or Hargreaves. He is the most unlikely person I can think of, but I've seen him look daggers at Mr Weston, though I can't imagine him putting one in him."

"I don't think I can either," Bobby agreed. "Do you know if any will has been found?"

"No, and Mr Anderson says he is sure there isn't one. He is going to assume Mr Weston died intestate. There'll be a lot of formalities to go through, I suppose. It'll be a long time before it's all cleared up and the estate is ready for distribution. A year perhaps, he says. He has asked me to stay on till it's all settled."

"Are you going to?"

"I expect so." She smiled faintly. "Mr Anderson is so afraid of my leaving that he has promised me a rise—ten shillings a week more."

"I'm sure you will be worth it," Bobby said. "I expect he would be rather at sea without your help. I hope," he added, rising, "that I haven't taken up too much of your time."

"It has saved me time," she answered quietly. "I was coming this evening to see you." He looked surprised, and she got up and went across to the table in the window where she had been working. From a drawer she produced box of chocolates. She handed it to Bobby. "It came this morning," she said. "By post."

"Oh, yes," he said, opening it. There were gaps in the top row. "I see you've sampled them," he said.

"I did not," she answered. "A puppy did. This puppy." She opened a small dispatch case that had been standing on the floor. Inside was a little dead dog, pathetic even in these days when death has grown so common. "It died quickly," she said.

Bobby looked at it, looked at the chocolates, looked at her. The quiet atmosphere of the room had grown tense again with the presence in it once more of death, of sudden death, man-given death.

Involuntarily he glanced at that length of the carpet where when last he had been in this room a dead body had lain. There might have been another lying there now, he supposed, if those chocolates had been eaten by her to whom they had been sent. Thomasine saw where his glance had gone and seemed to read his thoughts.

"Me, too," she said quietly. "Very nearly. Not quite."

"Poison," Bobby said.

"First the knife, then poison," she agreed. "And next?"

"Who should want to murder you?" Bobby asked. "Why?"

She did not answer that. She was closing the small dispatch case, hiding from view the little stiff body it contained.

"Don't tell Hargreaves, please," she said. "He would make an awful fuss. Or any of the others. It belonged to Hargreaves, but they all made a fuss of it."

"You have good nerves," Bobby said again, wondering how little she seemed moved by her escape, by her new knowledge that she had an enemy who hated or feared to the pitch of killing. "Have you said anything to any one else?"

"No," she answered.

"For the present it would be wiser to say nothing," Bobby told her. "I will detail a plain-clothes man to be at hand here in case he is needed."

"Oh, no, I don't want that done," she protested.

"I can't run the risk of a fresh tragedy," he replied. "You may be glad to have help at hand."

"I can look after myself, I don't want anybody's help," she answered, with all her old disdain. "Your policeman or a dozen of him wouldn't have saved me from those chocolates if I hadn't felt suspicious."

"No, I suppose not," he admitted. "What made you suspicious?"

"Well, I couldn't help wondering what it meant. A box of chocolates to-day is about as common as a box of diamonds. And nothing to show who it came from. Who did it come from? I don't know how many points that box would take. A good many, anyhow. I was quite sure it didn't come from Mr Franks. For one thing, I knew he had used all his points already, and besides, he wouldn't have sent them like that, without a word. The more I wondered the funnier it seemed. I suppose I was expected to eat one or two while I was wondering. Well, I didn't. I had a good look, and they looked as if something had been done to them. I cut one or two open, and there was a sort of white powder I could see inside. The puppy was in the room, being a nuisance. It was always tugging at your dress or scratching your stockings and making them ladder. I gave it two or three just to see, and it was dead very quickly. I was coming to tell you if you hadn't come here instead."

"I will try to trace the chocolates," Bobby said. "There is a packer's number. That may help. I don't suppose it will, but it may. I must get them analyzed, too. To make sure of the poison. I think it is arsenic. Perhaps we can trace that, though it's easy stuff to get hold of. I had better take the puppy's body, too. Hard luck for the little brute. It will be necessary to have proof the death was caused by poison and identify the poison."

"Well, don't tell Hargreaves," she repeated. "He would make the most awful fuss. So would all of them; they were all perfectly silly about the wretched little animal. They seemed to think I ought to like having my skirt torn and my stockings laddered."

"Can you think of arty one who might want to murder you?" Bobby asked.

"Gracious, no," she declared. "It's a mystery to me."

"Have you any enemies you know of?"

"Oh, dozens," she answered carelessly. "Only when it comes to trying to murder you—well, I think most of them would draw the line there. I've been trying to think. It's so soon after what happened to Mr Weston, you can't help feeling it's something to do with it, can you? One thing did strike me. If there's something I know or saw or heard, who ever it was killed Mr Weston may think would help you if I told you—well, that might be it, mightn't it?"

"Yes," Bobby agreed. "Can you think of anything?"

"No," she answered at once. "I've tried my hardest, but it's no good."

"Go over everything in your mind, every possible word and incident you can remember," Bobby said. Grimly enough he added: "Your life may depend on it."

"Yes, I know," she answered, apparently unmoved. "There's one thing. If you look at the brown-paper wrapper—here, I'll show you—it's been used before, and you can see where there's been an address written on it. It's been erased, but I've been trying to make it out, and it does look as if you could make out something that looks very much like 'Dan Edwardes, Esq.' "

"Yes, it does," Bobby agreed. "We can make certain. It won't be difficult to bring the writing up."

"Of course, that doesn't mean he sent it," Thomasine said. "I'm sure it couldn't be him. He didn't murder Mr Weston, did he? And he has never taken the least notice of me, beyond being civil and saying good morning and so on."

"Oh, no," Bobby agreed. "No. Of course not."

"Don't bother about any plain-clothes policeman," she added as he prepared to depart. "I can look after myself."

"You are a very capable young lady," Bobby agreed, "but you are also my responsibility. You must let me do what I think best."

He went away then, and in the hall found Hargreaves, looking very anxious and troubled, and one of the maid servants, looking even more troubled and anxious, and indeed not far from tears.

"Mr Hargreaves has lost his little dog," the maid explained. "We can't find it anywhere—such a dear little thing."

"A little Sealyham," Hargreaves said. "It knew us all."

"The only bit of happiness in the whole house," the maid declared, and went to pursue her useless search elsewhere.

Guilty as Bobby felt, he said nothing. A human life might be at stake, and his responsibility was heavy. He told Hargreaves a plain-clothes constable was coming, but Hargreaves hardly seemed to take it in. Evidently the only thought in his mind was concern for the little lost pup.

CHAPTER XXII
FISH SOUP

Bobby was in no happy mood as he left Weston Lodge Cottage. Twice death had struck in that room he had just quitted, once at a man, once at a woman, though this last time missing its aim to destroy a harmless puppy instead. A pity, he thought, that human hate and malice should have cut short that brief spell of innocent, playful animal existence. Sentimental, he supposed, and he did not usually count himself a sentimentalist. Indeed, he had always felt a touch of contempt for those who, as has been said, are inclined to spell "dog" backwards; and, anyhow, what he had to think of was this new imminent threat now disclosed. Perhaps, he told himself, the unease he felt was no mere sentimental regret for a puppy's death, but rather foreboding of ill things to come.

He stopped at the first road call-box he came to and rang up headquarters to give instructions for a plain-clothes man to be sent out to Weston Lodge Cottage at once, with orders to keep his eyes open, and more especially to keep them on Miss Thomasine Rowe. He also gave details of the packer's number found in the box of chocolates, these to be 'phoned on immediately to the firm concerned, with a request for any possible information that could be supplied.

"Tell them we want to know everything, down to the colour of the packer's eyes, if possible," Bobby said, "and tell whoever you send to Weston Lodge Cottage he is responsible for Miss Rowe's safety, and if anything happens to her, worse will happen to him."

"Though, of course," he reflected, "the ultimate responsibility is mine and not his at all."

Then he rang up Mr Anderson's office, got permission to post his man at the Lodge—"to watch developments", he said—and received a promise that Hargreaves would be told to make the necessary arrangements.

By the time all this 'phoning was finished, Bobby was ready for lunch. So he got something—not much—at a public-house he came across, one of those where the word refreshment is given as a rule a strictly liquid interpretation. Then he drove on to Mr Dan Edwardes's residence, a comparatively small but comfortable-looking dwelling. It was a converted farmhouse, centuries old, and still bearing its ancient name of Saxon Fields.

Bobby, whose appetite had been more whetted than satisfied by his recent meal, found his nostrils twitching as he alighted from his car at the house door, so fragrant and so savoury was the odour that issued from a window he judged to be that of the kitchen.

Before he could knock, Mr Edwardes appeared, in shirt sleeves, a large apron, a big spoon in one hand, beaming benevolently—or sardonically—through his thick, rimmed glasses.

"Ah, inspector," he said, "I saw you coming. I was wondering when I would see you again. Just in time for lunch."

"Thanks so much," Bobby answered. "I can smell something good. I've had my lunch already, worse luck," and how emphatically a stomach much worse than merely empty endorsed those last two words.

Mr Edwardes suddenly looked excited.

"Excuse me," he said. "A crisis, I think." He scuttled away, and as he did so called over his shoulder. "Come in. First door on your right. Shan't be a minute."

He disappeared in the direction of that savoury smell already noted. In more leisurely fashion Bobby followed the instructions given, and found himself in a small, pleasant dining-room, comfortably furnished, the table laid with small linen mats on shining mahogany, with silver and with glass that even Bobby, whose knowledge of glass was limited, could see was of rare quality. He was still admiring it all when Mr Edwardes appeared, carrying with care a small silver tureen.

"Excuse my running away," he said, setting down his burden, "but the fact is—a moment later and all would have been lost. It would have been too late to add the flavouring I had prepared." He shook his head gravely. "I had to choose," he said, "between some lack of courtesy to a guest and an insult to an ancient recipe."

"It certainly smells jolly good," Bobby agreed, as well as a watering mouth would permit.

"Fish soup," Mr Edwardes explained. "A recipe my father brought from Japan. Chinese originally. Everything they have in Japan came first from China. Only their brutality is their own, and that I think is primitive, not innate as with the German. So there may be hope for the Japanese. They have a B.C. mind, perhaps, but the Germans have a beastly mind, which is worse." He was bustling about as he chattered, laying a second place. "I am alone to-day," he explained. "My housekeeper is out and we've no maid. The last didn't hold with a gentleman never out of the kitchen, so she has gone into munitions."

"I don't think I've ever heard of fish soup before," Bobby remarked.

"Ah, we in the West have much to learn from the ancient wisdom of the East," declared Mr Edwardes. "Now, if you'll sit down, you'll be able to tell me what you think of it."

"Oh, thanks so much," Bobby said, sternly calling an eager and protesting stomach to order, "but I've had my lunch already."

Mr Edwardes gave him a quick look.

"Which means, I suppose," he said, "you don't want to accept hospitality from a suspect?"

"Have you been called suspect?" Bobby asked.

"I have much too high an opinion of your discretion, my dear Inspector Owen," Mr Edwardes told him, "to suppose for one moment that you would even hint at such a thing till you were ready to clap the handcuffs on. In the meantime"—he was beginning to apply himself to the soup—"you will excuse me? If I am to be marched off to prison, I may as well at least enjoy a last meal. Prison fare no doubt is excellent and wholesome, but probably there they would agree with our late maid and not hold with a gentleman who wanted to be always in the kitchen. Well, do I await arrest?"

"You must know perfectly well," Bobby said, a trifle sharply, "that there is no question of that just now. Why should there be?"

"I note the qualification 'just now'," Mr Edwardes observed. "As for 'why'—immovable object, irresistible force. As I said before, the immovable object goes. Natural to look to the irresistible force for the reason. When I saw you I made sure you had heard stories from the Mill."

"What stories?" Bobby asked.

"Preparations. Calling an extraordinary meeting. All that. I've had a meeting of the responsible heads, telling them what we are thinking of, and asking for suggestions. I've given them all a copy of that little book I sent poor Weston—'What It Will Be Like'. Most of them aren't a bit impressed. Too new. Won't work, they say. Indecent haste, too, some of them feel, with poor Weston not yet in his grave. There'll be an inquest, I suppose?"

"Formal proceedings only," Bobby said. "We shall have to ask for an adjournment."

"'To allow the police to complete their inquiries,'" Mr Edwardes quoted. "Sorry if you think I'm talking too much. I expect I'm nervous. I didn't sleep too well last night. Murder is a bit unexpected in an average life, and mine has been very average—too average, probably. There's going to be plenty of opposition to my new order—there always is to anything new—and I should like to see it in running order before there is time for any more trouble to develop."

"Do you expect any?" Bobby asked sharply.

"I didn't expect what has happened," Mr Edwardes answered. "Somehow I doubt if it is finished."

He got up and went away and came back with a salad.

"A groundwork of cheese," he explained. "A dressing of dried egg. Most of the green stuff from the hedgerows and byways. Very excellent, too. But no olive oil and only vinegar. Vinegar is an insult to any salad, but lemons can't be had, and I regard wine, which some recommend, as much too strong. So what else can one have?

Well, if you aren't here to arrest me and you won't eat with me, I wonder a little why you have come?"

"Well, it's really about chocolates," Bobby said. "Have you had any recently? A box or anything?"

"Chocolates?" repeated Mr Edwardes, looking very puzzled. "Do you mean—?"

"Just chocolates," Bobby said. "Cream. Caramel. That sort of thing. A box has been sent to some one connected with the case. I should like to know who did send it?"

"I didn't, anyhow," Mr Edwardes said. He pushed away his plate. He repeated: "Chocolates? Why should that interest you? You don't mean?"

Bobby nodded. He saw that Mr Edwardes had guessed the reason for the inquiry. A quick and alert mind.

"Poisoned," he said. "Arsenic, I think."

"Why do you ask me?" Mr Edwardes said. "I can understand about Weston. He stood between me and what my sons had asked of me. They are dead. Three dead men. Why not a fourth? you might suppose I had asked myself. But why should I want to poison any one else? Who is it?" Bobby did not answer this, and Mr Edwardes went on: "What makes you think it was me?"

"I haven't said I do," Bobby answered. "The brown paper wrapping had been used before. There was a name and address on it. There had been an attempt to rub it out, but all the same I think that name and address was your own."

"I can only say I know nothing of it," Mr Edwardes repeated.

"I am only asking a question," Bobby said. "An old address on brown paper is no proof that it was used the next time by the same person. But it is reason for a question."

"Yes," Mr Edwardes agreed. "Oh, yes. I see that. Yes. Poisoned chocolates. That suggests a woman, doesn't it? And the use of a knife suggested a man. Poison is a woman's weapon. A knife is a man's. Perhaps meant to deceive both times. Have you thought of that?"

"Oh, yes," Bobby answered. "Only it doesn't take you much further forward, does it?"

CHAPTER XXIII

NEW DEVELOPMENT

Next day the inquest was held and immediately adjourned, in order, as old Dan Edwardes had foretold, "to allow the police to complete their inquiries". Mr Anderson, as the solicitor in charge of the administration of the estate, was present, and afterwards spoke to Bobby, who had attended to give formal evidence.

"I'll walk along with you, inspector, if you don't mind," he said. "There has been a new development. I don't quite know what to make of it, but it's worrying."

"Definitely worrying?" asked Bobby, still under the obsession of that repetitive word.

"Oh, definitely so," declared Mr Anderson. "Definitely," he repeated, pleased to have been offered a word that he felt was so exactly the word required. "You know young John Wilkie? Not a very satisfactory young fellow, I'm afraid. But my late unfortunate client seems to have taken a certain interest in him. I understand there was some sort of not very clear connection by marriage, but no blood relative and no claim on the estate. He came to see me this morning. What it comes to is he says he believes it possible this is not after all an instance of o.s.p."

"Eh?" said Bobby startled, wondering if perhaps this was some variation of "O.B.E."

"Obiit sine prole," Mr Anderson explained, and Bobby remembered sufficient of his Latin to guess that this meant "died without issue". "I am gravely troubled," Mr Anderson went on. "The suggestion is that the deceased contracted a so-called irregular marriage in Scotland and had issue—a son. Naturally, in such case the said issue, if any, would have full right of inheritance. I am," repeated Mr Anderson, "disturbed."

"Did Wilkie produce any evidence?" Bobby asked.

"Naturally; the first point I raised. Wilkie's story is to the effect that my unfortunate client once stated to him, while in a state of annoyance with Mr Martin Wynne, one of the next of kin as I am at present advised, that that young man might find there were others who came before him. Also he said something about perhaps not having been so much of a bachelor as people supposed."

"Not much to go on," said Bobby. "Too vague."

"Oh, definitely," agreed Mr Anderson, and Bobby wondered uneasily if he had attached another victim to that all-pervading word's triumphant chariot. "Naturally I pointed that out. Wilkie agreed, but went on to say that the deceased at one time had interests in Paisley. He suggested that it might be worth while to make inquiries in that district."

"I suppose it ought to be followed up," Bobby agreed.

"That was my own feeling. I got through at once to the Glasgow firm with whom we are sometimes associated. They undertook to make inquiries. Naturally I shall require the most satisfactory proof. In any event, I feel the story must be probed."

"Oh, definitely," said Bobby mechanically.

"These so-called irregular marriages are most unsatisfactory," Mr Anderson declared. "I cannot think why they are permitted. A blot on Scottish law."

"Oh, well," Bobby suggested tolerantly, "I suppose the idea is that people marry themselves. The Church has only to bless their decision, and the State nothing to do but register it."

Mr Anderson didn't like this theory. He shook a doubtful head at it. Subversive, he thought. Bolshevism, very likely; and though he didn't know what Bolshevism was exactly, he did know that it was something very horrible and shocking—except when engaged in fighting Germans.

"I should hardly care to go as far as that," he said firmly. "Domicile. That's the crux of the question. If the woman, assuming for the moment that there may be some foundation for the story, was a resident of Paisley, domicile would present no difficulty in her case. But as regards my late client, clear proof would be necessary both of intention and of domicile. For domicile, residence thirty days before the date of the so-called marriage would be necessary. Intention, too. Very difficult at this interval of time. However, now the point has been raised it must be dealt with. Definitely."

"Yes, I think that's clearly necessary," agreed Bobby, dismissing the unworthy thought that a faint smile playing about the lawyer's lips, a certain touch of honey in his voice, came from the not too distant prospect of a long, even a very long bill of costs. "I'll get in touch with the Paisley police," Bobby offered, "and ask them to give what help they can."

Mr Anderson thanked him and confessed that it was partly in the hope of obtaining such assistance that he had spoken. They had reached by now the entrance to the county police headquarters. Mr Anderson shook hands and then, in the act of departing, turned and said:—

"Oh, in confidence."

Bobby waited, wondering what was coming, and if it would prove to be something all this had been leading up to.

"It has occurred to me ... I cannot say I was fully satisfied ... I experienced, in fact, a definite uneasiness," Mr Anderson continued. "The young man's manner struck me as embarrassed—even painfully embarrassed. I would not say suspicious. That would be going too far. No doubt it may seem to you a far-fetched, even fantastic conclusion, but it did occur to me, perhaps indefensibly, that possibly the young man meant himself, and that his intention is to claim to be the issue of the aforesaid marriage, and therefore first heir to the estate."

"I say," exclaimed Bobby, really startled, "that's an idea," and only just in time did he stop himself from rubbing his nose, a habit of which, under strict wifely instruction, he was endeavouring to break himself. But perhaps Olive would have been less insistent on this had she but heard the shrill whistle in which he now vented his surprise. "I never thought of that," he said, as the weird sound he had produced echoed down a startled street, and Mr Anderson positively smirked.

For he put trust in, and in general entertained, no idea that was not fortified by rule and precedent; and so was much gratified that this unaccustomed excursion of his into the realm of conjecture was apparently being received with respect and even favour.

"I never thought of that," Bobby repeated. "I do know he has told lies about his movements on the night of the murder."

"You think he may be the murderer, then?" exclaimed Mr Anderson excitedly.

"Oh, no, not yet," protested Bobby, noting that even the trained legal mind can jump to conclusions too hastily at times. "A case for reasonable suspicion only so far. A liar isn't necessarily a murderer, and sometimes a perfectly innocent man will lie himself into suspicion by trying to avoid it. A bit sticky, too, if a man known to be there or thereabouts at the time of the murder comes forward afterwards to claim to be the dead man's hitherto unrecognized son and heir."

"It is a point I considered," Mr Anderson replied. "It struck me, assuming the hypothesis I have put forward to be well founded, that possibly the statement made may be in the nature of staking out a claim with a view to future development when the situation might appear more favourable and safer. The investigation closed, that is, and all clues—the correct word, I believe—obscured by the lapse of time. One idea might be to delay the distribution of the estate."

"That might be it," Bobby agreed. "I suppose, anyhow, it will be some considerable time before the estate is ready for distribution."

"Oh, considerable," agreed Mr Anderson. "Except for Mr Martin Wynne, all the claimants are abroad. One or two are serving. It will be necessary to communicate with them all. In these present war-time conditions—well, twelve months or even longer is no unreasonable estimate. A most complicated affair," and though Mr Anderson did not smack his lips physically, Bobby was sure he did so spiritually.

"Always difficult," Bobby agreed, "to reopen a case once it has been closed."

"Fortunately," Anderson went on, "Miss Rowe, a most capable young woman, agreed to continue her assistance when I pointed that out. She had expected apparently there would be little need for her services and was already thinking about seeking fresh employment. I assured her there was no need. Indeed, I told her the period necessary might well extend over the year. In the present scarcity of competent clerical help it is a great relief that she consents to continue. I shall hope in due time to persuade her to join my own staff. A most striking young lady."

"Yes, isn't she?" Bobby agreed. "Every one feels that. I expect Mr Weston did, too."

"Naturally," Mr Anderson declared, once more shaking hands preparatory to departure, "if any such claim as seems to be foreshadowed is put forward, I shall contest it up to the Lords if necessary," and there came into his eyes such fire as one might expect in those of the warrior charging on the foe. "The whole thing," he said, "may turn out to be merely a form of blackmail—a claim put forward in the hope that a compromise may be agreed to in preference to undergoing the cost and worry of defence. No such agreed compromise will be effected with my consent," and again his eyes flashed fire.

CHAPTER XXIV
DRAWING NEARER

Waiting Bobby's return from the inquest was Sergeant Payne with a whole bundle of reports, fruits of that patient, all-embracing, sometimes even world-wide search, whereby the police organization digs up from here and there those small facts and no facts, it is the business of the detective to put together till they form, if indeed they ever do, the coherent pattern whereon action becomes possible. For, indeed, it may be the answers to the seemingly commonplace and unrelated questions put by ordinary police constables at John O'Groats and at Land's End which provide in the end the solution of the mystery in the Midlands. Just as in that great detective problem which is the universe, it is the patient work of the ordinary investigator here and there that in the end provides the material for the answer to the question posed.

"I've had a talk with the young fellow Franks had borrowed that half-crown from," Payne began. "I think we must accept his story. I've seen his young lady, too. She says the same. The lighting is pretty dim in a cinema foyer these days with all these restrictions, and fuel and light inspectors liable to pop in at any moment, but Franks spoke to them both, and they both know him."

"Did they speak to Miss Rowe?" Bobby asked.

"No, there's that," Payne admitted. "But the young chap said if Franks was there, Miss Rowe wasn't likely to be far away. Sort of joke, apparently. She never lets him out of her sight. Besides, they both say, anyhow, they saw her. Franks asked them to wait while he went to fetch her to speak to them."

"Did he?" Bobby asked.

"No, they didn't stay. Missed each other in the half light. The young man sticks to it it was her, though. His girl says the same. Describes her, too. Wearing a high-crowned hat with a tall blue feather and a caracal coat."

"Leaves a loophole," Bobby said. "Not completely satisfactory. Easy to make a mistake in bad light, and if Franks pointed to some one and said 'There's Thomasine. I'll go fetch her'—well, they could easily get the idea they had seen her. And stick to it."

"I think they would stick to it all right; I got that impression," Payne agreed.

"Anything in about the chocolates?" Bobby asked.

"No, sir, not yet—should be any minute," Payne answered. "There's a report in from London. They've confirmed Miss Rowe's story about giving a Japanese knife to a friend. They've got permission to send it to us for identification by the sellers."

"Good," said Bobby. "Of course, the story was bound to be true. Miss Rowe's not the kind of girl to tell a lie that could be so easily exposed."

"Queer coincidence," said Payne, "that Miss Rowe happened to buy the thing just before a similar weapon was used by the murderer."

"Striking coincidence," agreed Bobby. "Suggests anything?"

"Suppose," said Payne, "suppose it means the murderer is some one who knew of Miss Rowe's purchase and thought if he got hold of the same sort of knife and used it, it would throw suspicion on her."

"Who could that be?" Bobby asked.

"Well, there's Martin Wynne," Payne suggested. "He was having a lot to do with Mr Weston over the shares business. I can't think of any one else."

"Your favourite suspect?" Bobby asked.

"Oh, I wouldn't say that," declared Payne hastily. "All the same he does well out of it—gets a big slice of big money. Of course, there's Mr Edwardes owned up to having Japanese curios and says he doesn't know how many, and there's young Wilkie all mixed up with a knife-throwing act."

"Have to check up on that," Bobby agreed; and went on to tell Payne of Mr Anderson's recent communication.

Payne was very interested.

"Looks like we've got something there," he said. "There was that envelope-—marked 'papers re Aggie' and no such papers in it, only ten fifty-pound notes. If there's some young fellow who believes he is Weston's son, he might be keen on getting hold of papers to prove it."

"So he might," agreed Bobby.

"How about this, sir?" Payne went on, thinking hard. "This young Wilkie chap is Weston's son and believes he is legitimate, as being born of an irregular but legal marriage in Scotland. Weston won't acknowledge him. Tried him out once, caught him pinching the firm's cash. Made him sign a confession and packed him off with a small allowance. Wilkie isn't satisfied and threatens to raise a stink. Weston gets papers ready to show Wilkie he's all wrong about thinking there ever was a legal marriage. And he puts in the money, too, five hundred pounds, by way of keeping Wilkie quiet. Weston doesn't want a stink, do him no good, especially if he wants to stand for Parliament again. Wilkie gets mad; perhaps thinks the papers shown him are faked, which they may be. Anyhow, there's a quarrel, and it ends up with Wilkie sticking a knife into the old man and clearing out with the papers 're Aggie', faked or genuine; and if they are genuine, perhaps he means to fake 'em in his turn. How about it, sir? Holds water?"

"Well, it's jolly ingenious," Bobby said warmly, "and it brings the bank-notes and the 're Aggie' envelope into the picture, which is more than any theory of mine has managed to do. Yet all the time I've felt they were significant, even the key to it all. I can see holes in your idea, though. May be able to stop them perhaps and make it water-tight. We'll have to start a careful search of birth and marriage records. Question there," added Bobby, looking very thoughtful, "is: Must police funds stand the expense? Or can we push it on to Anderson?"

Payne was little interested in this point, since he would neither pay himself nor have to explain to an economically minded Watch Committee why police expenses were so high.

"You think there are holes, sir," he hinted.

"Psychological stuff," Bobby said. "Of course, you can never be sure you know any man—or yourself either—well enough to be quite certain what he'll do next. But I can't see Weston in the role of black-mailee—if there is such a word. What he liked was getting a hold on other people. He dominated others, he wasn't one to allow himself to be dominated. Why he even," said Bobby, bristling all over, so that Payne got quite frightened, "had the cheek to try to boss me. Some fat-headed idea or another that I had got mixed up in politics and that was going to give him a hold."

"Can't understand that, sir," declared Payne, on appeasement bent. "I'm sure I've never heard you say a word about politics."

"I should hope not," said Bobby in such a tone Payne was almost afraid he was going to be reduced to the ranks then and there. By way of diversion he said as quickly as possible: "That summer-house, sir, you said I was to look for, in the Weston Lodge Cottage grounds, you remember?"

"You found it, did you?" Bobby asked, forgetting at once a grievance that still rankled, even though the person responsible therefor was dead. "Any dabs?"

"Yes, sir. It's there all right, clean away from the house, all among trees, so you can't see it, almost on top of the lane that runs along at the back there. Not much used, apparently, all dusty, and dabs as plain as you could want. I can't think how you knew."

Payne paused, evidently hoping for an explanation, and Bobby said apologetically:—

"Oh, well, that was simple enough. Martin Wynne got back home in the small hours. But it had been raining hard here, and yet apparently he hadn't got wet, as the servants at his boarding-house hadn't noticed wet clothing or muddied boots or anything like that. I had seen him that evening, so I knew he had neither overcoat nor umbrella. And I knew Miss Olga Severn had been waiting for him. It was a fair guess they had had a talk together and under cover. What I want to know is, what did they talk about?" and hearing this, Payne plainly lost at once both admiration and surprise, so that once again Bobby reflected how mistaken it was to offer explanations making simple a result that otherwise could remain mysterious and awe-inspiring.

"I take it you did find both Wynne's dabs and Miss Olga's?" Bobby added.

But Payne shook his head, a little pleased that this time at least his senior had not scored.

"A man's dabs all right," he said, "but we haven't got Wynne's to check up on. And a woman's too. Might be a child's, but probably a woman's, only not the same as those on Miss Olga Severn's vanity case."

"Oh, no, I didn't think they would be," Bobby said, and this time did not explain; nor had he the opportunity, for now they were interrupted by the arrival of the report of the officer charged with the inquiry into the provenance of the box of poisoned chocolates, the poison now identified as arsenic.

It was to the effect that the firm of manufacturers concerned had replied that a packer's number identified the packer only, not the box. They could say, however, that the packer concerned had done no work for them for some two months, having left to join the A.T.S. They could also say that out of the last consignment of boxes she had packed, one, and one only, had been sold in the Midwych district. It had been used to make up a lot of a dozen sent to Lewis and Lawrence, confectioners, of Midwych High Street, in part fulfilment of an urgent order for a couple of gross. Since then they had been able to supply no further boxes of that style and quality to any retailer anywhere, owing to the drastic restriction order now in force.

A visit in search of further information had therefore been paid to Lewis and Lawrence, where the incident of the arrival of a dozen chocolate boxes in response to an urgent order for two gross-was keenly remembered. It was also remembered that all the boxes had been sold the same day, and the name of one customer was also remembered.

"Mr Weston himself it was," Payne said, watching to see how surprised Bobby looked. "They knew him quite well—of course he was well known in Midwych. No way to identify the actual box, though the price is the same, but there's a note still in their books of who he said it was to be sent to—"

Payne paused, hoping Bobby would say "Who?" Instead Bobby said:—

"To Miss Olga Severn?"

"That's right," Payne said, disappointed at such a lucky guess. "What's it mean?"

"Means, I think," Bobby said frowningly, "means we are drawing nearer to the heart of things."

CHAPTER XXV

MISSING CHOCOLATES

A 'PHONE RING interrupted them. It was from the head of the department where Ronald Franks worked in the big engineering concern employing him. The departmental head seemed in a very bad temper. Bobby could not at first make out why. Presently it appeared that there was a big important and pressing Government contract on hand. To complete it, every available pair of hands was needed, was indeed necessary, and how was it to be finished in time if Inspector Bobby Owen encouraged every man he could get hold of to throw up his job and join the army? What was the good of an army without equipment? demanded the 'phone angrily. So Bobby said he didn't know the answer to that one, and anyhow he had no idea what the departmental head was talking about. So the departmental head said he was talking about Ronald Franks. Not, he admitted frankly, that Franks was anything to make a song about in the ordinary way. But just at present a deaf and dumb cripple, blind from birth, would be welcome, and after all Franks was a degree or two better than that. The departmental manager explained that it wasn't only Franks, it was the example. If Franks was to be encouraged to get released, half the younger men would claim release as well and all of them would be unsettled. Output would go down, the war would be lost, and the whole blame would rest on the shoulders of Inspector Bobby Owen of the county police.

Bobby, guiltily aware that he had already nearly lost the war by using too much water his bath, protested feebly. He knew nothing about it, he had encouraged neither Franks nor any one else to seek release, and if he had, it would have made no difference. Release, call up, non-release all of it no affair of the police.

Unconvinced, and still grumbling, the departmental head rang off, and Bobby told Payne what it had all been about, and Payne rubbed his nose, having picked up from Bobby the habit Bobby was attempting, by order, to abandon.

"What's it mean?" he asked. "That little twirp—why, the army wouldn't look at him."

"Oh, I don't know," Bobby said. "They'll look at most these days—and sometimes even turn a twirp into a man."

"I suppose," admitted Payne, "they could train him to peel potatoes. My young brother says soldiering and peeling potatoes are all one. Sounds as if Franks had been using your name—like his cheek." Payne paused. "Look here, sir," he said. "If there's anything wrong with that alibi, and the light in a cinema foyer isn't too good these days, and he may have got that pal of his to tell lies to help him out—well, I mean to say, is Franks doing a bunk?"

"Looks like it," said Bobby. Then he said: "What from?"

"If it's him he's scared," Payne answered. "I mean to say—if he's guilty. You wouldn't think, not to look at him, he had the guts to steal a copper out of a blind man's cap, but you can't ever tell. You wouldn't ever expect a young lady like Miss Rowe to pick on such as him for her best boy."

"No, you wouldn't," agreed Bobby, and sat for some time lost in thought.

Then he put through a call to Weston Lodge Cottage. Hargreaves answered it. Bobby explained he wanted to speak to Miss Rowe, and when she answered, he told her he had been informed from the works where Mr Franks was employed that he was leaving to join up. Did Miss Rowe know if this was true? Because, if it was, Bobby would have to get in touch with Mr Franks and ask him to sign a formal deposition. Once in the army, Bobby remarked, a man might easily be lost for good, so far as personal contacts were concerned.

Thomasine, evidently disturbed, her husky, distinctive voice less steady than usual, replied that it couldn't be true, because Mr Franks was in a reserved occupation. She knew he would have joined up long ago had it been permitted, but he was doing far too valuable work to be spared. His departmental head considered him his key man, without whom the whole department would have to be re-organized. She was meeting Mr Franks later on, she added, and she would ask him about it.

So Bobby hung up, smiling sweetly, for he thought Mr Franks was going to hear things, and just possibly, as a result, he thought he himself might come to hear things, too; and Payne repeated thoughtfully that the biggest mystery in the whole thing was what a slap-up girl like Thomasine Rowe could see in the bit of chewed-up rag that called itself Ronald Franks.

"Reminds you of something the cat's brought in," he said. "Why, wouldn't want to be found dead near him."

"Well, I daresay she wouldn't either," Bobby observed; and a little later, after Payne had left him in order to see if Olga Severn could give any further information about the box of chocolates, there came a long-distance call from the police in South Wales. It was to the effect that a paragraph had appeared in the local press recounting that Monsieur Ivan Janovitch—in private life, Ted Jones—of the Great Knife-Throwing Act "Miss and Death", now performing with such sensational and record-breaking success at the Magnificent Theatre, had been the victim of a recent burglary. Not only had his wife lost jewellery of a stupendous though unspecified value, but also among other articles stolen, had been a Japanese dagger, formerly used in the amazing knife-throwing act already mentioned. Mr Janovitch was gravely disturbed lest this stolen Japanese knife might turn out to be the weapon used in the recent murder of a prominent industrialist. There was more to the same effect, including a passing mention of where and when the sensational &c. &c. knife-throwing act could be seen the following week.

"Publicity," said the South Wales police disgustedly. "That's why he went to a reporter before he came to us. We told him off good and hard, but what's he care? He's got his free advert, and very likely that's all there's to it. And if we prosecute for a public mischief, it'll only be more free publicity. You can't," said the Welsh police sadly, "you can't do much to a man who lives on publicity."

Bobby agreed; agreed, too, that very likely there was nothing in it beyond publicity hunting, but you could never tell, and when presently he left to go home, he found Franks waiting in the street outside.

Very reproachfully, almost with tears, Franks wanted to know why the inspector had given him away to Thomasine; and Bobby explained he had been rung up by Mr Franks's boss, so it was evident Mr Franks's information had ceased to be confidential. And why, Bobby asked, this sudden desire to join up? Franks replied that he had been thinking about it long enough. He added resentfully that "she"—he seemed to think the pronoun enough for identification—had been on at him already, and anyhow what had it to do with the police?

"Murder investigation," said Bobby briefly.

"Well, it wasn't me; you know that," Franks protested. "Nothing to do with me. How could there be when I was at the Super Superb? I've got a witness, and you know it."

"Jolly good alibi," Bobby admitted. "But you can never tell with an alibi. The light allowed in a cinema foyer to-day isn't much more than darkness made visible. There are such things as disguises. I've known witnesses to be mistaken. Or merely trying to do a pal a good turn. Or even bribed."

"My God," gasped Franks, "you don't . . . you can't . . . mean . . ."

"Just what I say," Bobby told him. "Only that, and nothing more—or less. Until the facts are established, I have to consider every possibility. Of course, if you can tell me anything more . . . anything to help to make it clear what really happened."

He paused, waiting. Franks stood there with his mouth opening and shutting. Bobby said:—

"Shall we go inside?"

Franks stared at him, looked round wildly, then turned his back and fairly ran for it. At the corner of the street he ran straight into the arms of Thomasine Rowe. He was hurrying by, almost as if he were too disturbed to see her. She caught him by the arm, and together they vanished. Bobby lighted a cigarette and waited. He thought there might be developments. He had not to wait long. Only a few minutes elapsed before Thomasine, magnificent in wrath and indignation, came swinging round the comer again. She saw Bobby and marched upon him. Evidently his recent 'phone call had brought her hot foot to Midwych, as he had thought it might. What, she demanded, had he been saying to Mr Franks?

"I was telling him," Bobby explained, "that if he knows any-thing—"

"He doesn't," she interrupted fiercely.

"—it would be wise to let me know," Bobby went on, ignoring her interruption. "Don't you think so?"

"He knows nothing," she repeated, staring at him angrily. "How could he when we were at the cinema when it happened?"

"Yes, there's that, isn't there?" Bobby agreed. "And no one can be in two places at the same time."

"There's a witness," she told him. "It just happened he saw a friend he owed some money to and he went across to pay him."

"Bit of luck it happened that night," Bobby observed.

Again she stared at him, long and challengingly.

"I don't know what you mean," she said at last. "Mr Franks is very highly strung. He is extraordinarily sensitive and delicate. I suppose you think that makes it easy to bully him into saying anything you want him to? Only a brute would try."

"I suppose so," agreed Bobby. "You know, sometimes I feel I am a bit of a brute, and then I'm sorry I'm a policeman, and then again I feel there's no thrill in all the world like the pursuit of a murderer—your wits against his, your life against his, life for a prize, and one little bit of the world at least made safe for ordinary people. A worthwhile job. Because, you know, sometimes assassins strike twice."

Thomasine greeted this last remark with something as much like a snort as one could expect from a lady.

"You leave that poor boy alone," she said. "A coarse, brutal character like yours can't understand the delicacy and sensitiveness of his," and again Bobby noted with wonder the deep tenderness in her voice.

Head over ears in love with him and only the good Lord knows why, he thought, and made no attempt to defend himself against her wrath. All the same, he hoped she was wrong; he hoped he understood Ronald Franks much better than she did. He said:—

"You haven't mentioned that chocolates affair to any one, have you?"

"No. But I wish you would take that man of yours away," she said petulantly. "He is only a nuisance; just sits there like a great goop."

Bobby was pleased at this moment to observe the "goop" in question peeping cautiously round the corner of the street.

"I'm sorry you find him a nuisance," Bobby said, "but after what's happened, we have to think of your safety. Really, he ought not to let you out of his sight."

Miss Rowe looked contemptuous. The "goop" had withdrawn his cautious head by now. Miss Rowe said:—

"He gets all excited if I even look out of the window, but I came away by the back door and he didn't know."

"Too bad," said Bobby. "By the way, we've had those chocolates analyzed. Arsenic all right, and lots of it. But it seems the amount the puppy took was about the total amount in each separate one of the top row of chocolates. And there are six chocolates missing."

"Oh, yes," Thomasine said. "I threw some away. I remember. Into the waste-paper basket. Some I cut open and there was that same funny white powder in them all. Afterwards, after you had gone, I remembered about them, and I thought it wasn't safe to leave them there, so I went into the kitchen and put them in the fire."

"Oh, yes, that explains it," Bobby said; and to himself he wondered if this were the truth or if—but he did not much like to think of alternatives.

CHAPTER XXVI
LOGIC

As HE made his way homewards that evening, Bobby was still thinking uncomfortably about these four women who seemed by the logic of events and by their own emotional entanglements to come in turn, one after the other, into the limelight of suspicion. First, the dark and enigmatic Thomasine with her strange obsession for the seemingly commonplace and unattractive Franks. Bessie Bell, too, her fierce blonde beauty and her air of stark defiance—against what? And Florence Severn, the athlete, hovering in the background like a hawk waiting to swoop—upon whom? Finally, her niece, Olga, welfare officer, upon whom the twists and turns of the investigation seemed ever and anon to throw fresh gleams of suspicion, only for them to fade away again almost at once—but did they?

It was after dinner that Bobby began to set himself in real earnest to try to think out his problems. Over the meal Olive had presided with smug triumph, not only because a long cycle ride had tested and proved true a strange rumour she had heard about a far-away small-holder who had a hen, an aged hen, a very Methuselah among hens, he might be willing to sell—as he was, and never mind the price—but also because by her most recondite and delicate arts she had made it seem almost young again. In fact, a veritable miracle of rejuvenation. So now, that achieved, she was ready to turn her attention to the perplexities and the difficulties with which Bobby found himself confronted.

"Four women and four men," he said gloomily, "and if it's a case of a pair of them teaming up together—well, almost any variety of complication is possible." He began to tick them off on his fingers. "First the men," he said. "Take old Dan Edwardes. Do respectable old gentlemen, hitherto leading blameless lives devoted to Greek grammar and cooking, take to murder?"

"What has age to do with murder?" Olive asked; "and does respectability count when you have lost three sons?"

"I don't know," said Bobby. "There are his dabs on those glasses we found to show he was with Weston late that night. He hasn't said a word about it. If he is innocent, why not?"

"If he is guilty, he wouldn't," Olive said, "and if he is innocent he may not want to draw suspicion on himself while he is trying to put through his new plans for the Weston West Mills. I think he feels it's something he owes his sons, and he won't let anything interfere with it."

"Perhaps he hasn't, not even a life," Bobby said. "All the same, would any normal man commit murder merely to put right what he has come to think of as a social wrong?"

"Is any old man normal when he has been sitting brooding over the loss of three sons and now he's left alone?" Olive asked. "Bobby, if you prove him guilty, I'll never forgive you."

"If he did this thing," Bobby answered gravely, "he must answer for it to the law. Neither you nor I have the right to condemn, but neither have we the right to absolve."

"Well, I don't believe he did," Olive retorted, shifting her ground. "Besides, he hasn't been sitting and brooding; he's been cooking. I expect that's kept him sane, even though it's enough just now to drive any one mad."

"You're being inconsistent," Bobby pointed out. "No logic."

"You and your logic," said Olive, and metaphorically threw logic out of the window. "I wonder," she added thoughtfully, "if he's such a howling swell at cooking, what he would have thought of that old hen—before and after," and if it hadn't been Olive, one would have said that she smirked.

"That chicken—or hen—has no after," Bobby reminded her. "Besides, the evidence isn't so very strong. We do believe he was the last person in Weston's company—unless he himself really is the murderer. We think he may be unbalanced mentally after what he's suffered. We know Weston bitterly—passionately—opposed his plans and he was just as strongly—passionately—bent on carrying them through. We know that now Edwardes will get his way—in the only way in which he could get it. By Weston's death. And though we can't prove it, the murder weapon may certainly have come from his collection. Not too good when you think of it like that. It may be when he thinks of his sons and of all the others all the world over, another death may not have seemed to matter so very much. I'm afraid we can't leave him out."

"He has always lived so quiet a life," Olive remarked musingly. "I think sometimes if things break loose inside you, they break loose all the more because of that. Like pent-up waters through a broken dam."

"If there were nothing else, if he were the only one," Bobby decided, "there might be grounds for an arrest. But, then, he isn't. There are the others. Martin Wynne."

"I've never seen him," Olive remarked. "Didn't you say he was very good looking?"

"That," said Bobby severely, "has nothing to do with it." Without paying any attention to Olive's murmured and nearly inaudible "Oh, but it always has," he continued: "He was on bad terms with Weston, too; pretty hot they were when I heard them. Then the dabs in the summer-house do suggest he was hanging about fairly late that night, and what for?"

"I thought you said there were dabs to show a girl had been in the summer-house, too," Olive reminded him. "Mightn't that be the 'what for'? I've heard it is sometimes," she added demurely.

"If it was only a spot of courting by night," Bobby asked, "why that night, and why a damp, neglected summer-house in some one else's garden on a rainy night?"

"When it is what you call a spot of courting—and I do think that's a horrid vulgar way to talk, and you might just as well say if it was a true lovers' meeting," Olive said, "I've been told that then its sometimes 'Who cares?'—time, weather, place, or anything."

"Yes, but this isn't true love," Bobby protested. "It's murder. That's different."

"True love as well, perhaps," Olive said, and Bobby frowned.

"If it is, it's a complication," he said.

"It always is," said Olive. "The most complicated thing in the world. Crime is always simple, love isn't—ever."

"I don't know what you think you're getting at," Bobby grumbled uneasily. "Anyway, you're growing too complicated for me. Come back to facts. Martin Wynne gets a big slice of the estate. He had access to Japanese knives at Edwardes's place, he is liable to crazy notions, as witness that crazy story he told about the message he had from a dead woman in the stratosphere."

"How do you know it's a crazy story?" Olive asked. "You weren't there. Of course, he is an inventor. I remember Mrs Klein—"

"Who's she?" asked Bobby, stricken by a sudden fear that Olive was about to introduce a new suspect.

"Mrs Melanie Klein," Olive explained. "She writes about children's psychology and understanding them. I've a book of hers."

She produced it. Bobby looked at it, and said thank the Lord he left all that sort of thing behind him when he left college, and what on earth did Olive want with stuff like that, and Olive took the book from him and showed him a passage to the effect that strong desire could overcome will and training and conscience, too, and that artist, scientist, inventor, might take any road, even that of murder, which seemed to lead towards the wished for goal.

"I think she is right," Olive said. "If you want anything passionately—how to fly in the stratosphere, for instance, or to carry out plans which you think your dead sons wanted—I think a life may come to seem a small thing if it's in the way. I'm afraid you must keep Martin Wynne at the back of your mind."

"I'm not sure he isn't in the front of it," Bobby said gloomily. "There's a jolly good case."

"It would be better," Olive said, "if he wasn't so good looking."

"There's a woman all over," declared Bobby tolerantly. "As if his looks mattered one way or another. Now, let's come to Franks. A bit of chewed-up rag, Payne calls him."

"What about his alibi?" Olive asked.

"I know," Bobby agreed. "It bothers me. Sound as a bell. Direct evidence of eye-witnesses—Reynolds and his girl. No reason why Reynolds should tell lies to help Franks. Intelligent young chap, good character, no special pal of Franks, not in the least likely to tell lies to help a murderer to escape. All the same, that half-crown business does seem to be a bit too pat. We've got to accept it, and yet I feel sure there's a catch in it somewhere. And why is Franks so keen on joining up all at once? Doing a bunk, Payne says, but why?"

"I think I could guess," Olive said. "But only a guess. What about Mr Wilkie and his story about Mr Weston having married and there may be a son? If there's any truth in the knife-throwing artist's story, Mr Wilkie may have got hold of a Japanese dagger, too."

"The whole thing seems lousy with Japanese daggers," Bobby complained. "Perhaps the murderer knew it, and that's why one was used. Between them Mr Anderson and Payne drew up a pretty strong case against Wilkie; and if we could identify him with Weston's hypothetical son, it might be good enough."

"Why son?" asked Olive. "If he really was married and had a child, why not a daughter?"

"Well, you know," Bobby said slowly, "I never thought of that, not once." He began to look excited. "It's an idea. Thomasine Rowe. Could that be why Weston engaged her? Wanted to have his girl by him, and though she is such a good looker, she sticks to it he never tried to make love to her. Bit queer, with his reputation. Might explain it, though, if it's like that. Or Bessie Bell? Is that why he got her there? I can't trace any hint of their ever having had anything to do with each other, and she says she has no idea what he wanted. She looked scared to death that night, though. Or Florence Severn? But it can't be her. She's too old."

"Is she?" Olive asked. "What are the dates?"

Bobby started to rub his nose, recollected himself, stopped, and whistled instead.

"Good gracious!" said Olive, startled, and Bobby continued:—

"She says he had asked her to marry him. Every one seems to have thought that's what she was after."

"It might be what she wanted was for him to acknowledge her," Olive said, "and the story she told you was because she knew of the gossip and wanted you to accept it. She might think a disinherited, abandoned daughter too much of a likely suspect and an expectant wife no suspect at all."

"It's got to be considered," Bobby agreed. "I can see another year or two spent looking up births, marriages and deaths. Irregular marriage in Scotland, though. No official record. Illegitimate child. Father may be entered unknown—sometimes women won't give away their lovers, and sometimes they are promised money not to. And we don't know the mother's name. Except Aggie at a guess. Not much to go on, and not much help anyhow. If you ask me, I should say the niece was a good deal more likely. It was Weston gave her her job, and we mustn't forget that vanity case."

A knock at the front door interrupted them. Bobby went to answer it, as he and Olive were alone in the house, Olive's only domestic help being an elderly lady, who, with fine impartiality, "obliged" Olive and the vicar's wife each three days a week, thus keeping as she hoped on the right side of both church and law. Cautiously Bobby opened the door, alarmed lest any ray of light should escape and thus bring upon him the wrath of the air-raid wardens, who, and well he knew it, would chuckle for a week if they had the luck to catch a police inspector bending. A voice he recognized said:—

"Is Mr Owen in?"

"Miss Olga Severn, isn't it?" Bobby said. "Come in, please."

Carefully he adjusted the black-out curtain after her entry. He ushered her into the small dining-room and as he did so, she said:—

"I was on my way to a welfare concert at the General Aircraft factory."

"Oh, yes," Bobby said. "Where Mr Martin Wynne works?"

"Yes. I thought I would stop on the way to tell you. It's about a box of chocolates. One of your men has been asking me about Mr Weston giving me one. He didn't say how he knew, but it's quite true."

She paused as if expecting or hoping for an explanation. Bobby said:—

"When we are making inquiries in a case like this, all sorts of things turn up. Sometimes they are important. More often they aren't. But we have to follow them up. You never know."

"Your man wanted to know what I had done with them," she continued. "I don't know why. I didn't do anything. I didn't want to send them back. It would have made Mr Weston awfully angry, and I might have lost my job, and I didn't want to. I like it. When I saw who the chocolates came from, I just put the box away. I've just moved from aunt's and my things are all anyhow still, but I said I would try to find it. Well, I can't. I rang up my aunt, but she doesn't know anything about it either and she is sure it isn't anywhere there. I can't think what has become of it. That's all I wanted to tell you. I must go on now, or I shall be late."

Bobby did not attempt to detain her. But he thought he knew only too well what had become of it. He followed her into the dimly lighted entrance hall. There she was half hidden in the shadows, and the thought came to him that her soul and her mind were as hidden from him as was here her outward appearance. He said:—

"Did Mr Weston often send you chocolates?"

"No, never before. Only that once."

"Was there any special reason this time?"

"I think," she answered in a low voice, "it was because he wanted me to marry him."

CHAPTER XXVII
SIGNIFICANT FACTORS

BOBBY WAS going back to rejoin Olive when the 'phone bell rang once more. This time it was Sergeant Payne, reporting on inquiries he had just completed. These included much of the information Olga herself had just given. They proved in addition that both Thomasine and Franks had been at work at the hour at which the post-mark showed the box of chocolates to have been sent off from the central Midwych post office. But that office was only a few yards from the Wych and Wych Arms, so that Bessie Bell could easily have slipped out to send it off without her absence being noticed. Then both the Misses Severn, both Florence and Olga, had been in town that day, the one shopping, the other on some errand connected with her welfare work. Also both Wilkie and Mr Edwardes were masters of their own time. Further, Martin Wynne, as a research worker, was freer than most from the ordinary discipline of office or workshop, and would have had no difficulty in leaving his desk—or rather his drawing-board—without his disappearance attracting any attention.

"Looks," Bobby said to Olive after he had rung off, "as if any one of them could have sent the thing. Except Thomasine and Ronald Franks. Which doesn't mean any of them did, of course. No one at the post office remembers anything about it. Not likely to.

Again, who ever is responsible may have got some one else to do the actual posting."

"You never really thought it was Miss Rowe herself, did you?" Olive asked.

"Oh, no," Bobby agreed. "You can never tell, though. It had to be considered. Anyhow, she and the young man are both cleared as far as that goes. She couldn't herself, and I can't see her employing any one else. A self-reliant young woman. Still, we are broadcasting an appeal to any one who posted a package addressed to Weston Lodge Cottage to come forward. I don't expect any result."

"Why should any one want to poison her?" Olive asked.

"Well, there's the suggestion she made herself—that she knows something. Or if she's the mysterious missing heir there've been so many hints about, and if some one knows it, then it might be an attempt to put her out of the way. That brings in Olga Severn again. She means to marry Martin, but wants him as part heir to the Weston estate, so tries to wipe out Thomasine to make sure Martin gets his share. Pure guesswork. Thomasine is a bit of the dark horse in the case. Only the private secretary, apparently, but was she more? Self-contained, enigmatic. Formidable in the sort of dark restraint she shows. There's this against her—she has lied twice over in two instances. At least, unless her suggestion is valid and it was Olga Severn I heard that night, deliberately imitating her. Anyhow, the other lie is patent."

"Yes, I know," agreed Olive thoughtfully. "One lie, perhaps." With a slight gesture Olive dismissed one lie as merely an example of human frailty. "But twice, I don't like twice. Besides, what possible motive—unless she really is the possible, improbable lawful heir."

"No birth certificate to check up on," Bobby said. "Born abroad. There are points against her, serious points. Familiarity with Weston's affairs, the house and the domestic arrangements generally. And I don't like the coincidence of her buying a Japanese dagger so short a time ago. Of course, she has her explanation—pat, almost too pat, like the repaid half-crown that clinches their alibi. She is in the picture all right, and though it's not evidence, I don't much like either that odd little incident I told you about the first time I saw Franks."

"I should put that out of my mind if I were you," said Olive firmly. "Far too flimsy."

"It worries me," Bobby repeated. "How on earth can you account for her having fallen for a nonentity like Ronald Franks?"

"The attraction of opposites," Olive suggested. "Mother instinct, too. Every woman is a mother. Girl babies grab at dolls before they can walk or talk. A husband is only a bigger and more troublesome child she has to look after, worse luck." Here Bobby interposed a murmured "Don't mind me", and Olive didn't, but went on: "Thomasine is an unusual type. She feels—and is—different. She feels—and is—superior in many ways to most young men. But all they see in her is a pretty girl, different from other pretty girls only in being prettier than most—a striking girl, as you told Franks. But when she meets him she fascinates him, she finds she can dominate him, she feels she can express herself through him as a mother expresses herself through her child, he becomes her child. And men may think women are a poor, weak, soft lot, but steel is butter to a woman when it comes to protecting her child."

"Psychology," said Bobby, with a certain doubt in his voice.

"Theft is only theft," Olive replied, "but there's always psychology where there's murder."

"Um umm," said Bobby. "If it comes to psychology, what about Bessie Bell? Quite a little history there of readiness to resort to violence. There's something she wants to keep quiet, too, or why did she go in such a funk to see Weston when he sent for her, and why her secret excursions on her days off? We'll have to try to follow her, but it won't be easy. She is very much on her guard. And you can't shut your eyes to the possibility that, having a secret to keep, she struck to guard it still."

"Do you believe Olga Severn," Olive asked abruptly, "when she says Mr Weston wanted to marry her?"

"If it's true, it may explain why she and her aunt have quarrelled," Bobby said. "We've traced the chocolates to her, but we can't prove some one else didn't get hold of them, poison them and send them to Thomasine. The snag there is that neither Olga nor her aunt will let us take their finger-prints and the careful English law won't let us insist. And if we got them by too barefaced trickery, and that came out at the trial, ten to one the jury would say it wasn't fair and acquit on the spot. There are times when British ideas about fair play do tie up a poor, hardworking policeman. Anyhow, both of them were very much on their guard, and I should guess Miss Olga has cool, dry fingertips and doesn't make dabs easily; except on nice dusty surfaces, for instance. But the trouble is that those we found in the summer-house don't agree with those on her vanity case, which, however, do agree with those in the knee-hole of the writing-desk. So far, though, no way of pinning them on either of the Severn women—or on any one else for that matter. Anyhow, as they both say Weston had proposed marriage, one of them must be lying."

"Why?" asked Olive.

"Oh, well," said Bobby doubtfully.

"Two strings to his bow," said Olive, "and meant neither, perhaps, except—well, except as an opening gambit. He was that sort, wasn't he?"

"Oh, well," said Bobby again. "Well, we may have hit on the reason aunt and niece quarrelled, and perhaps also why Miss Florence Severn let her ring slip off her finger the first time I saw her."

"Wasn't that just because it was too big and didn't fit?" Olive asked.

"I think perhaps it was because it did fit in another sense," Bobby answered gravely.

Olive looked thoughtful, and then said, yes, there was that, when you came to think of it. Then she added that in her opinion, they had better now go to bed, as they had talked quite long enough without getting much further forward. But Bobby said he would sit up a little longer and try to rack his brains a little harder still. It was indeed getting on in the small hours when at last he went upstairs, where he found the light still on and Olive wide awake. She said:—

"I've been thinking."

"Any result?" asked Bobby.

"A headache," said Olive sadly.

Bobby sat down on the edge of the bed and looked equally sad.

"I've been trying," he remarked, "to pick out the significant factors."

"What are they?" asked Olive. "I don't see how you can tell in such a confusion of things that may mean a lot or may mean nothing at all."

Bobby began to enumerate those he had tried to select, holding up successive fingers as he mentioned each one in turn.

"First, Weston got both Martin Wynne and Bessie Bell to his house on the night of the murder, which seems to suggest there's a link between them.

"Second. He got me there, too—like his confounded cheek—and that suggests he thought the link, whatever it was, was a police matter. Thirdly. He had the—the—"

"Damn cheek," suggested Olive. "I know that's what you want to say, so you may as well get it out."

"Thank you," said Bobby, deeply appreciative of such wifely tact. "He had the—as you say—to hint he knew how to make himself unpleasant to policemen who didn't do what he wanted. Suggestion is he wanted to scare Wynne and Bessie by using my presence as a kind of hint of making a criminal charge, but at the same time didn't want to press it, and wanted to be sure I wouldn't either. So the thing is to find out what he knew or thought he knew. All probable and improbable records are being searched, but so far without any luck, and it's not likely they themselves will tell."

"Well, why should they?" asked Olive, very reasonably, and Bobby went on, unheeding:—

"Fourth. Mr Edwardes was there also the same night, but much later. That, suggests Weston meant either to tell him what he knew about Wynne, or more probably he hoped to be able to say he had nobbled Wynne, who held the, so to say, balance of power, and so had hamstrung Edwardes's plans for the new deal at the Weston West Mills."

"And how much further forward," asked Olive, "does all that take you?"

"Not an inch," admitted Bobby, "so far. But I think there's just a faint suggestion of a background appearing.

"Fifthly. We found an envelope marked 'Family Papers—Re Aggie', but containing only bank-notes. Query: Who was Aggie?"

"Aren't you being," Olive asked, "a good deal better at asking questions than at answering them?"

"Find the right questions," retorted Bobby sententiously, "and you get the right answers.

"Sixthly. We found a confession of theft and embezzlement signed by John Wilkie.

"Seventhly. Weston had sent for him, too. That suggests Wilkie also was to be made use of. And here you get the general conclusion that Weston had in hand some complicated plan to upset the new deal Edwardes proposed. But there's no certainty that this plan was the direct cause of what happened. It may be that some one else knew about it and saw a chance to twist it to another purpose."

"Complicated cross purposes," commented Olive.

"Oh, it's complicated all right," declared Bobby. "A bundle of clues all pointing different ways. But did Wilkie know why he had been sent for? Was he afraid Weston was going to use that confession? Or even that fresh embezzlements had come to light? It's quite plain he lied when he said he reached Midwych by the train due in at four that morning. He was certainly on the spot much earlier. And what for?"

"How do you know?" demanded Olive.

"Oh, come," protested Bobby. "You can be quicker in the uptake than that. Stands out a mile. Gives him a motive if he thought he was going to be prosecuted. But there's still another person we know was on the scene that night. Olga Severn. She spoke to me, you remember, mistaking me for Wynne. Which looks as if she knew what was going on and was waiting for Wynne so she could hear the result. I take it she and Wynne are in love. If it was Olga who was in the summer-house with him till all hours that night, the presumption is they had something important to talk about. Not a very long shot to suppose it was connected with whatever it may be Weston thought he had found out about Wynne and Bessie."

"Can they be married?" Olive asked.

"No telling. The records have been looked up without result. Anyhow, if they are, why should that give Weston a hold on them? Why should that make Weston think he could threaten police action?"

"Don't forget either, you don't really know it was Olga Severn in the summer-house," Olive warned him.

"What we do know, anyhow, is that the dabs in the summer-house do not agree with those on her vanity case, but the vanity case dabs agree with the ones on the panelling of the knee-hole of Weston's writing-table. There I think—I think—I think—" said Bobby very slowly, "I think we come to the crux of the whole business."

"I don't see why," protested Olive, really puzzled this time.

"Because," explained Bobby, "Miss Florence Severn is now having that ring of hers altered to fit, so it won't come off her finger so easily any more. We know that because she's being watched."

"Oh, well, yes," said Olive, considering this. "Yes, I see. Only— well, I still don't see how you are going to get over the Rowe and Franks joint alibi."

"A snag," Bobby agreed. "A big snag. That brings up another important point. She seems to be passionately in love with Franks, but is he with her?"

"No," said Olive. "Fascinated," she suggested.

"That's how I see it," Bobby said. "Rabbit and boa constrictor."

"Poor Thomasine," said Olive.

"You mean, poor Ronald Franks, don't you?"

"No," said Olive. "I mean what I said—poor Thomasine."

"Oh, well," said Bobby doubtfully.

"She has great love for him," Olive said, "and he has little or none for her. That is not only tragedy. It is a cause of tragedy. I think perhaps she knows deep down inside her how little he really cares, and, Bobby, I begin to think that it's there is the root of it all."

Bobby looked at her uncomfortably.

"I believe I had the same idea, only I didn't want to," he said. "All the same, he is altogether under her influence, whether it's love or merely fascination. She can make him do anything she wants."

"What is there she could want to make him do?" Olive asked uneasily, for she thought she knew.

Bobby, profoundly disturbed, was beginning to walk up and down the room.

"What it all adds up to," he said, "is where are the half-dozen poisoned chocolates missing from the box some one unknown sent Thomasine Rowe?"

CHAPTER XXVIII

BOBBY PERTURBED

It was, indeed, the thought of those missing chocolates and of the purpose for which they might be destined that was chiefly troubling Bobby all through the routine of ordinary work demanding his attention during the earlier part of the following day.

True, the careful analysis he, with Olive's help, had made of the known facts—relevant and irrelevant—enabled him to feel he saw at last a reasonable pattern of events beginning to emerge. But small was the gain, small the advantage, when there lay so heavy on his mind the threat of yet more tragedy to come.

"What we think we know," he said to Payne, whose mood was almost as gloomy as his own, "is no more evidence than what the soldier said."

"What isn't evidence," Payne pointed out, "is often much better evidence than what is."

Bobby nodded assent to a platitude of police experience, and later on was informed that Mr Edwardes had called and was asking for an interview.

"Good," said Bobby; who always felt it was promising when possible suspects came forward of their own accord to make statements which might be true, when they were useful, or might be false, when very likely they would be more useful still.

So he had Mr Edwardes shown in at once, and Mr Edwardes told him smilingly that now everything was settled at the Weston West Mills for the establishment of the new "common good" order.

"I've set up a trust," he explained. "I call it 'common good' rather than 'common wealth', because good is more than wealth and a better thing to aim at. So now I shan't care so much if you do want to arrest me. I take it I am still under suspicion?"

"Why not?" Bobby asked, thinking the time had come to apply a little pressure; "when we know you were with Weston late on the night of the murder and you have tried to keep it secret."

"Oh, you know about that," Mr Edwardes said, looking very surprised. "How do you know?" Bobby did not answer. Mr Edwardes went on: "I thought if you knew, you would think it proof. I did mean to tell you finally. You won't believe that now, but it's true. I made up my mind I would get my trust going first. After that, I shan't care so much, one way or another. By the way, I didn't kill Weston. I suppose you think I should say so anyhow. He was perfectly all right when I left. But I think he was expecting some one. While we were talking we had a drink in the dining-room, and all the time he was listening and watching, watching the door of the study opposite and listening. It was plain he was expecting something or some one. I knew enough of his reputation to guess it was a woman. No business of mine. He began to be anxious to get rid of me, too, though he had asked me to come."

"Did he say why?"

"He hinted that unless Martin and I withdrew our plans for the Weston West Mills, he would ruin Martin."

"What did you say?"

"I said that was his affair and Martin's, not mine. I think he hadn't expected that." Abruptly Mr Edwardes paused and added: "Don't think I'm trying to push suspicion off myself on to Martin. I'm not."

"If you had your drink in the dining-room," Bobby asked, "how is it the tray and glasses were in the study?"

"I don't know; I can't explain that," Mr Edwardes answered. "Throws doubt on my story, I suppose. I can't help that."

Bobby made no comment, though he could see a possible explanation. The assassin might easily have opened the study door to listen if any of the inmates of the house had been disturbed or were stirring. On seeing a tray and recently used glasses through the open door of the dining-room, the idea might easily have been conceived of carrying them into the study, so as to point suspicion in another direction. In a way, all this seemed to support rather than to throw doubt on Edwardes's story. Mr Edwardes went on:—

"I didn't come here to talk about that. John Wilkie called to see me this morning."

"Yes?" said Bobby encouragingly.

"Primarily to borrow another ten pounds," Mr Edwardes continued. "Apparently he has been cultivating Franks. He seems to think Franks is the murderer. Improbable in my opinion. Wilkie has been standing him drinks. That's what's become of the first ten pounds I lent him, he says."

"Doing detective work on his own account?" Bobby asked.

"Yes. He says he knows you are trying to get him. A mistake on your part, if you are. Dishonest and a rogue, no doubt, but I can't think he would commit murder." Edwardes paused to frown angrily, and then went on: "He says you've warned him not to leave Midwych. But he says you didn't tell him how he was to live. Actually he has been living on my ten pounds. He says he won't be safe till you've found the real culprit. So he has been having a try on his own account."

"Stupid of him," Bobby said uneasily. "It's dangerous to go hunting a killer—very dangerous without experience or help. He's got to stop it."

"I hadn't thought of it like that," Edwardes said, and looked uneasy too. "Perhaps that's what it means. He told me some vague story I couldn't make head or tail of about how soon there would be more trouble, and something about poison."

When he heard this last word Bobby sat upright and looked startled. Mr Edwardes saw, and said quickly:—

"Oh, you understand?"

"I don't. I wish I did," Bobby answered. "I must get hold of Wilkie and find out what he does mean."

"He promised to come with me to see you," Mr Edwardes said. "He was to meet me at the 'bus terminus. He wasn't there. I waited a little and then rang up home. I thought he might have gone there by mistake. He hadn't, but there was a 'phone message from him to say he had found out something important and was following I would know who. Franks, I suppose."

"The young fool," Bobby muttered and felt more uneasy still.

He picked up the receiver of the 'phone on his desk and asked to be put through to the works where Franks was employed. He was informed in reply to his inquiry that Franks was absent through illness. A medical certificate had been promised, but had not yet arrived. So Bobby sent for Sergeant Payne and set machinery in motion for finding and bringing to headquarters either or both, preferably both, of the young men in question.

"You are perturbed," Mr Edwardes remarked, when all this had been arranged. "You say you don't understand the reference to poison, but you are perturbed."

"There's been one death in this affair," Bobby said briefly. "I don't want another."

"No," agreed Mr Edwardes and added slowly: "You think Wilkie is in danger?"

"I don't know who is in danger," Bobby answered. "I wish I did. But I think there is danger somewhere—to some one."

"You think—" began Mr Edwards and then paused. "It's no use asking that," he said. "You wouldn't tell me. Poison. That suggests a woman. Doesn't it? When I heard Weston had been stabbed, I thought that meant it was a man. And I thought I knew who."

"Martin Wynne?" Bobby asked.

"How do you know?" Mr Edwardes asked. "You seem to know what I think without my telling. I don't know how. Why should you think I suspected Martin?"

"I take it you had never heard of Franks and you didn't know of Wilkie's return. But you did know Weston had been talking of ruining Martin Wynne. Plain whom you would suspect—provided you were not guilty yourself."

"Well, yes, there's always that, isn't there?" admitted the other.

"Are you sure you are being quite frank with me even now?" Bobby asked. "Fresh discrepancies in the Weston West Mills books have come to light, haven't they?"

"How on earth do you know that?" demanded Mr Edwardes, looking so taken aback Bobby was forced to smile.

But this time he thought he wouldn't explain. If his lucky shot—it was not much more—increased his prestige in the other's eyes, so much the better. Not that the guess or deduction had been difficult. There was the rather angry recent reference to Wilkie as "dishonest" and a "rogue" which had sounded an opinion recently acquired or at any rate recently and strongly reinforced. Mr Weston's death and the formation of the trust for carrying out the new arrangements had very likely involved a fresh examination of accounts. Again, Bobby had long felt that Wilkie's uneasy wanderings in the vicinity of Weston Lodge Cottage on the night of the murder proved that Mr Weston's unexpected summons had very much disturbed him; and why should such a summons have made him uneasy rather than hopeful of a return to favour, if there had not been some fresh misbehaviour Wilkie feared might have come to light? All this had flashed through Bobby's mind in an instant; on it he had hazarded his remark, and now it seemed he had been right. But all he said was in a very severe tone:—

"You keep too much back. You are hindering rather than helping. Why?"

"There's no proof Wilkie is responsible for the deficit we've found," Mr Edwardes protested. "It was certainly either Wilkie or Mr Weston himself. The latter doesn't seem likely. But we can't tell, and I didn't see any reason for saying anything about it. It's a considerable time ago. If you were suspicious of Wilkie, it was hardly fair to rake up more stories about him. At least, that's my view."

"It strengthens motive," Bobby said. "If there was still more embezzlement to come to light with possible prosecution as a result."

"Others had motives," Mr Edwardes said. "I admit I had, for one. But it's a long way from motive to action. At first I took it for granted the murderer was a man. But now there's a hint of poison—well, poison is more a woman's weapon, and Weston had given many women cause enough. I knew he had been threatened."

"Who by?"

"He didn't say, all he said was that a vixen had been threatening him, but he knew how to tame her. He said he might be getting on in years, but he was still strong enough to be a match for any woman."

"Are you still holding things back?" Bobby demanded angrily. "He did give a name, didn't he? Bessie Bell, the head barmaid at the Wych and Wych Arms."

Mr Edwardes looked more and more startled.

"How do you know?" he asked, bewilderedly. "You seem to know it all without being told."

"Never mind how I know," retorted Bobby, though indeed the reference to being still a physical match for any woman only made sense as in connection with Bessie, more especially as Bessie had been present that night.

"I don't think I need have troubled to come to see you at all," Edwardes said, a little resentful, a little amused, very much more than a little puzzled. "I thought you ought to know that Wilkie was hinting at poison. I thought a knife meant a man, and I thought poison suggested a woman. But it seems you knew already, and you knew the man and you knew the woman. I might as well have stayed at home."

"You've tried to hide too much already," Bobby said, still severe. "You've not been helpful. But a man may use poison and a woman a knife. All a question of means and opportunity. A knife in the hands of a woman can kill as easily as can poison given by a man. What we want to know now, is, against whom is this threat of poison aimed and why?"

But on that point Mr Edwardes had nothing to say, though he did express a hope that it wasn't himself. He said uneasily he supposed his action with regard to the new arrangements for the management of the Weston West Mills might upset some people and disturb some personal interests. He added that he supposed perhaps he had acted in a high-handed, even unfair, manner in taking advantage of the kind of interregnum caused by the murder, to push through his plans.

"More motive, I suppose," he said ruefully, and so departed, leaving Bobby to his own troubled thoughts.

CHAPTER XXIX
OLIVE VISITS

HARD UPON Mr Edwardes's departure appeared Payne, curious to know the purpose of the visit. To him Bobby repeated the gist of the story he had just heard, and Payne looked very doubtful and suspicious.

"Showing himself a bit worried, isn't he?" Payne asked. "Bad conscience? What about it's being the murderer not this time visiting again the scene of the crime, but haunting the police instead?"

"Possible," agreed Bobby. "Fear complex, making him feel he must know just how much he has to fear."

"At the Mills they are saying he's never been quite right in the head since he lost his boys," observed Payne thoughtfully. "There's some new scheme he has on they don't think much of. Eye-wash, they think. They are all making good money now, so why worry? It's some idea he has of letting them choose their own bosses, but you have to pass an exam first before you are eligible. They are all up in arms about that. They say they aren't a pack of kiddies."

"People always hate new ideas," Bobby said. "Quite right, too. Most new ideas are only silly fads. Never mind that, though. Not our pigeon. What we've got to do quick as we can is to get hold of Wilkie—and of Franks, too. Looks bad, poison coming into the picture again."

"Poison means woman," Payne declared with emphasis. "And there are four of them."

Bobby nodded assent, wondering to himself which one of them was indicated; which one had the temperament of the poisoner; whether, too, a woman was designated as prospective victim?

Useless questions, till more was known whereon an answer could be based. The day dragged on with still no hint of any answer growing plain, with no news either of Wilkie or of Franks. All Bobby found himself able to do was to increase the strictness of the watch being kept on those under suspicion, and none knew better than he how easy it is to evade a watch whereof the person under surveillance is conscious.

Earlier than usual, depressed and uneasy, Bobby left headquarters and returned home, fearful of what the night might bring, for the feeling was strong upon him that a climax approached. Olive, a little surprised to see him home so soon, told him she herself had only just got back from town.

"Shopping," she explained, and added with a slight swagger: "While I was there I dropped in at a pub for a drink."

"You did—what?" Bobby asked, staring. "What on earth for?"

"There," complained Olive. "If a man tells you he dropped in at a pub for a drink, you don't say 'What on earth for?' do you?"

"Well, no," admitted Bobby. "That's different."

"That's a man all over," said Olive bitterly. "They can do what they like. We've got to explain. It was a very nice pub, too, except for the smell and the way people stared and it's all being so technical. What's a bottle-and-jug department?" Without waiting for an answer, she went on: "Besides, Miss Bell looking as if she had half a mind to give me a good smacking like the one she gave the girl who is Miss Severn's maid now."

"Do you mean you've been talking to Bessie?" Bobby demanded, more and more bewildered.

"About you," Olive explained. "I suppose the port wine I didn't drink because I thought there was a mistake somewhere and they had given me red ink instead, must have gone to my head. Because I said the most reckless things about you."

"Look here," began Bobby, alarmed.

"I just didn't care," Olive went on unheedingly. "I told her that as a man, or even a husband, you probably rated above the worst known, and that any one could see she was in trouble, and that if she would come here one evening and tell you all about it, she would be doing the most sensible thing in her life, even though that wasn't saying much."

"What did she say?" Bobby asked.

"Nothing."

"Will she come, do you think?"

"I don't know. I think perhaps she might."

Bobby tried to explain to Olive that she mustn't do things like that. He had an uncomfortable picture in his mind of one of chose missing chocolates dissolved in the glass of port Olive had described as so strongly resembling red ink. Just as well she hadn't tasted it, perhaps, even though there was no reason to be suspicious. Meekly Olive listened to his homily, and, lifting large, innocent eyes, promised faithfully never to do it again—unless, of course, she simply had to. Bobby was continuing with eloquence, when Olive, who had heard enough, interrupted with the sudden remark that that day she had also seen Thomasine Rowe for the first time. Bobby was launching into a fresh and more fervent remonstrance when again Olive interrupted.

"Quite by accident," she said; "and I didn't speak to her. I had to go to the W.V.S. depot in Market Street and she came in. It was about a subscription Mr Weston had promised them and they had been wanting to know if they were to get it. I didn't speak to her and I don't suppose she noticed me. But I noticed her. And her hat—"

"Why her hat?" Bobby asked. "Was she wearing a caracal coat, by the way?"

"An intelligent question," Olive said approvingly, "but not so very intelligent. She was. And it looked new—even brand new. But it was her hat I noticed."

"What about it?"

"High-crowned. Great tall blue feather. It didn't suit her a bit. It was awful. On her, I mean. She must have known it, too. You could see at a glance she had real clothes sense. Everything just right, from her shoes—shoes are awfully important—to her make-up. Smart without even ever so tiny a hint of being too smart. And then—that awful hat."

"Well, but—" began Bobby, who did not at first see much to interest him in this question of taste in attire.

"My good lad," said Olive, gently reproachful, "are you really so slow in the uptake that you can't—see?"

She shook her head sadly and retired, leaving Bobby to wonder afresh why he was thus being called upon to consider the strange and multiple reasons which may dictate feminine choice of a hat. Then it began to dawn upon him as Olive, in the kitchen, prepared to wrestle, like all her sister housewives, with the daily task of turning rations eternally the same into a dinner reasonably different.

This time, however, she abandoned the effort almost at once, and when she returned to Bobby, she showed a face so flushed, a look so strange, that he for a moment yielded to the unworthy suspicion that possibly the port, untasted because it looked so like red ink, had been exchanged for something stronger, of which the effect was only now becoming evident.

"I want to show you something," she said, and even her voice had changed—a little hoarse it had become, and uneven.

She led the way down a short passage to the kitchen and for a moment stood on the threshold as if unwilling to enter. Bobby, looking over her shoulder, saw that the window was wide open, but noticed nothing else.

"What is it?" he asked.

Olive moved across to a small table with an enamelled top on which she usually carried out most of her culinary preparations. On it now were various spoons, dishes, basins, and so on. With a touch of resentment in her voice, for Bobby was a precise sort of person, and once or twice, when visiting the kitchen, had carefully placed back in their places on the shelves ingredients or utensils waiting to be used, Olive said:—

"You may think I'm untidy, but I do know when some one has been in my kitchen."

"Why?" Bobby asked. "Do you mean now?" and he looked round as if to see if any one were hiding anywhere.

"I was mixing dried egg when I heard you come in," Olive said. "I left it on the table there. It's been moved. Some one's been in and moved it. Look." She pointed to a few grains of powder that lay by the side of the basin she indicated. "Where does that come from?" she asked. Her voice became a little shrill. "Who has been putting something in my egg?" she asked. "What for? What is it?"

Bobby bent to look more closely. He noticed some tiny brown fragments mingled with the grains of powder. Chocolate, he thought, the brown fragments looked like. He wetted a finger and tasted one of the grains of powder.

"I think it's arsenic all right enough," he said.

CHAPTER XXX
NURSING-HOME

OLIVE, DEEPLY though she had been shaken for the moment, had by now recovered much of her self-possession. She was looking out through the window into the garden where once had been wont to flourish the roses that now had been displaced by the homely cabbage, though indeed these served more for the nourishment of innumerable caterpillars than for any marked addition to the food stores of the country. But, separating the garden from the road, there were still rhododendron bushes serving as a hedge to preserve privacy. From, through, and behind these, it would have been easy to keep observation on the house.

"Perhaps some one was hiding there," she said.

Bobby said he would go and look, though by now the gathering darkness was making close examination difficult. He came back and said:—

"Can't see much. Ground's hard, for one thing. Getting dark, too. Will you be all right if I have a skirmish round?"

"Yes, of course," Olive answered. "I'm not afraid now. It was only thinking I might never have noticed." She conjured up a faint and watery smile. "I never thought perhaps some day my cooking might kill you, Bobby dear."

Bobby gave no answering smile. He was in no mood for it. Telling Olive briefly to lock door and window and keep them locked till his return, he went out. Everything was quiet and deserted, as before the dying day people fled to the refuge of their homes against the coming of the darkness of the black-out. Small probability of any hurrying, fugitive form having attracted attention when all alike were hurrying, all fugitive. But he knew that the constable patrolling this beat, a steady, reliable man, an old pensioner called back to war service, was due to pass the corner about now.

Possible that he might have seen something. At any rate he could be asked and at the same time be warned to increase his vigilance. Bobby began to walk in that direction. To his surprise he found that he was at one and the same time perspiring slightly and shivering. A paradox. Danger for himself in a man-hunt he accepted as natural and even desirable. It was only danger gave dignity and value to the pursuit, as indeed it is only danger that gives dignity and value to life. In the actual moment of danger, too, he had always found a touch of exultation, even of an ecstasy that came perhaps from the release of all his energies, of a total energy to full intensity of being. In recent months, too, duty had often called him out at night, knowing well that on his return he might find the warden's post where Olive worked smashed to nothingness with all in it by some stray bomb. But that was a public risk, shared by all, an accident of war, death for some as the price of general survival. To it, too, there was an answer. Even now, as he walked, he could hear the distant muttering far overhead that told of the wrath of England gathered there to strike afar. But this that he had just experienced was a private and a secret peril, unforeseen, aimed at one who trusted him and only because of him was involved in it. He felt glowing fierce within himself a hard core of deadly anger such as he had never known before.

When he reached the corner where the road he was following met the main highway, he found his man already there, busily engaged making entries in his note-book. Seeing Bobby coming, he saluted and said:—

"Them motorists again. No respect for law and order. If I had my way—"

He paused, not quite sure what his way would be, or else searching for one sufficiently drastic. Bobby asked:—

"What's happened?"

"Car," explained the constable, "not immobilized according to regulations. Was taking particulars of same when lady arrived. In answer to inquiry, admitted same was hers. Lady then administered severe push, same being unexpected, and while recumbent on back in ditch, entered car and drove off, disregarding instructions to stop same and return."

"You've got the car number?" Bobby asked.

"Oh, yes, sir," the man answered, and, becoming less official, went on: "I got that down O.K. and was asking for her licence, when all of a sudden like she gave me a shove over, which a lady didn't ought, and there was me flat in the ditch and her doing a speed act."

"I suppose it wasn't any one you knew, was it?" Bobby asked.

"Oh, yes, sir," came the unexpected answer. "Quite well, sir. Miss Bell it was, what serves in the saloon bar at the Wych and Wych Arms in town."

Bobby went back to the house, feeling more uncomfortable even than before, a vivid memory in his mind of that glass of port, which, owing to its resemblance to red ink, had so fortunately remained untasted. By 'phone he set in motion a county-wide search for Bessie's car. There was, he hoped, every chance that it would soon be reported. A car is noticeable in these days of deserted roads. It may even be stopped on general principles to make sure the driver has a right to the use of the petrol he is consuming. Nor was this hope deceived; for presently the 'phone rang and there came through a message to say that a car bearing the required number was standing deserted in the road at a spot about twenty-five miles distant—so Bessie had evidently driven at speed—and described as only a few hundred yards from Milton Pagney railway station and directly outside the exclusive and expensive nursing-home known as Pagney Manor.

"She would get there just in time to catch the London train," Bobby said. "It's a slow train. She could leave it anywhere it stops. Jump for that matter at the Singlewhurt curve before the tunnel. They slow up there to twenty miles or less. I suppose she left her car at a distance so as to attract less attention."

"There's the nursing-home, too. She may know some one working there," Olive said. Then she said: "I don't believe it was her."

Bobby said nothing, but looked gloomy. That untasted glass of port was still in his mind. Presently he said:—

"You had better come, too. I'm not leaving you alone with God knows who prowling round."

Olive had strong nerves. She had proved it in early days before her marriage. She had had need of them then, she had had need of them again in recent months, as indeed had had every other British woman when came the Germans, exultant and joyous and busy, because as yet Britain the Unready had such small power to reply. All the same she was glad of Bobby's suggestion. The friendly, familiar kitchen, her daily workshop, had taken on a strange and sinister air; no longer did it seem a centre wherefrom issued the stuff of life, but instead was dark and heavy with the shadow of treacherous, lurking death.

Bobby issued a few more directions over the 'phone and then they started out in his small two-seater. The moon was not yet up and the darkness had grown intense, so that he had to drive with caution. It was more than an hour before he reached the Milton Pagney station. But there he found no trace of Bessie. None of the railwaymen had seen anything of any one answering her description, nor was her striking personality one to be easily overlooked or forgotten. It seemed clear she had joined no train at Milton Pagney.

So Bobby decided as a forlorn hope to inquire at the Pagney Manor nursing-home.

"Not much chance of any luck," he remarked. "If she had meant to hide there, she would hardly have left her car right outside. Making it a bit too easy. Still, we'll ask."

He left their own car by the roadside near Bessie's, for the heavy gates admitting to the drive, though not locked, were both closed and cumbersome, and it seemed less trouble to walk the short distance to the house rather than to open them. There was a short delay before Bobby's knock and ring were answered, and then it was a nurse who opened the door, for by now it was late and the household staff had gone off duty. She did not look best pleased at being disturbed at such an hour and looked even less so when she knew their errand was simply to inquire for a Miss Bessie Bell, of whom she had never heard. In fact, Bobby had to display his official card to check a distinct tendency to bring the interview to a close by a firmly shut door. In any case the nurse was certain there was no one of that name among the patients or belonging to either the nursing or domestic staff. But she hesitated when Bobby briefly described Bessie.

"Mrs Abel's like that," she admitted reluctantly, "and Mr Abel calls her Bessie."

In fact it was soon apparent that Mrs Abel and Bessie Bell were one and the same and that Mrs Abel—or Bessie Bell—had arrived at the nursing-home only shortly before and was still there.

"But you can't possibly see her," the nurse insisted. "The doctor sent for her because poor Mr Abel isn't likely to live much longer. She is with him now. It may be all over any hour almost, or he may take a turn for the better. It all depends."

It was a case of infantile paralysis, the nurse explained. A bad case. Now complications had set in. There was small hope of recovery, though the end might be postponed for a time. Bobby asked if he might see the doctor in charge. Not too willingly the doctor appeared, complaining this was no time for police inquiries. Bobby was obliged to produce again his official card, at which the doctor sniffed contemptuously. This wasn't Germany, he pointed out, Bobby wasn't Gestapo, Mrs Abel was at the death-bed of her husband. She was an admirable woman for whom he had the greatest respect. He had good reason to believe that only Mrs Abel's own earnings had provided the necessary fees to pay for the sick man's treatment during recent years. The home had done what it could to make it as easy for her as possible, but all the same expenses were necessarily high, and Mrs Abel always wanted the best. Nor had she ever once pleaded poverty or asked for any special consideration.

"Wants to do it all herself," the doctor said. "A proud woman. Proud as hell. In my job you see the worst side often enough, but you see the best as well sometimes, and you see it in Mrs Abel. You ought to watch those two look at each other when she goes into the room on her weekly visit. You may be all the police in the country, but I'm not going to have her worried just now."

The doctor grew quite flushed and excited. He said he must protect his patients. Bobby said he was very sorry but unless Mr Abel was actually dying he must insist on a personal interview. It was essential he should know if Mrs Abel and Miss Bessie Bell were one and the same. If necessary, he would wait all night. In that case, he would have to send to his headquarters for help, which would mean stationing constables on guard both front and back of the building. This made the doctor more angry than ever, but Bobby made it clear he intended to do what he said. The prospect of having the place picketed by police patrols did not appeal, as Bobby had known it would not. The doctor showed signs of hesitation, and Bobby repeated it was necessary he should see Mrs Abel sooner or later and he thought himself it had better be sooner. Finally the doctor, though still indignant, gave way, and went off to ask Bessie if she would leave her husband for a few minutes. When he had gone Bobby looked somewhat ruefully at Olive.

"Thinks I'm a brute," he said. "I suppose I am. Murder's a brutal business."

"I expect it's true, what he's been saying," Olive said.

"So do I," Bobby agreed. "But I must be sure. I can take no one's word unconfirmed."

Olive did not reply. She was thinking of her pleasant little kitchen and of those few grains of whitish powder spilt near the egg she had been preparing, and of how now it seemed to her her kitchen would never again seem quite the same.

The door opened and Bessie stood there, no longer fierce and defiant in her lusty strength, no longer self-confident and proud. Humbly she said:—

"Now you've found me, can't you wait to take me till John is dead?"

CHAPTER XXXI
FAITH

Bobby long remembered their slow drive home that night, the heavy darkness brooding all around like a thing tangible and felt. His mind was uneasy, his sense of duty troubled, his duty that for him came before all else. It added to his unease that he knew well how much his decision to act as he had done had been influenced by the mere fact of Olive's presence. Not that she had uttered a word, made the least sign. She had taken care not even to look at him. All the same, all the time he had known what she was thinking, willing, wishing, hoping. Like tangible things, those thoughts of hers, those emotions, willings, hopes, had beaten upon his mind, bending it as it were, bending it by some strange force of sympathy and understanding to ultimate consent. Grimly Bobby asked himself what he would have thought and said if he had heard that one of his subordinates allowed himself to be accompanied by his wife on an official errand, had moreover endured her mute influence on his conduct. Would he have accepted the excuse of fear for her life and safety? He didn't know. Olive's voice broke suddenly upon his thoughts.

"You know very well," she was saying quietly, and more as if she were speaking to herself than to him, "you wouldn't have done anything else, even if I hadn't been there."

Bobby was so startled that as nearly as possible he jerked the wheel over to send them into the ditch by the side of the road. So all the time she had known exactly what was in his mind. How? he wondered. But, then, she often did. He said moodily:—

"How am I to tell it wasn't all a put-up job? That doctor eats out of her hand. How do I know Abel wasn't simply putting on an act? How do I know any of it's true?"

"It's all true," Olive said. "I know it is."

But Bobby knew that wasn't so. She didn't know. It was faith she had, not knowledge. He wanted knowledge. The sort of knowledge that you can put down on paper and tie up with red tape in a neat bundle. Official knowledge. Facts. Hard, solid, sensible facts, quite unaffected by such considerations as long years of devotion to a sick man, of toil and self-denial to give him comfort, of presence at, or absence from, a death-bed.

"She says she came to our house to-night to tell me all about it, because that's what you advised her to do," Bobby went on. "Well, perhaps. She says she saw some one in the kitchen but it wasn't you, though she doesn't know who it was, so she thought you had a visitor and that made her change her mind and go off again—pushing my constable into the ditch on the way. Well, perhaps. Or perhaps it was for another reason she came and she herself was the woman in the kitchen. I always knew there must be something between her and Martin Wynne, but if it's true she married him before she married this Abel person, then it may be true, too, that she thought I had followed her to arrest her for bigamy and nothing to do with

Weston's murder. But if it's like that, why is there no trace of any such marriage anywhere?"

"You must look again," Olive said. "Look where she said."

Bobby went on unheedingly:—

"If Weston had got hold of any such story, possibly he was using it to put pressure on them both. Provides strong motive for getting rid of him. If Bessie were charged with bigamy, that would put an end to her power to go on paying the nursing-home fees and Abel would have had to go. Public assistance." Bobby paused and looked at Olive: "Didn't you tell me once," he said, "that if a woman found the man she loved weak, or in trouble—or ill—then he became her child, and for her child a woman would do anything, dare anything? Right or wrong no longer counted."

"If I did, I wish I hadn't," Olive said.

"Martin Wynne as well," Bobby continued. "If he's in love with the little Olga Severn girl, and there was a previous marriage with Bessie, and Weston knew—well, there you are again. Weston has to disappear or Martin's chance with Olga goes."

Olive said abruptly:—

"All that doesn't bring in the envelope you found—the one marked about some one called Agnes and with the bank-notes inside."

"May turn out to be just a side issue," Bobby said. "You can't tell. Not in the picture at all, perhaps."

Olive did not reply, and the rest of the journey was completed in silence. On their arrival they found the constable of the "push-over" incident waiting at the garden gate.

"'Phone bell's ringing, sir," he explained. "I came back this way and I iheard it. I knew as you were out chasing after that there hussy, so I thought I would wait in case of being wanted when you got back. There it goes again," he added, "every quarter hour or so it goes regular like."

Bobby told him to wait, and went in to find out what was the cause of this persistent ringing. More trouble, he told himself uneasily. He picked up the receiver and heard the voice of Hargreaves, the butler at Weston Lodge Cottage. Hargreaves said that the constable on duty there that night had been taken ill with pains in the stomach and was now unconscious. The doctor had been rung up and prescribed treatment which had been ineffective. He had been rung up again and had promised, very unwillingly, to turn out. He had not, however, yet arrived. Before losing consciousness the sick man had asked that Inspector Owen should be informed, and accordingly Hargreaves had been ringing up at regular intervals, but without a reply till now.

"I've been out on duty," Bobby said briefly. "I've only just got back. Have you rung up county police headquarters in Midwych?"

It had not occurred to Hargreaves to do that. The constable had only asked for Inspector Owen to be told. He had said nothing about headquarters.

"When was he taken ill?" Bobby asked, and got the more or less expected answer that it was an hour or two after supper.

"What did he have for supper?" Bobby inquired next, and again got a not unexpected reply. The supper had consisted of bread and cheese and cocoa.

Easy enough, Bobby reflected, given the opportunity, to slip a doctored chocolate into a cup of cocoa.

Had Bessie, he wondered gloomily, been at Weston Lodge Cottage before coming on to his own home?

An inquiry whether there had been any callers during the evening, or if any strangers had been seen near the house, brought the reply that Miss Severn, the younger Miss Severn, had been in to see Miss Rowe, with whom she had had a chat. Just before supper-time, Hargreaves agreed, in reply to a further question.

"I'll come along at once," Bobby said. "Meanwhile, ring up the doctor again, and if by any chance he hasn't started yet, tell him it may be urgent, that you suspect arsenic poisoning, and ask him what to do."

"Arsenic," repeated Hargreaves, sounding more bewildered than shocked. "What arsenic?"

Bobby wasted no time trying to explain. He told Hargreaves to try again to get in touch with the doctor. On his own account Bobby gave a few elementary first-aid suggestions—an emetic, the administration of magnesia—and added:—

"Send one of the maids to see if Miss Rowe is in her room."

This demand completed Hargreaves's disarray, so much so that Bobby half expected to hear that Thomasine had been given the magnesia and a visit made to the sick constable to see if he were still in bed. However, presently some one did come to the 'phone—one of the maid-servants apparently—to say that knocking at Miss Rowe's door got no answer.

"Break down the door, then, if she doesn't reply," Bobby ordered. "Lose no time. She may have had cocoa for supper, too."

"She always has," came the startled reply.

Bobby repeated that he would get to Weston Lodge Cottage as soon as possible. Olive had been listening to all this, and from Bobby's questions and brief remarks had guessed what was happening. When Bobby now hung up the receiver, she said:—

"Bessie can have had nothing to do with all that."

"Why not?" Bobby asked. "She had a car. It's only a few miles."

"Suppose Miss Rowe is not in her room?" Olive asked.

"May mean anything," Bobby answered. "She may have had some message calling her away. She may have gone out for her own reasons. She may merely be sound asleep. Or," he added sombrely, "the cocoa she had for supper may have been a stronger brew."

"I don't understand what it all means," Olive said, and she shivered slightly.

"It may mean anything," Bobby said again. "Perhaps that the waters are getting deeper, but all the same that shore is nearer. Only I've a feeling that when we do reach shore, it may be to find a dead man or woman lying there."

"Who?" asked Olive, though barely above her breath, but Bobby made no answer, merely said that he must hurry away.

He stood for a moment, asking himself if there was anything he could have done that might have averted the coming tragedy of which he felt with apprehension the near approach. He could not think so. Not within the limits of his recognized authority and duty. In England one may not act upon suspicion, mere suspicion, nor even upon certainty unless in support thereof can be marshalled those plain facts which alone allow action infringing upon private right. Better the skies should fall than that an innocent person should be—inconvenienced. An improvement on the old Roman maxim no doubt. Or was it?

Leaving that question unanswered, he told Olive to go and get some rest. The still-waiting constable he installed in the kitchen, telling him to wait there till either Bobby returned or till he was called on the 'phone. Help might be needed, Bobby told him, and did not, even in his own mind, admit that he did not mean to leave Olive without protection. He persuaded himself it was as useful and sensible to leave the man there, in reserve, so to say, as to take him with him. Nor had the constable any objection to spending duty time, not trudging his beat, but instead in a warm, comfortable kitchen and with full permission to smoke or to make himself a cup of tea if he liked.

CHAPTER XXXII
LOST TORCH

As HE drove on his way through the long, dark night, Bobby's uneasiness transferred itself from Olive, now in safety, he hoped, to Nicholls, the constable he had established at Weston Lodge Cottage and now in danger, as it seemed, of his life. Why, Bobby asked himself, had this attempt on the man's life been made? Whose interests could it serve? The attack on himself—and incidentally on Olive—he could understand. His death or even his prolonged illness would have delayed and confused the whole inquiry, very likely have rendered it finally ineffective. But the death or the incapacitating of a man like Nicholls would make little difference to the course of events.

Did it mean that the murderer, feeling, as Bobby told himself he must feel, the slow, inevitable drawing near and nearer still of the pursuit, was now striking out in blind and reckless fury, ready in despair to pile death upon death?

If it were that, what might be happening next? and with this fear in his mind Bobby drove faster still, dark as was the night, with the moon not yet risen and the skies overcast.

Fortunate that in these days most roads are bare of traffic, and so he was able to maintain his speed without accident or incident. Near his destination he had, however, to slow down, and even once or twice to stop and alight to make sure of his whereabouts. He knew that at one point, if he could find the opening, a footpath led from the road he was following past the back of the Weston Lodge Cottage grounds to join another road that served the district in which old Mr Edwardes lived. If he could find it he could leave the car by the roadside, follow the lane till he got to the fence bordering the Weston Lodge Cottage grounds, climb through, and reach the house more quickly than by the road and the front approach up the long and twisting avenue. It was more by good luck than anything else that he did presently see his dimmed headlights shine on the stile where the footpath entered the road. There on the grass border he left his car and, torch in hand, ran on up the path.

He knew he had first to pass a dense spinney and then he would come to a fence over which he intended to climb or jump into the grounds rather than waste time looking for the small gate that he believed was somewhere further on at the end of a path leading to the house.

The fence presented no great difficulty, but when he had clambered over and was hurrying forward he heard footsteps. He paused to listen. A voice called softly:—

"John. Is that you?"

"Who are you?" Bobby called back, and, taking a step forward, stepped into nothingness.

He very narrowly escaped a broken leg. Only by a violent effort did he save himself, and in so doing he let his torch fly out of his hand. The voice he had heard before said:—

"Hurt yourself? I heard some one coming. I turned back."

Bobby, a little dazed by the suddenness and violence of his fall, got slowly to his feet.

"Where's my torch?" he said. "Who is it?" he asked again. "Mr Edwardes?" he asked, for he thought he recognized the voice. "Why are you here?" He made a step or two forward, suspicion sudden in his mind. "Have you been to my house, too, to-night?" he asked

"Your house? No," Edwardes answered. "You're Owen, aren't you? Inspector Owen. What's brought you here so late?"

"I asked you that," Bobby said. "I'm here on duty. Why are you? You called me John—what John? John Wilkie? Are you waiting for him? Are you expecting him?"

"I am looking for him," Edwardes answered.

"A bit late?" Bobby suggested. "Why here?" Then he said: "Did you see where my torch fell?"

"You'll never find it," Edwardes told him. "I lost mine here in the same way the night Weston was murdered—fell into the ditch trying to find the way out of the grounds. That's a slit trench you fell into. The Home Guard did some practising here, and that's a relic. Regular death-trap in the dark. Are you hurt?"

"Shook me up a bit, that's all," Bobby answered; and felt he was lucky, for the trench was both deep and narrow, and he might very easily have hurt himself badly. "Scratched my nose a bit." He was still looking for his torch. "The blessed thing can't be far off," he said irritably.

"Lucky it's no worse," Edwardes said. "I nearly put my eye out when I fell." He went on: "I thought perhaps your people had my torch. A policeman went by, but he didn't take any notice. I didn't think he knew me. I wondered if that might be one reason why you suspected me."

"What time was this?" Bobby asked.

"I don't know—some time between eleven and twelve."

"You didn't hear the church clock strike?"

"No. If I did, it didn't make any impression. I wasn't listening. I was grubbing round trying to find the torch."

"If we had found it, could we have told it was yours?" Bobby asked, still vainly searching for his own.

"You always can, can't you?" the other retorted. "Finger-prints, that sort of thing."

Bobby let this assumption go uncontradicted. He was thinking how odd it was that in this moment of haste and urgency Edwardes should be offering him unsuspected testimony of innocence. For this story of the fall, of the lost torch, of the so nearly injured eye, was corroborated by the earlier tale told by Constable Clerke, now discharged, who had spoken of fall and lost torch and damaged are all happening as the clock struck the hour which other testimony showed was about the time of the murder.

"Why did you think Wilkie might be here?" Bobby asked. "Why are you looking for him here?"

"I suppose I had better tell you," Edwardes said. "I had made up my mind I had to. He came to see me this evening. I was out and he asked if he could wait. My housekeeper left him in the lounge. He said he would like to go upstairs for a moment and he did. Presently he said he couldn't wait any longer and he went off. After he had gone she found one of the attic doors wide open. When I got back she told me. I went to have a look. One of the daggers is missing from my father's collection of Japanese weapons."

"Are you sure?" Bobby asked. "You told me once you didn't know exactly what you had."

"I've listed them since," Edwardes answered. "The weapons, I mean. All of them—spears, swords, the whole lot. I scratched a tiny number on each one. It's knife number three that's gone."

"We had better get on to the house," Bobby said.

"Yes," agreed Edwardes. He said: "Martin Wynne had lunch with me. He went upstairs, too. By himself."

"We had better be quick, hurry," Bobby said. "Martin Wynne," he repeated. Then he said: "I never hear anything in this case but I'm told something else that makes it all different." He said again: "We had best hurry," for it seemed to him he was conscious of an inner voice, urging haste.

Yet it was not easy to hurry in that black and baffling night. If Mr Edwardes had not been with him and had not known better than he did the topography of the place, more than once he would have been completely at a loss, now that he had no torch to help him. Mr Edwardes, hurrying along at Bobby's side, for he, too, seemed to feel the need for speed, said, panting a little:—

"I tried to get another torch after I lost mine, but I couldn't. No batteries to be had." Then he said: "Did you ever hear Weston was married twice? There's gossip he was and that he had a child by the first marriage he never acknowledged."

"If it's true, it might help to explain some things," Bobby answered. "We've been working on it, but we can't get confirmation. Only gossip. I've noticed a possible family likeness. Not much, but it's there."

Mr Edwardes gave a sort of gasp of surprise and stopped dead. Bobby told him impatiently to come on. Edwardes said:—

"Not that way. The kitchen garden's over there; you'll be on top of the cucumber frames in a moment." He took Bobby's arm and turned him to the left. "This way," he said and went on: "Anyhow, Weston was no more John Wilkie's father than I am. I knew both his parents."

"Oh, Wilkie," Bobby exclaimed, surprised, for it was not Wilkie he had thought was meant. "Do you mean Wilkie believes that he is Weston's son?"

"Apparently it's been hinted to him that he may be. He won't say who it was. I don't know where you see any family likeness. I don't I don't think he much believes it himself. Only of course if it were true, he could claim the estate. So he hopes it is. I told him it was all nonsense. But if he believes it, it shows he isn't the murderer. He would hardly kill the man he thought might be his father."

"Why not?" Bobby asked. "Parricide is possible. Besides, if he didn't know ... if he wasn't sure. . . ."

"You do suspect him, then?"

"I didn't say so," Bobby replied. "Suspicions don't matter. I need proof."

"He thinks you suspect him," Edwardes repeated. "He's pretty badly frightened about it, too. He expects to be arrested any moment. He says he was with Hargreaves, in Hargreaves's room, when it happened. The murder, I mean. He said it was no use telling you, you wouldn't believe it; you would only say he and Hargreaves had made it up together. They were standing at the top of the stairs in the dark when they heard it—heard Weston's last cry, I mean. But they didn't know what it meant, and when it was all quiet again Hargreaves let Wilkie out by the back door. He had borrowed ten shillings from him—Wilkie from Hargreaves, I mean."

"Why on earth" began Bobby furiously, but Edwardes cut him short.

"Why didn't they tell you?" he completed Bobby's sentence. "No one's keen on telling detectives things certain to bring them under suspicion. I felt like that myself. When you know the police are searching-for clues, you aren't in any great hurry to present them with one leading straight to yourself."

"Which means," Bobby explained, "that when the police get hold of it, as they always do, then it becomes ten times more suspicious. I had practically ruled Wilkie out. Now I suppose I must put him back again. Do you know anything to suggest there's any truth in this story of an earlier marriage?"

"No. I don't believe it for a moment," Edwardes answered at once. "Weston was much too careful. I think it's because it got about he was living with some woman in Scotland when he had business interests there. Probably somebody said that perhaps there was a Scots marriage and that you only had to say you were married up there and then you were. I should guess that's what started the story. Possibly the woman put the tale about herself."

"Who was she?" Bobby asked.

"I've no idea, I never heard," Edwardes answered. "Quite likely she had a child. Wilkie thinks so, and tries to think the child might be himself. Wishful thinking, with an eye on the Weston estate. That's all. Except that I believe her name was Agnes."

"Oh yes, Aggie," Bobby said.

While they talked they stumbled on their way as best they could, and now they were so near the house they could distinguish its vast outline as a dull, dark shadow against the greater darkness of the night. A gust of wind stirred the still air and moved, it seemed, the black-out curtain over a window at the ground floor, for a thin, bright beam of light shot out.

"That's the study window," Bobby said. "Isn't it? It's open."

The wind blew again. Again the thin shaft of light shot out, reaching to their feet. They had passed by on their way round to the front of the house, but now they both turned. Mr Edwardes said:—

"I think it's the study. I think the window must be open. The wind blew it open."

Bobby did not answer, but he began to run, following the light that lay like a guide on the ground. Edwardes followed. They reached the spot and found the french windows were ajar. Bobby pushed them back, pushed back the black-out curtains, entered. Edwardes followed. There was light in the room. The door of the great safe swung open. Before it, almost on the exact spot where Weston's dead body had lain, lay the prostrate form of another man.

"Martin Wynne," Bobby said. Then he saw close beside a heavy walking-stick, one of the kind known as "penang lawyers". Its solid silver head was stained with blood. He recognized it at a glance. "That's yours, isn't it?" he said to his companion, and once more suspicion rose in his mind.

CHAPTER XXXIII

NO ONE THERE

FOR THE moment, however, all suspicion had to be laid aside while attention was given to the injured Martin, whose heavy, laboured breathing suggested concussion.

"He's not dead, is he—not another?" Edwardes asked, and when Bobby, kneeling by the injured man, shook his head, Edwardes added: "Hadn't we better move him somewhere? There's a couch in the next room."

"Not yet," Bobby said. "A doctor's been sent for. Better leave him here till the doctor comes. It's concussion, I think. I don't think we can do anything for the present but make him a bit more comfortable and keep him warm. Things happening to-night," he added slowly. "What was he doing here?"

"That's my stick," Edwardes said abruptly.

"Yes, I know," Bobby said.

"He didn't take it, I know that," Edwardes said. "I saw it after he left, after lunch. How did it get here?"

"You might ring the bell, will you?" Bobby said, without attempting to answer this question. "Or open the door and shout. Very likely they're all upstairs. We want blankets and a rug or something to keep Wynne warm."

Mr Edwardes obeyed both injunctions. A startled Hargreaves appeared, uttering loud exclamations of surprise and dismay. Engaged with the sick man, neither he nor the maids had heard anything. He went off to get the rugs asked for, and a loud knocking at the front door announced the arrival of a sleepy and disgruntled doctor, somewhat pacified, however, by finding he had two patients to attend to. First he glanced at Martin and approved Bobby's first-aid treatment of rest and warmth. Then Hargreaves was told to stay with Martin, and Bobby led the doctor upstairs, where both the cook—Mrs Parham—and the housemaid were hovering excitedly. Leaving the doctor with the sick man, and with the housemaid to get him anything required, Bobby asked Mrs Parham to show him the room occupied by Thomasine Rowe, who in spite of all the noise and excitement had not appeared. Mrs Parham led him down the corridor into another crossing it almost at right angles, and indicated a closed heavy looking door of solid mahogany. Bobby gathered that repeated knocking had failed to secure any response and that his injunction to break the door down had apparently been regarded as too drastic for a respectable, properly conducted household. Nor indeed had any of the three of them, Hargreaves and the two maids, much idea of how to set about such a job, or much time to consider it, with all their excitement and concern over the sick constable. Bobby, however, had had in his time traffic with some of the more expert and experienced practitioners in the burglary profession, and he had little difficulty with the lock though it was as solid, substantial, and well made as the door itself. In two or three minutes he had it open, and he was in no way surprised to find within the room no sign of Thomasine, no hint of what had become of her or where or why she had gone. Bobby's face was grave. He found her absence ominous. Mrs Parham, who had begun to chatter expressions of wonder and surprise, grew silent under the dimly felt influence of his apprehensions. Bobby said to her:—

"Apart from my man's illness, have you seen or heard anything out of the way to-night?"

It was with some hesitation that she acknowledged presently that Wilkie had been an earlier visitor.

"I heard his voice," she said. "I didn't see him clear, but I knew his voice. He was here just like that other time."

"What other time?" Bobby demanded. "The night of your master's murder? You never told me that before—suppressing evidence," he added sternly. "That's serious."

"No, it isn't, then," retorted Mrs Parham with spirit, as befits a cook who knows her value in the social scale, "because it's what I didn't know till the other day along of doing out Mr Hargreaves's room, and there was Mr Wilkie's cigarette case he told us he had lost; and if I knew Mr Hargreaves had some one in his room that night, I knew it couldn't have anything to do with the poor master being murdered, because they were both, the two of them, standing there at the top of the stairs when I heard the master cry out, and you said it was his death-cry, poor man. So why should I say a word? and I never did or would, when it was nothing to do with any murder, but against strict orders and as like as not cost Mr Hargreaves his place and no character, too, very like, if Miss Rowe got to know, and her a proper cat as ever was."

"You should have told me," Bobby repeated as severely as before, but Mrs Parham only looked defiant and said something about not being one to get others into trouble.

Bobby did not attempt to reply. It couldn't be helped now, though Mrs Parham's story seemed to provide Wilkie with a satisfactory alibi for the moment of the murder. It would have saved some trouble if he had known before, but that was about all. For the moment he was less interested in the past than in the present and the future, and more especially in what had been happening here in the last hour or so. What had Wilkie been doing here, if Mrs Parham's story could be trusted? Was it Wilkie who was responsible for the injury to Martin Wynne? By what agency had Mr Edwardes's walking-stick got to Weston Lodge Cottage, if Martin had not brought it himself? What had Martin been doing by the open safe? And Thomasine—where was she? He threw another doubtful, questioning glance around the room, as if to try to find there the answer to all he wished to know, and no answer was given him. Mrs Parham saw that quick and apprehensive look, saw what doubt and quick fear it expressed, said hurriedly:—

"Has harm come to the poor lamb, too? Can't you do something to help?"

Bobby noticed that the "proper cat if ever there was one" had turned into a "poor lamb" now, and he noticed, too, that the help Mrs Parham wasn't one to give to the police, she was ready enough to demand. But that was a not unusual attitude. He told her to see if the doctor wanted more help, and himself went downstairs to find the telephone. Ringing up headquarters, he asked for assistance to be sent at once. Mr Edwardes heard him telephoning and came to join him.

"The doctor says your man will be all right; he thinks he has got rid of most of the poison," Mr Edwardes told him. "And he says Martin will be all right with rest and quiet. He's bandaged his head. The injury is only superficial. What's it all about? What's it mean?"

"I don't know," Bobby said. "I think I know who murdered Weston and why, or why should ten fifty-pound notes have been left lying untouched? But to-night's a nightmare I see no sense or reason in as yet. Unless it's murderer's panic," he added sombrely, "and that is always bad."

"What murderer?" Mr Edwardes asked. "I don't know how my walking-stick got here. Does that make you think of me again? At any rate, I suppose it clears Martin, doesn't it?"

"I thought what's going on to-night," Bobby said slowly, "cleared Martin Wynne and you, and John Wilkie, too. But I'm not sure now. I'm beginning to wonder if I've been on the wrong track all the time." He paused, frowning and uneasy. He said: "I'm going to Miss Severn's place—Mayfield. Down the road. Will you come? I might need help."

"A polite way of saying you want to keep me 'under observation'?" asked Edwardes, with that faint touch of irony in his voice Bobby had heard before. "Certainly I'll come. But why Mayfield? Why Miss Severn?"

"Thomasine Rowe isn't here," Bobby explained. "I want to know where she is—and why," he added under his breath.

"Oh, Miss Rowe," Edwardes echoed. "Martin can't have come here for her? Nothing between them. It's Olga Severn he is interested in."

"Or Bessie Bell?" Bobby said, wondering if Edwardes knew anything.

He did not seem to.

"The Wych and Wych Arms barmaid?" he asked. "Why . . . what about her? . . . this isn't a love story."

"I've thought sometimes," Bobby retorted, "that that's just what it is—that it is even more a love story than a murder tale. But I'm not sure yet where love and murder cross."

He went to find Hargreaves and borrow a torch. Hargreaves managed to find him one, though with a battery nearly exhausted. It was the best he could do, Hargreaves said, and he thought it would last. By its light occasionally switched on Bobby and Mr Edwardes hurried together down the long, dark avenue and the road beyond till they reached the gate admitting to the Mayfield garden. Through it they passed and came to the front door. Bobby knocked. He found the bell and rang. They heard its shrill summons echo through the house. He knocked again and the sound was loud in the quiet, still night.

No answer came and Mr Edwardes said:—

"I think there can be no one there."

"We'll try the back," Bobby said.

They groped their way round the side of the house through the quiet garden where the long shadows of the night crept away before the flickering light of their torch. The last glimmer that it gave before the battery expired showed them the back door and showed them that it hung open.

"I wonder how long that's been like that," Bobby said. Impatiently he put the useless torch back in his pocket. "No luck with torches to-night," he said, hesitating on the threshold.

"Why are you afraid?" Mr Edwardes asked.

CHAPTER XXXIV
INTERRUPTED MEAL

BOBBY DID not answer. Indeed, it was a question he had but half heard, nor had he been aware of the hesitation, of the tremor in his voice that had told how much he feared what that dark and silent house, that open door swinging slowly to and fro in the still night air, might presently reveal.

He entered and Mr Edwardes with him. He told Mr Edwardes to close the door so that they might light up safely.

"What is it here?" he asked. "Electricity? Gas? What?"

"Oil lamps," Edwardes replied. "Miss Severn wouldn't pay to connect up with the company's main cable."

Bobby had some matches in his pocket. He struck one, and by its small light saw they were in a bare passage. On one side was a door. He opened it. Within was the kitchen. He struck another match and saw the table was laid for a meal. There was a lamp on the table. He lighted it. Now he could see that places had been laid for two. But only one plate and cup had been used. Apparently the meal had been interrupted, for there was uneaten food on the plate, unfinished drink in the cup. The chair opposite was standing at a little distance and sideways, as if it had been pushed hurriedly and violently to one side. The picture in Bobby's mind was of some one who in the middle of a meal had risen and gone in haste. Why? There was a jug on the table, half full. Bobby picked it up.

"Cocoa," he said, and his voice was troubled.

"Why not?" Mr Edwardes asked. "A pedestrian drink, no doubt, but grateful and comforting."

Bobby was smelling, tasting—this last cautiously. He could find nothing suspicious. Edwardes, puzzled and curious, said:—

"Is cocoa something new and strange to you, inspector? A fresh experience in the dailiness of daily life?"

"My man at Weston Lodge Cottage had cocoa for supper, too, tonight," Bobby answered.

Mr Edwardes looked startled and drew away a little from the table, as though suddenly it gave him fear. Then he said:—

"I've trodden on something squashy."

Bobby took the lamp and looked. He saw it was a chocolate on which the other had put his foot. Bobby asked him to sit down, and Mr Edwardes watched with grave attention while Bobby scraped with care from shoe and floor every atom and remnant of the chocolate, preserving them with equal care in a small box. Then, together with Edwardes, who had asked no questions but seemed to understand, he searched the rest of the house and found nothing of interest. There was no sign of Florence Severn, nothing to show where she had gone or why. The bed was untouched, though preparations for the night had apparently been begun, since between the sheets was a newly heated hot-water bottle. But nothing to suggest why the house had been left thus, deserted, a meal on the table, the door open. But then, as they were descending the stairs again, it occurred to Bobby to look in the letter-box. Within was a postcard. It was from Olga, and was to the effect that she might be kept late at work, but would try to be at Mayfield as soon as possible. Slowly Bobby read it aloud.

"Came while Miss Severn was out, I suppose," he said, "and she never thought to look—if she came back, that is. Perhaps she never did."

"She must have," Mr Edwardes pointed out. "She had supper."

"Probably," Bobby agreed, "but nothing to show who made that meal or ate it. It might be some one else. Did Olga come as she said she would?" he mused. Very carefully he put the card away. "May carry dabs," he said. "Neither of them, neither Miss Olga nor her aunt, would give me their dabs. There should be some on the crockery in the kitchen. They would help."

"I think I heard some one come in," Mr Edwardes said.

Bobby stiffened to attention. The utter silence in that deserted house seemed less intense now. No recognizable sound, indeed, hardly a sound at all, rather a sensation, as though a sound had been, had passed, had left the air a little troubled. Bobby put down the lamp so that its light should not show, convey no warning, and softly as he could tread moved on tip-toe down the hall towards the back, whence that faint tremor in the air had seemed to come. But before he had gone half-way he heard a door open and shut, the back door, he knew instinctively. Then he ran, leaving caution, reached the back door, tore it open, ran forward a few yards, stood listening intently for some hint by sound or sight that he might follow.

Useless. Only silence and the black night, and in that darkness what hope in pursuit? Though he made the effort, he had soon to abandon it, helpless in that dense obscurity. Not even so much as a sound of retreating footsteps could he catch. The fugitive had understood that night, not speed, was his—or her—best friend, and so had put faith not in haste, but in silence.

Bobby groped his way back to the house. Mr Edwardes was waiting at the door. He said:—

"I didn't bring the lamp. I suppose there's still the black-out to remember." Then he said: "You know all this is getting on my nerves. Who was it?"

Bobby said crossly that he didn't know. How could he? He added that in his opinion blind man's buff was a much over-rated amusement. He returned for the lighted lamp, and, defying the black-out regulations, went out again. He found nothing, and, as the weather had been dry, and outside the back door the path was paved, he doubted if even in broad day there would have been any footprints to help. He went back into the house and into the kitchen, and looked at the crockery still on the kitchen table. Nothing to show anything had been touched, but now on a chair he noticed a man's hat.

"Was that there before?" he asked Edwardes, who had followed him into the room.

"I don't think so," Edwardes said, looking at it. "I don't know."

Bobby picked it up. It was a light-coloured felt of the type worn by many men at present. There was nothing to give any clue to ownership.

"A small size," Bobby said. "Six and five-eighths. Mr Wilkie has a small head, I think. About his size, isn't it? Anyhow, it's a man's—"

"Did you think it might have been a woman we heard?" Edwardes asked.

"Why not?" Bobby asked. "It's late. Past bed-time. And two women out somewhere—we don't know where or why. Thomasine Rowe and the elder Miss Severn. And Olga Severn, for that matter, who sent a card to say she would be here, but no sign of her. Has she been, I wonder? And if she has, where is she?"

In a low voice Mr Edwardes said:—

"Don't look round, but there is some one peeping in at the window, and I think it is Ronald Franks."

CHAPTER XXXV
GAOLER NIGHT

"OH, WELL," Bobby said, careful not to turn his head in the direction of the window, "just wait here a moment, will you? and I'll show you."

He hoped this vague, ambiguous remark would both arouse Franks's curiosity, if he were really listening at the window, and at the same time put him off his guard.

He went out of the room, closed the door behind him, all with a show of indifference, and then leaped into sudden energy as he raced down the passage, and round the side of the house to the kitchen window.

Useless again. No one was there, and he thought that very likely it was only his imagination that made him fancy he heard a faint ironic laugh somewhere out there where the darkness lay, covering all the land. He went a few yards in one direction and then in another. He heard no sound, he could see nothing, nothing save the vast blackness around. To a fugitive this night was like the cloak of invisibility old tales tell of, wherein those who possessed it could wrap themselves, and so pass unseen, safe from all pursuit. He went back to the house and found Mr Edwardes in the doorway, this time holding up the lighted lamp.

"Black-out or none," he said, "all this is a bit too much."

"A lamp's no help," Bobby said. "You can't run carrying a lamp. Not like a torch. A lamp only means you are not seeing, but seen."

Edwardes took the lamp back into the kitchen and then returned to where Bobby still stood in the doorway, staring out into the night. In the distance they heard the rumble of a passing train. A searchlight shot across the sky, darted to and fro, and vanished. The distant sound of the passing train, the dancing light above, both seemed to intensify the dark and sombre silence around.

"No good standing here," Bobby said. "No help, no hindrance to what is happening out there," and he nodded towards the depths of the night, but made no effort to move, oppressed as he was by a dreadful helplessness.

"No," agreed Mr Edwardes, "no," but he, too, stayed, staring and listening, and they both watched the searchlight as it came again and went dancing up and down the heavy skies, as though waiting for the stars to come out and play.

Abruptly and not far away, more or less from the direction where an orchard lay at the end of the Mayfield garden, they heard a shrill young voice that cried: and, they thought, with terror:—

"Aunt Flo., Aunt Flo., where are you?"

"That's Olga Severn," Bobby said. "Or is it?" Then he shouted: "I am coming. Wait for me."

Therewith he plunged into the darkness, running in the direction whence the voice had seemed to come, shouting again as he went. But almost at once in that baffling darkness he lost his way. He found himself tangled up with raspberry canes and then blocked by a hedge that seemed to run in circles, round and round on every side. He broke through it and ran on and came to another hedge. Through that, too, he forced his way, and came presently to a brick wall, though he knew for certain there had been no brick wall anywhere around Mayfield. Yet there it was as though it had sprouted magically in the night, solid and real, too high to climb, stretching interminably away on either hand, a nightmare wall, since it was where no wall could be. Then he realized what had happened. He had broken through the same hedge twice, once outwards, once back again, having somehow turned right round in the dark, and now here he was back at Mayfield again, brought up short by the wall of the house. He heard footsteps. It was Mr Edwardes. Mr Edwardes said:—

"Is that you? It is you, isn't it? I heard you coming back. Did you find her?"

"How can any one find anything in this darkness?" Bobby asked irritably. "It's like looking for a needle in a haystack when you can't even find the haystack." Then he said: "She never answered. Why didn't she answer? She must have heard."

"I suppose she didn't want," Mr Edwardes said, a reply which did nothing to soothe Bobby's irritation.

"I'll have another try," he said. "You stay here. Show a spot of light. Never mind the black-out. Put the lamp just inside the open door. It'll be a guide, and there aren't any Germans about to-night," and even as he spoke far off the sirens wailed above the sleeping town of Midwych. "There," said Bobby, with intense exasperation, "it only needed that."

For a moment or two he stood hesitating. But the warning might come to nothing. It often did. One waited for the message of the guns before taking action. If their voices sounded, he would have to drop everything and go where the need would be more urgent. Mass murder must take precedence of a mere private killing.

"What about the lamp now?" Edwardes said.

"Better not show it," Bobby said. "You never know. If the raid develops I shall have to go. If it doesn't I'll be back here."

With that he plunged again into the darkness, going more cautiously now. He was not sure how far the Mayfield garden extended, or whether the orchard he remembered was part of it or no, nor was he sure whether it lay in the straight line or to one side. There were open fields beyond, he remembered, and he thought there was a small spinney to one side a little further on, between Mayfield and Weston Lodge Cottage, provided, too, he fancied, with an undergrowth of blackberry bushes—difficult going there, he supposed. He came to the hedge that had confused him before. But now he had a better idea of his whereabouts, having proceeded with greater care. Once more he scrambled through, to the even greater detriment of his clothing that to-day is not only clothing, but coupons as well. Not far off he saw a torch flash in and out. He made his way towards it, came to another hedge and, coupon-conscious now, shirked another scramble. He wondered if he dared risk a jump in the dark, take off and landing both concealed. He heard footsteps and the torch shone again. A voice said:—

"Is that you, Wynne? Is it you?"

Bobby did not answer. He had had too much experience this night of vanishings and disappearances into that too convenient darkness. By good luck, the questing beam of the torch, though it had failed to find him, had shown him a gap in the hedge through which it seemed easy to pass. Unhappily, the swiftly passing light had not shown a strand or two of barbed wire wherewith an effort to close the gap had been made. It caught his trousers and ripped them more than many coupons could atone for. In anguish of spirit more than of body, though his leg was bleeding from a long red scratch, he commented aloud on such ill luck by the use of one expressive word. At once the beam of the torch settled upon him.

"Oh, you," the voice said, half in relief, half in apprehension, and Bobby knew it for that of John Wilkie.

"Why are you here?" Bobby demanded sharply, old suspicions flaring up.

"I'm looking for Martin Wynne," Wilkie said. "Have you seen him? He was at Mr Edwardes's place when I got there, and he said he was going on to Weston Lodge Cottage. But they hadn't seen him there, so I thought I would try Mayfield and I couldn't get any answer, and just now I thought I heard some one calling, but I don't know who."

"Why are you looking for him?" Bobby asked.

"Well, why shouldn't I?" Wilkie retorted. "He's up to something, he knows something, if you ask me. I thought I would follow."

"Why did you take a Japanese knife from Mr Edwardes's collection this afternoon?" Bobby asked abruptly.

"How do you know?" Wilkie asked, surprised. "Who told you? I thought I had better have something."

"Why?" Bobby demanded again.

"Well, some one got killed not so long ago," Wilkie retorted. "If there's another I don't mean it to be me. Martin Wynne took a walking-stick of Edwardes's—one with a nice heavy handle. I noticed that."

"You're not being frank with me," Bobby said. "You are keeping things back. I think you'll have to be held for questioning."

"A fat lot of good that'll do you," retorted Wilkie sulkily. "I'm not keeping anything back. I don't know anything to keep back, for that matter. I'm only trying to help. I'm as keen as you are on finding out who did it—killed Mr Weston, I mean. I know people think it was me, and so do you. What sort of chance of getting bookings do you think I'll have if a story like that gets about? You don't know how stage people gossip. If it's any one, it's Martin Wynne."

"Wynne has been attacked to-night, knocked out," Bobby said, wondering if this were news or something Wilkie had the best of reasons for knowing already.

"Has he, though?" Wilkie said, and sounded surprised enough. "Who did it? Not me, if that's what you're hinting at." Wilkie lowered his voice. "Are you sure, or was it faked? I mean, how about his having knocked himself out? If you ask me, it was he did in his uncle. There's something he had got hold of—Mr Weston about Martin, I mean. That's what he was always scheming for—to get to know something about you so you had to do what he said. Power. That's what he wanted—to feel he had power and you had to do what he told you. Then it was all right if you did what he said. Something about Martin and the barmaid at the Wych and Wych Arms. Anyhow, that's my idea. Bessie's not like most girls—stand up to any man she would and give as good as she got. Or better. I wouldn't put it past her and Martin to have done that other job and then fixed it to-night for her to lay him out so as to put you off."

"Well, it's an idea," agreed Bobby, without mentioning that it was one he and his assistants had often canvassed as among the possibilities to be considered. Nor for that matter did considerations of time and place to-night put it beyond possibility. Bessie could well have reached Weston Lodge Cottage before he got there, and Bobby was much inclined to believe that the doctor at the nursing-home would always be willing to swear an alibi or so for her. Bobby continued: "I think Mr Weston had a hold on you, hadn't he? Not only for what he knew, but for what he might still find out. The Weston West Mill books have been gone through again, you know."

"Nothing fresh there any one could prove," Wilkie declared hastily, and once more Bobby thought he heard a faint sound, as of some one who moved at a little distance.

But he was not sure, it might well be only the murmur of the faint breeze that sometimes stirred, only to die away again. Or one of the creatures of the night, busy about its own concerns. Helplessly he stood and stared into the black obscurity that held him as in a prison from which there was no escape, since where he moved, it moved with him baffling and impenetrable. He said:—

"Have you seen anything of Franks?"

"Franks? No. Is he here, too?" Wilkie said, and, as if with some vague idea of looking for him, switched on his torch once more and flashed the ray around.

"Don't do that, didn't you hear the alert?" Bobby exclaimed, and snatched the torch away and switched it off again.

"I forgot. Anyhow you can't look for any one without showing a light," Wilkie grumbled. "I thought I heard some one about here. That's why I came. Then I heard you. I thought it was you I heard, but if Franks is here, perhaps it was him. Over there it was."

Bobby took a step or two in the direction indicated, though still he would not show a light when for all he knew some German, with engine cut off, might be gliding down, finger on bomb release, ready to launch it in the direction of any gleam of light he saw. As he moved he said to Wilkie:—

"I'm pretty sure it was Olga Severn I heard call out, and if Franks is about here, too—"

He left the sentence unfinished, but Wilkie completed it—to Bobby's equal surprise and unease.

"If he is, he's not alone," Wilkie said, "and you had better get a move on. Because I think there's things happening that had best be stopped—if it's not too late."

"What things?" Bobby asked, and Wilkie answered:—

"I don't know, but you said just now I wasn't being frank with you and I was keeping things back, and so I was, because I didn't know what they meant or how you wouldn't twist them against me or how much you knew already. But now I'll tell you what I saw a minute ago, and if you don't believe me it's gospel true all the same, so help me God, unless I was dreaming, as I thought almost I was."

Bobby waited till Wilkie began to speak again, in a slow and hesitating voice, as though he himself were still not persuaded of the full reality of what he had seen.

"It was some one running I heard first, and I knew, I don't know why, that it was some one terribly afraid. I switched on my torch, and it was Florence Severn, and by the way she ran she made me think of a rabbit with a weasel close behind. I could see that she was afraid and that she had no hope as she slipped and dodged through the trees. And when the light from my torch caught her she cried out, not very loud, but twice over, and she put her hands over her eyes as if she knew it was the end, for I think she did not know it was me, but thought who ever followed her had found her. But then she cried out again and began to run once more, and I saw Thomasine Rowe. She had a strong torch in one hand that she kept flashing in and out, so that sometimes I saw her plainly as she ran in between the trees and sometimes she was just a shadow there. In one hand she held this torch and in the other hand she had a handbag and a knife—a Japanese knife like the one belonging to Mr Edwardes I borrowed to-night. It was frightening somehow, because they looked so different, the handbag like any handbag any woman carries and the bare knife in the same hand—and her face was like the fires of hell. What were they doing, running like that, through the trees in the night, one behind the other, and why?" He paused and then he said: "I suppose you think I invented all that to put you off or something?"

"No, I don't think that," Bobby said; and once more he was conscious of an immense frustration, for what could he do, and how could he tell what was happening or not happening out there in that baffling, impenetrable darkness that held its secrets more securely than ever could have done high walls or triple gates?

The picture in his mind was vivid of the two women running thus in the darkness of the lonely night—pursuing and pursued. He felt he could reconstruct now what had happened at Mayfield. Florence Severn, waiting for her niece, the niece she had hated as a rival but to whom she had turned in her fear, had heard a knock or a ring and had answered it, thinking it was Olga come at last, but finding there upon the doorstep, not Olga, but Thomasine.

A moment of fear, Bobby supposed, but perhaps a fear only fully understood in time for that flight from kitchen within to the night without, whereof it seemed Wilkie had witnessed a phase that might by now have worked itself out to its destined end.

"Was it you they were running away from, trying to hide from?" Wilkie asked.

"I don't think so," Bobby said; and fingered his torch, wondering if he dared use it yet, or whether he must still consent to be the prisoner of the night. No gun-fire had yet sounded; but who could tell what death was not lurking up there in the skies, ready to launch itself at any moment on any glimmer of light that showed, just as who could tell what grim, strange tragedy was not being enacted in the shelter of this all-pervading darkness, where two women had vanished in dreadful flight and pursuit more dreadful still.

"If you saw them running by," Bobby said, "it can't be either of them you heard or thought you heard near here. So who was it?"

"You said something about Ron Franks?" Wilkie said. "Do you mean he has something to do with it? Could it be him?"

Bobby's mind was busy for a moment or two before he answered. The chance was slender; but in this extremity of doubt and helplessness, any chance was worth taking. Making his voice loud and clear so that it should travel as far as possible through the silent night, he said:—

"Oh, that's certain, and he'll hang, that's more certain still."

"Oh, I say, come now," Wilkie muttered; "do you mean—hang?"

"I mean the rope is around his neck and there's nothing to do but pull it," Bobby answered, still in the same clear and strong voice. "A pity, too, but there you are. Nothing can save him—unless of course even now he tells what he knows. Though it'll be too late for that soon, because we know it nearly all by now."

"Oh, I say, come now," muttered Wilkie, and felt rather than saw Bobby's fierce gesture to him to be silent.

They waited. At a distance they heard the sirens again calling, this time to tell the countryside that peril had passed for the time.

They waited still, and heard at last what Bobby had hoped for—the sound of stealthy movement near by, a low branch brushed aside, the grass rustling at the contact of careful feet.

"That's you, Franks, isn't it?" Bobby said. "Well, are you ready to speak out? I think you have no chance unless you do."

He flashed the torch. A shadow drew nearer, shuffling and uncertain, became plain in the beam of the torch. Franks said:—

"You can't bluff me, you can't touch me. I had nothing to do with it. I didn't know a thing about it. You know yourself I was miles away—at the cinema. There's witnesses saw me there. You can't make anything of that."

"Conspiracy," Bobby answered. "In conspiracy all concerned are equally guilty. Another conspiracy to-night, perhaps, or why are you here? Or not a new conspiracy, but just the old one going on?"

"There's no conspiracy," muttered Franks, but his voice was uncertain. "Why should there be? What about?"

"To prove your claim to be Mr Weston's legitimate son, and so heir to his whole estate if he died without a will," Bobby answered.

"I—I don't know what you're talking about," Franks muttered, and the ray from Bobby's torch showed him dabbing at a perspiring forehead. "I—there wasn't any conspiracy," he muttered again.

"If there wasn't," Bobby said, "why all that careful planning of an alibi at the cinema when, exactly in the way in which the conjuror forces a card on people, you forced recognition on your friends of another girl, whose hat and coat Thomasine Rowe had copied and wore, and who you had made sure beforehand would be there that night. You pointed her out in the half-light of the cinema foyer as Thomasine, they recognized hat and coat and so thought they recognized Thomasine. So you had two honest independent witnesses to swear to an alibi, and though we never accepted it for a moment, it would have been hard to disprove. Good enough to make a jury doubt. Only there was the weak point that the other girl's hat didn't suit Miss Rowe—not her style, so why was she wearing it? Miss Rowe has what women call 'dress sense', and there had to be some strong reason to make her wear what she must have known was an unbecoming hat. That was what made me sure the alibi was faked."

"All that's only talk," Franks said, trying to bluster, but his voice was hoarse and indistinct. Then it grew shrill, high. "You can't prove anything," he cried. "I've never said I thought he was my father."

"Oh, yes, you have," Bobby said, speaking with more confidence than he really felt, for though he was sure of his facts, he knew there was still much for which he had none of that proof a court of law demands. "It was plain from the very beginning there was that sort of idea floating about, and it was plain Mr Weston knew it, or why that envelope marked 'Family papers, re Aggie and child', and why did it contain bank-notes but no sign of papers? Were the bank-notes a bribe—or perhaps a trap? Mr Weston was hardly the sort of man to leave important private papers lying about in a safe to which his secretary must have had frequent access. If there really were a living child, presumably he or she was one of those concerned, and of them all you were the only one showing any family likeness—the very first time I saw you I noticed hat, especially the mouth and nose. Mr Weston was your father, wasn't he?"

"Yes, he was," Franks answered defiantly, "and he did me out of my rights just as he did my mother, too. They were married all right, Scots fashion, perfectly legal; she told me so herself. Only I had to have lawyer's proof; and when I wrote to him, all I got was my letter back, torn in half, and saying if I wrote again he would put the matter in the hands of his lawyers. There's a father for you. God, how I hated him! And I told Thomasine, and she said she would get the proof for me, and then we could marry, and I didn't much want, but she had a way with her so you couldn't call your soul your own when she was there, and I never dreamed she meant to do what she did, or she had that knife with her, or that was what she wanted it for, when she made me buy it."

"You bought it?" Bobby asked sharply.

"At Farquhar's, in the Strand in London," Franks admitted. "She made me. To make sure I was in it, too. She had one already, but she said we must each have one. She talked about all the things we could do when we had made Mr Weston acknowledge me. She made me buy her a swanky ring, too—took nearly every penny I had. More. What did she care so long as she had her ring? I couldn't stand her really, the way she bossed a chap; you couldn't dare call your soul your own. Made you sick the way she thought she owned you. That ring—cost the most out of all they showed us, but of course it was the one she had to have."

He stopped abruptly, and through the darkness, from very near at hand, there came a long, low, fluttering sigh, and then a gentle sob, a half-heard sob, as it were of faith and hope and love all together gone—and for ever.

"Miss Rowe," Bobby called. "My God, she heard you," he said to Franks, and as he dashed away into the darkness, calling, shouting, flashing his torch, he heard Franks's last protest:—

"I didn't know ... I didn't mean ... I couldn't help ..."

CHAPTER XXXVII
CONCLUSIONS

IT WAS towards morning when Bobby, unshaven, dishevelled, worn out, half dead with fatigue, at last reached home. Olive, who also had not seen bed that night, heard the car and came running to the door. Bobby was in the act of half leading, half carrying Florence Severn from car to house. To Olive he said:—

"She's pretty well done in. Collapsed. The doctor will be along presently. Do what you can till he turns up, will you? She's been out all night. It was hours before we could find her. In a ditch. Unconscious."

Olive asked no questions. She had the rare quality of preferring action to chatter. While she did her best with her unexpected and only half-conscious guest, Bobby, in reckless mood, not caring a hang about the consequences to the war, filled his bath with a good ten inches of water, and just revelled in it. Indeed, for the customary two pins he would probably have made the depth a foot. Then he shaved and changed, wondering ruefully whether those trousers of his were repairable—coupon shortage was acute, he knew, in the Owen household—and finally sat down to breakfast, looking, as Olive remarked thoughtfully, rather more like the man she once had known, and rather less like a dilapidated scarecrow found by accident in the remotest corner of a rag-and-bone dealer's yard.

Bobby acknowledged the compliment with a bow—his mouth being too full for speech. Presently, however, between two fresh forkfuls, he asked:—

"How is she?"

"Asleep," Olive answered. "Restless, though. She keeps tossing and turning and muttering to herself. I've left the door open so we can hear if she moves."

"She has been babbling incoherences all the way," Bobby said. "I had to bring her here. At Weston Lodge Cottage they have their hands full, what with our own man and Martin Wynne, who got himself knocked out last night. I want to get a statement from Miss Severn if I can."

"What has happened?" Olive asked.

"Thomasine Rowe has poisoned herself," Bobby said. "Using the chocolate creams stuffed with arsenic with which Miss Severn first tried to poison her, and then in turn Thomasine Miss Severn last night. Olga Severn is still missing. She was somewhere around last night, but we can't find her. I hope to God no harm has come to her. Her aunt knew Thomasine meant mischief and sent for her for help, and Olga came. Apparently she went first to Thomasine to find out what was really happening. I don't suppose Thomasine told her anything much, but the visit frightened Thomasine, and probably that is why she tried to put us out of action. Olga may have threatened to make her aunt tell me the truth at last. It was certainly Thomasine whom Bessie Bell saw in our kitchen. What happened next I don't know. I wish I did. I think Olga must have sent for Martin. He got a crack on the head for his pains, and he'll be laid up for a day or two. Nothing serious. Mr Edwardes has gone home to bed. He took Wilkie with him. Franks is being held for the present. Bessie Bell is still in the nursing-home. I rang them up to ask. Mr Abel died during the night."

"Did Thomasine know you knew it was her?" Olive asked. "Is that why she . . .?"

"There was more to it than that," Bobby explained gravely. "She heard us talking in the ordered—Wilkie was there. He had got it into his silly head that Martin Wynne was guilty, and he was trying to play detective on his own—apparently not without some sort of hope that somehow he might be able to establish a claim for himself on the Weston estate. He kept flashing his torch, and naturally that served as a kind of rallying point for us when we were chasing each other round and round in a night as black as the inside of a blind man's hat. Thomasine left her hunting of Florence Severn whom she had followed out there in the dark to kill, and crept up to listen. None of us heard her, but she heard Franks giving her away to save his own skin and telling us all how little he had ever cared for her. I think it broke her up, to realize all she had done for him and how ready and eager he was to throw her over. She had suspected before, perhaps, and now she knew. Her world crashed. We found her at last, but she died while we were carrying her to the house. Perhaps she wouldn't have hanged. Not premeditated murder, I think. She took the Japanese knife with her that other night as protection, without any intention of using it, even though she had put an edge on it herself where she lodged with the village carpenter. Anyhow, it would have meant penal servitude for life, and I don't think she would have stood up to that very well. A bad business. She had the makings of a fine woman, an unusual woman. A fighter through and through. She might even have escaped conviction. I think she would have faced it out to the last. Only for hearing the way Franks talked about her. That broke her up. She had lost her soul for his sake, and all he could think of was to whine about the money he had had to spend on buying her a ring."

"I suppose you can't get him hanged instead, can you?" Olive asked wistfully.

"I don't think so," answered Bobby, almost as regretfully. "Nothing to show he had any reason to suppose there was anything more on hand than an attempt to get hold of private papers he hoped would prove his legitimate birth."

"Is it quite certain?" Olive began.

"Florence Severn was an eye-witness," Bobby told her.

"Is that why Thomasine tried to kill her?"

"Not altogether. Miss Severn tried to poison Thomasine with those chocolates, and Thomasine began to think it was one life or the other."

"But are you sure Miss Severn sent them? Why did she?"

"It always lay between the two Severn women—the aunt and the niece—and if only Miss Olga had let us take her dabs we should have known it much sooner. Even yet we haven't hers—at least, not to swear to. But we have the aunt's, and they are identical with those on the inside panel of the knee-hole of Weston's writing-table. She was hiding there when—she's a small woman—when the murder was committed. She had watched Olga slip away from Mayfield. So she jumped to the conclusion that Olga was off to visit Weston on the quiet, as she herself had been used to do. She tried to follow. She lost Olga in the dark. Later she went to the house, and when she found the windows of the study open, as once they had been left open for her, she was quite sure it was Olga who was expected. She slipped in and hid, intending to confront the two of them—Weston and Olga—to take them in the act, as it were. I don't know what she thought when not Olga but Thomasine came creeping in. Probably she was merely puzzled. But she lay still and watched and saw what happened. In her surprise and horror she betrayed her presence. Thomasine—one murder was enough—she couldn't face another— tried to make herself safe by forcing Florence to sign a confession that she herself was guilty. Futile in one way. It would have deceived no one. But it did serve to make Florence keep silence—for a time. Afterwards, when we asked so many questions, she began to work herself into a panic for fear Thomasine should use the confession. And at last she made up her mind to try to get it back at all costs."

"The chocolates she poisoned and sent to Thomasine?" Olive asked.

"Yes. Mr Weston had sent them to Olga in the first place. Olga wouldn't touch them, and left them behind when she left her aunt's. So Florence made use of them. She thought Thomasine had the confession hidden in her room, and she meant to offer to help in nursing her, and so get a chance to look for it. From what she's been saying in her half-delirious state, I think her idea was only to make Thomasine ill, not to kill her. Willing to take the risk, though. Her life or Thomasine's, she thought, and Thomasine thought much the same."

"Poison is awful," Olive said, shaken still when she thought of what had happened in her own kitchen, "but I almost think that that spying on her niece was worse. I suppose it was jealousy, and jealousy makes you forget everything."

"Fear, too," Bobby said. "She began to think she might have left finger-prints where she hid under the desk. Now-a-days every one has heard of finger-prints. That was at the bottom of all that about Olga's vanity case and her own ring. She got hold of the vanity case, put her own dabs on it, and hid it where it was sure to be found. That was to suggest the knee-hole dabs were Olga's. To stop our finding out they weren't, she persuaded Olga not to let us take hers. As an additional precaution she put on an act about her ring she pretended was too loose on her finger and let me see it come off. If we managed to identify the knee-hole dabs as hers, she had her explanation pat. Oh, yes, she meant to say, my ring came off, and I had to crawl under Mr Weston's desk to pick it up. Plausible enough for a jury, I expect, but so plainly put on for my benefit I was sure it meant she knew something and had something to hide. It fitted, if the ring didn't."

"It was rather clever of her," Olive said reluctantly, "to think all that out."

"It's all been very clever, it's because it was all so very clever I was able to see through it," Bobby said. "Life is more simple. Weston himself was so clever he himself laid the trap that caught him. Baited it, too. One of his more elaborate schemes. I imagine there is little doubt of Ronald Franks being really his son. No telling for certain, but it seems likely. Franks's mouth is Weston mouth and his nose is the family nose. When there was so much talk of unacknowledged illegitimate children, I remembered the vague sort of likeness I noticed the first time I saw him, though I couldn't quite place it then. Illegitimate, no doubt, and other illegitimate children as well, I expect. Weston didn't intend to have anything to do with any of them. Probably he never knew for certain if any of them were really his. Franks's mother told him there had been a marriage—Scots fashion. Trying to excuse herself and keep his respect, perhaps. No one will ever know. Anyhow, the boy got a dusty answer when he wrote to Weston. But he remained convinced he was legitimate, he made himself acquainted with all his supposed father's doings, when Thomasine Rowe became private secretary he managed to make friends with her. She seems to have fallen for him pretty heavily—goodness knows why. What on earth could a fine, strong, virile girl like her see in a twerp like Ronald Franks?"

"Strong and virile," Olive said. "That's just it. She wanted a child—subconsciously. Without what the B.B.C. lady the other day called 'two years of nappy-washing'. So she chose Franks instead."

"Well, I don't know," said Bobby doubtfully. "I suppose extremes meet. Opposites attract and all that. Besides, if she established

Franks's claim—and especially if Mr Weston died without making a will, and she knew he hadn't and didn't mean to—then she would be the wife of a rich man in full control of a big business and she in full and complete control of him. I take it she had no thought of murder when she started out that night. To strong, young people, an elderly man like Weston seems as good as dead already. But she made the mistake, the clever ones always make. She under-estimated other people. She never realized how quickly Weston knew all about her interest in his past life and her friendship with the Ronald Franks who had written to him. He knew most of what was going on round him; and when he knew Franks and Thomasine were in league, he realized why the extremely pretty girl he had chosen to work for him kept him so very much at a distance, and he saw his chance to get his claws on her. But he, too, did a spot of under-estimating. He didn't realize how strong were her passions, how fierce her energies, how deadly her will. First of all he got rid of Florence Severn. Anyhow, he was tired of her. To put her off his real plans he let her think there was something between him and her niece, Miss Olga, and indeed he made a few tentative passes at Olga, hinting at marriage. His favourite opening gambit, by the way. Probably, too, he had some idea of making in that way a kind of flank attack on Martin. He knew Martin was in love with her.

"All this was enormously complicated by the sudden threat to his position as dictator in absolute control of the Weston West business. He tried to weave the two threads into one, and with some success, though in the end with a success that cut the thread of his own life.

"First, as if by accident, he let Thomasine get a glimpse of an envelope endorsed 'Family papers—re Aggie and child'. She knew Aggie was the name of Franks's mother. But it held no such papers, for none existed. It held instead ten fifty-pound bank-notes. Then one day he sent her off early, telling her at the same time that he was having Martin Wynne to dinner, and that afterwards they were going on to visit Mr Edwardes to talk it all over with him. That was to make her think the coast would be clear. And he had seen she had had a chance to have a duplicate key made for the safe. She ought to have seen things were being made altogether too easy for her, but she walked unsuspectingly into the trap. And when it sprang she took her own way out, a way that he had never thought of.

"Weston had got rid of Martin according to plan, and he sat there waiting for Thomasine. As it happened, I had let him know his bait was already being sniffed at. I told him some one had been in his room. Thomasine, of course, having a preliminary look round. She had been giving Franks his last instructions when I heard them talking before she sent him off top speed to fix up the alibi she had planned. It had to be accepted for him because it really was genuine, and it would therefore, she hoped, be accepted for her also. Meanwhile Weston had an unexpected visitor—Mr Edwardes, anxious to know the result of the talk with Martin. And, when leaving, Martin met Olga, who was anxious, too, to know the result of the interview with Mr Weston. Martin had been faced with the older man's knowledge of his affair with Bessie Bell. Martin knew Bessie was going to be there. She had told him she had been sent for. He managed to make an excuse to get a word with her at the window of the room where she was waiting. He more or less defied his cousin, and when Olga met him he told her all about it. They stayed till the small hours talking in the summer-house and sheltering from the rain; and though we found dabs to show Martin had been there with a woman, there was nothing to identify the woman—both Olga and Florence Severn having taken precious good care we never got any of their dabs. Meanwhile Weston gave Edwardes a whisky and soda in the dining-room, and Edwardes has told us how all the time Weston seemed on the alert, listening. So he was. He got rid of Edwardes as soon as he could, and still waited till he heard sounds to tell him Thomasine was there, in the study, at work, trying to find the papers she hoped would prove her boy's claim.

"A dramatic moment when those two faced each other. The safe was open, she had in her hand the bank-notes she must have been puzzled to find where she had expected birth and marriage certificates, or at least letters of proof. He must have thought he had her utterly in his power, that now she would have no choice. He had only to give the alarm and there she was, caught in the act, stolen bank-notes in her hand, the safe wide open. He thought she had no way of escape. She had. The Japanese knife. With that she struck.

With that she saved herself and lost herself, exchanging the lie of attempted theft for the truth of accomplished murder."

CHAPTER XXXVIII
CONCLUSION

FROM UPSTAIRS Florence Severn was calling. They went to her. She was sitting up in bed. She said wildly:—

"Thomasine Rowe wants to kill me. Don't let her. She ran after me. Do you know why?"

"Because you saw her kill Mr Weston," Bobby answered.

Florence looked at him bewilderedly. She sank back on her pillows. She said:—

"Oh, you know. How do you know? How long . . .?"

"Oh, for long enough," Bobby answered. He went on talking. He felt the best way to win her confidence, to persuade her to talk herself, was for him to continue to talk and to let her understand how much he knew already. He was anxious to hear her own story of the previous night's events. He said: "From the very beginning there was a good deal to suggest her guilt. Little things. Uncertain things. Things all pointing the same way, and yet never enough to make up certainty. Once she told me murder wasn't murder when it was self-defence, and I thought, 'Perhaps you struck in self-defence'. Once I called her, to Franks, 'a striking' young lady, and I thought he was going to faint. A casual word, but I wondered if it had called up an image in his mind of her—'striking'. She was curiously callous about the death of the little dog she gave those chocolates to. It had been a nuisance, and she had removed it, and that was all. I wondered if she would be as callous and indifferent about removing other things in her way. Then I knew she had lied twice. First about being near the house the time I heard her voice in the grounds. But that might not have meant much, and she put up an ingenious explanation. She said perhaps Olga had imitated her voice. So I couldn't be absolutely certain. But I could be certain that her alibi was faked. Ingenious, though, in its way. Because she had managed to get it supported by two honest, independent witnesses. But I knew it was faked. She spoke of sheltering from the rain on leaving the cinema, and I knew, because I had been in town late, that it was a clear, moonlight night when the cinemas closed.

It rained earlier at Weston Lodge Cottage, but the rain-squalls only struck Midwych much later, between three and four. Wilkie made the same mistake. When he got the message that Weston wanted to see him again, he thought it might mean his other thefts had been discovered. He tried to find out on the quiet from Hargreaves. When he heard about the murder, he panicked. He had been in the house at the time secretly, there was the motive of the possibly newly discovered embezzlements, he felt sure he would be suspected. Self-conscious as only a third-rate actor can be, it always seemed to him he must be the centre of attention. As a matter of fact Weston had only wanted him back as a handy tool to use in the fight for the control of the Weston West business. He panicked badly. He tried to fake an alibi, too, by being on the platform when the early express from the south arrived and making a scene with the guard as if he had just arrived by it. In point of fact he had arrived the previous evening. He gave his story away just as Thomasine did by a blunder over the rain. He said he had been out in it and got wet through. But there was no rain after about four in the morning, and if he had come by the train he said—arriving at half-past four— he couldn't have been out in it. He persuaded Hargreaves, too, to keep silent about his presence, and even to make a show of hostility by repeating gossip he thought I was sure to hear in any case. So, though psychologically he didn't seem much like a murderer, he had to stay on the list. Just as well, perhaps that Mrs Parham, the cook, saw both him and Hargreaves standing together at the top of the stairs at the moment of the murder. He didn't know that, and she didn't say anything, chiefly for fear of getting Hargreaves into trouble. Of course, from the very beginning it was plain some one had been hiding in the study some time. But nothing to show who or how long, or what, if anything, had been seen. Only when the poisoned chocolates arrived—though at first I thought Thomasine might have sent them herself to herself—did I begin to guess what had really happened there in the Weston Lodge Cottage study, after the murder."

"It nearly drove me mad," Florence said slowly, "to feel she had my confession and might show it any moment. I thought if I made her ill I could offer to nurse her and that would give me a chance to get it back. Only she was so clever. She didn't eat any of the chocolates, and I knew she knew I had sent them, because I could see how she was watching me—watching and waiting. I was afraid, and I sent for Olga to come back, and when I heard some one at the door I thought it was her. But it wasn't, it was Thomasine. She looked at me and I looked at her, and she said could she come in, and I didn't say anything, I just banged the door, and I locked it and I bolted it, and then I felt safe, and I went back to the kitchen and she was there. She had run round the house and got in by the back door. She showed me a great knife she had with her, and she showed me some of the chocolates I sent her and she said 'Which?' So then she said 'Which?' again, and I didn't say anything because I couldn't, and she held out one of the chocolates, and I knocked it out of her hand and I ran and she ran after me. Always she was close behind, but it was dark, dark, and she never found me. But now she will."

"Not now," said Bobby, "for last night she killed herself."

It took a little time still to persuade her she was safe, but at last she seemed more composed and slept. Bobby and Olive left her then. Going downstairs Bobby remarked:—

"Not what you would call a fine character. I suppose you can make excuses for her—desperate with fear. Half crazy with panic."

"Do you think Thomasine really meant last night to kill her?" Olive asked.

"Who knows?" Bobby asked. "Quite possibly at first it was partly an attempt to frighten her into submission again. The rather melodramatic knife or poison offer—Queen Eleanor and Fair Rosamund style—does suggest that. But later, in the dark, running in the night, in the orchard, she meant to kill all right. The killer's look. Plain enough. Not a pretty sight, not a pretty memory, those two women running, to kill, to escape."

"What will happen to her?" Olive asked. "Florence Severn, I mean."

"Well, I don't quite know," Bobby answered hesitatingly. "We know she sent Thomasine the poisoned chocolates, because she has just said so. But only a verbal statement, and one made in an excited, rather hysterical condition. Could be repudiated all right. No other proof. I could make out a case to submit to the Public Prosecutor, and I suppose I shall, but I don't think they will authorize proceedings. I certainly shan't press it. Then, again, she is clearly guilty of withholding evidence, but I can't see any one wanting to prosecute in the circumstances. She was under pressure. Good counsel would get a jury sympathizing at once, and probably a 'not guilty' verdict. No, I think nothing will happen, and personally I should say she's had a bad enough time. No more than she deserved, but no need to rub it in."

"What about Ronald Franks?" Olive asked.

Bobby shrugged his shoulders. An answer with which Olive seemed satisfied. All he was worth and all that was necessary.

"Mr Wilkie?" she asked next.

"Oh, well," Bobby said, and again it was an answer that seemed sufficient.

"Mr Wynne isn't much hurt, is he?" Olive asked next.

"Oh, no. Probably it was Franks laid him out with a whack from behind. Not worth going into further. Common assault, that's all. As I see it, Olga must have rung Martin up when she got her aunt's S.O.S. Apparently he followed Wilkie to Weston Lodge Cottage, trying to find out what it was all about. Olga had told him about her aunt's confession. He thought it might be in the safe. It wasn't locked. Nothing in it of any value since Weston's death. He started to look. But if the confession wasn't there, the poisoned chocolates were, and Thomasine heard him, and thought it was the chocolates he was hunting for. So she made Franks knock him out from behind, using Mr Edwardes's stick Wilkie had left behind him. It was Wilkie who took both the missing Japanese knife No. 3 and the walking-stick from Mr Edwardes's house. He believed he was on the track of the criminal, and he wanted to be well armed. In his excitement he left traces of himself everywhere he went—the walking-stick at Weston Lodge Cottage and his hat at Mayfield when he was still trying to find Martin."

"I suppose it all means everything is over between Martin and Olga," Olive said sadly. "I'm so sorry. Can he get a divorce? I suppose it was because of their being married, and his trying to use it to blackmail Martin into doing what he wanted, that Mr Weston brought you into it?"

"Probably," Bobby growled, still sore, still unforgiving. "Bluffed Bessie I was there to take her into custody if he said so, and she knew what that meant to the dying man she loved. I don't suppose she knew bigamists aren't arrested offhand like that. She was scared all right. And Martin Wynne was in a nasty spot. No wonder he was so excited and upset. Unless he gave way, the whole story would come out, and the woman who was legally his wife, whom he still felt in a way bound to protect, whom he had taken 'for better or worse', to whom he was still handing over a good part of his earnings, would have to face prosecution, and perhaps a term in gaol. She was still his wife, and he didn't like the idea of being called on to appear as chief witness for the prosecution. That's what he and Olga were talking about half the night through in the summer-house. But I'm afraid it's bound to happen now."

"You don't mean Bessie will have to be brought up for bigamy, do you?" Olive asked, dismayed.

"I don't quite see how it can be helped," Bobby answered. "Can't suppress facts. There it is. Plain case of bigamy."

Olive looked very worried, and said it was a shame. Bobby patted her on the head—a gesture which always annoyed her, it seemed so patronizing, and if he did happen to be a few inches the taller, no need to show off—and said that that was that—meaning bigamy—and she asked him what was the good of being practically Chief Constable if he couldn't arrange a little thing like that, and wasn't he sorry for Bessie? So he said he was, but that made no difference, and if he was practically a Chief Constable, he only got an inspector's salary, so now he was going to snatch an hour's sleep before going on to headquarters. If Olive, in the meantime, could think of any way of bilking the bigamy laws, she was to let him know and he would be all for it.

Olive said thoughtfully that never before had she realized how absolutely Brutal and Unfeeling men could be, and it would be a most awful shame if Olga and Martin could only be married at the expense of sending Bessie to gaol, and she had never heard of anything quite so heartless, and anyhow—this with satisfaction—he couldn't have his nap now, because here were Martin and Olga themselves, coming up the garden path, evidently to have a talk, and if he, Bobby, failed to find with them some way of what he so coarsely called 'bilking the bigamy laws', then he wasn't the man she thought.

Bobby promised to do his best, admitted the newcomers, and listened gravely to Martin's stammering confession of how he had married Bessie when he was an undergraduate at Oxford and she a barmaid at a small inn not far from the city.

"I thought you most likely knew all about it by now," Martin explained, "so we made up our minds I had better come along and make a clean breast of it."

Bobby agreed gravely that when people reached the conclusion mentioned they often came to a similar decision.

"It didn't take us long," Martin continued, "to find out we had made fools of ourselves, but there we were—tied up and no way out. Uncle Weston got to know, and tried to put the screw on. I expect it was Wilkie told him. Wilkie was up at the time, and I always had an idea he knew about me and Bessie."

"It always seemed likely there was something of the kind," Bobby remarked, "but I can't understand why we failed to find any trace of your marriage. We made a pretty thorough search everywhere."

Martin permitted himself a faint smile at the memory of past astuteness.

"We fixed that all right," he said. "It wouldn't have done for either of us to let it be known. Besides, we were both under twenty-one by a few weeks. A pal of mine, Len Bolton, an Australian, awfully nice chap—R.A.F., killed in the Battle of Britain—had the idea. He lent me his birth certificate. Bessie borrowed her elder sister's, Jane. Jane is dead, too, poor girl—killed in an air raid. But of course it was all O.K. and perfectly legal, so long as we both knew what we were doing. Len made us write letters to each other so that should be quite clear."

Bobby sat silent for some moments, struggling with an emotion too deep for words—far too deep indeed. His prolonged silence, the intense feeling his expression showed, finally alarmed them both.

"What's the matter?" asked Martin.

"Aren't you well?" inquired Olga.

"No," said Bobby, turning on her a glittering eye that made her fairly jump. To Martin he said bitterly: "Nothing's the matter. Why should there be? Merely I don't know how many of the marriage laws broken and your marriage about as valid as a Vichy law."

"Why not? Of course it is," declared Martin stoutly. "We both knew."

"That," explained Bobby, "is why. Because you both knew. If one of you hadn't known, then it would have held. As you both knew, you were merely acting a sham, for which," said Bobby, glaring, "you both have incurred and deserve all manner of penalties. And I hope you get 'em too, hot and strong," he added viciously.

"I still don't see it," Martin complained. "We both knew, so what's the harm?"

"The harm is, you were fooling the law," Bobby snapped.

"Well, why not?" asked Martin. Then he added thoughtfully: "If you can."

Bobby, again overcome by emotion, again found himself speechless. Olga broke a silence that had become a little dreadful by saying:—

"You mean they weren't ever married—not really. Either of them? Then there isn't any bigamy or anything?"

"No," said Bobby, "especially anything," and he relapsed into gloomy silence as he thought of all the work and expense and time spent trying to trace this marriage that had been no marriage.

"I still don't get it," Martin said.

"Simple enough," Bobby told him. "I mean simple to any one gifted with intelligence above that of a sub-normal, lame dog born deaf and dumb."

"Meaning me?" asked Martin anxiously.

"Yes," said Bobby.

"Oh," said Olga.

"People who break laws the way you broke them—wholesale, that is," Bobby explained, "can't be allowed to claim their benefit. You staged a farce, and you can't be allowed to pretend it was real. If one of you hadn't known, then the thing would have held, because for him or her it would have been genuine, and the other couldn't be allowed to wriggle out."

"Oh, well," admitted Martin reluctantly, "if you put it like that. Bit upsetting, though, to find you aren't married when you thought you were. Anyhow, if I'm not married now I soon shall be." Then he seemed to remember something. "What are we in for?" he asked. "You said 'penalties'? What are they likely to be?"

"They ought," said Bobby fervently, "to be penal servitude for life at the very least. But I'm not sure how to proceed. You've made a verbal statement with no supporting evidence. If you choose to hand me a written statement with details that can be checked, I'll consider it. Even then all you could give me proof of is that two persons—both now dead—were married at a certain time and place. What proof is there they weren't? I don't at the moment see how I am to get evidence to show those two persons were in fact two other persons."

"We but . . ." said Martin, trying to think this out.

Olga was quicker.

"If Martin and Bessie don't say anything, then no. one else can?" she asked.

"Not so far as I can see," Bobby agreed.

"Then it's all right, and they are quite safe, both of them?" Olga insisted.

"I very much regret to say," Bobby told her, "that from the most barefaced and deliberate defiance of the law ever known, they will most probably escape scot free"; and how fiercely he scowled, for all his most deeply rooted official instincts were deeply, deeply hurt.

They were interrupted by a knock at the door, and Olive appeared.

"Headquarters—on the 'phone," she announced, and when Bobby went to answer the call she asked anxiously:

"What have you been doing?"

Bobby looked at her gloomily.

"Bilking the bigamy laws," he answered, and she clapped her hands and cried with delight:—

"Oh, I'm so glad, and I think it's rather nice it's all ending in a love story."

A little later, as he and Olive watched their two visitors walking away together, Bobby said reflectively:—

"It's all been a love story from the start, only in different keys. Lawless love in Mr Weston. Calf love with Martin and Bessie. Money love in Florence Severn. Possessive love in Thomasine Rowe. No love at all in Ronald Franks. Self-sacrificing love in Bessie for John Abel. And now normal love in Martin and Olga—and so good luck to them, even if they have fooled the law and got away with it."

THE END